**Praise for the first Ladies of St. Jude's Abbey
novel, *A Knight Like No Other***

"Historical romance at its best!"
—May McGoldrick

"Lively and entertaining!"
—Margaret Evans Porter

"Fast, fresh and fun!"
—Mary Jo Putney

One Knight Stands

Jocelyn Kelley

A SIGNET ECLIPSE BOOK

SIGNET ECLIPSE
Published by New American Library, a division of
Penguin Group (USA) Inc., 375 Hudson Street,
New York, New York 10014, USA
Penguin Group (Canada), 90 Eglinton Avenue East, Suite 700, Toronto,
Ontario M4P 2Y3, Canada (a division of Pearson Penguin Canada Inc.)
Penguin Books Ltd., 80 Strand, London WC2R 0RL, England
Penguin Ireland, 25 St. Stephen's Green, Dublin 2,
Ireland (a division of Penguin Books Ltd.)
Penguin Group (Australia), 250 Camberwell Road, Camberwell, Victoria 3124,
Australia (a division of Pearson Australia Group Pty. Ltd.)
Penguin Books India Pvt. Ltd., 11 Community Centre, Panchsheel Park,
New Delhi - 110 017, India
Penguin Group (NZ), cnr Airborne and Rosedale Roads, Albany,
Auckland 1310, New Zealand (a division of Pearson New Zealand Ltd.)
Penguin Books (South Africa) (Pty.) Ltd., 24 Sturdee Avenue,
Rosebank, Johannesburg 2196, South Africa

Penguin Books Ltd., Registered Offices:
80 Strand, London WC2R 0RL, England

First published by Signet Eclipse, an imprint of New American Library,
a division of Penguin Group (USA) Inc.

First Printing, October 2005
10 9 8 7 6 5 4 3 2 1

Acknowledgments

Thanks to Normand Beauregard of Swashbucklers' Ink who shared his amazing knowledge of the quarterstaff with me, so that Elspeth Braybrooke's many tricks with it are truly possible.

Thanks to Darren Lemieux and Robert Waite of the British School of Falconry, where I could experience for a short time the thrill Tarran ap Llyr knows by having a hawk sit on my wrist.

Gentlemen, thank you all for answering my many questions. This book would not have been possible without your patient and knowledgeable answers.

Chapter 1

W atch out!"

Elspeth Braybrooke ducked as an inch-thick staff swung over her head. If it had struck her, she would have been left senseless or worse.

With a shout, she raised her own staff and knocked the other one away before it could complete its arc. She twisted it, sliding her hands to one end of the almost-six-foot-long staff as she straightened. Bringing it down with all her strength on the other staff, she heard a grunt. She pressed her attack, not giving her opponent a chance to take the offensive again.

The staff blurred in front of her as she whipped it around her adversary, striking at the back of the knees and lifting just far enough to send her student crashing to the ground. She leaped around the prone girl. Gripping the staff on either side of the girl's neck, she did not push down in the fatal move.

Standing, Elspeth held out her hand and brought her opponent to her feet. As the girl bowed, her face was flushed with exertion and excitement.

"Show me how you did that twist, Sister Elspeth." She panted, but her eyes glowed with anticipation.

Elspeth returned the bow before smiling at the girl and

the five others who had been watching. "On the morrow, Sister Dominique. If we linger longer, we will be late for vespers. It is nearly sunset, so the service should be starting soon, and you are exhausted. A single swing of the staff will probably knock you off your feet."

Sister Dominique wiped the sleeve of her practice tunic across her forehead and against her blond hair that was jeweled with sweat. "If you say nothing to the abbess, she might not notice that we missed vespers."

"But we have Evensong tonight, and I love to hear the choir sing the Mass. And if the abbess discovered you had not attended Mass during Lent, she would be very disappointed in you."

"True," Sister Dominique said, making a face and then laughing.

"Hurry and clean up. I will meet you there. I don't want to miss a single moment of the singing." She pointed her staff toward the chapel, a graceful building with arched windows and a bell tower reaching toward the sky. Inside there was a simple peace that came from the rows of columns supporting the roof. No pews broke the floor's expanse from door to altar, because the sisters stood during Mass.

The girls stacked their staffs before walking toward the chapel. Their giggles and light voices drifted back to Elspeth.

As she gathered up the practice sticks her students used during their daily lessons, she knew she would have to struggle to stay awake during the church service. She had been teaching since dawn, which came earlier and earlier each morn as winter surrendered to spring.

Crossing the practice area behind the refectory, Elspeth hummed the song she hoped would be sung tonight. The melody was complicated, but when the choir performed it, the notes swirled gloriously around the nave. She wished she could sing in the choir. She had no time for it with her teaching. Maybe it was for the best. Singing with others never seemed to work, for her voice yearned to follow the song in her heart, which was not always the same one the choir sang.

She went down the steps into the undercroft. She kept the staffs her students used among the Abbey's other supplies. It was dusky within, and she heard skittering among the small stones scattered across the dirt floor.

"Don't eat too much, little mouse," she said with a laugh. "Save some for those of us who have worked hard today."

The abbess had chided her often for talking to everyone and everything she met, but Elspeth could not break herself of the habit. She leaned the staffs against a wall not far from a small window.

A shadow crossed the window, and footsteps hurried down the stone steps. A silhouette looked into the undercroft and called, "Sister Elspeth?"

"Back here," she replied to the sister standing in the doorway. "Back here with my friend the mouse."

"*She* is here!"

Elspeth stiffened. She knew the same words were being whispered with identical awe through every corridor of St. Jude's Abbey, rushing from the gatehouse to the chapel. They would be shared in the dorter where the sisters slept and in the refectory where they ate. In the stables and in the antechamber of the abbess's rooms, they would be repeated.

"*She* is here?" Elspeth asked, her voice dropping to a whisper.

Not a single soul within the Abbey's walls needed to ask who *she* was. Elspeth was sure every heart beat with the same excited rhythm as hers. Every breath was held in anticipation. Since the founding of St. Jude's Abbey by Eleanor, wife of King Henry II of England, the queen had come to the Abbey only once. Yet, each woman cloistered behind its walls knew that this unique abbey would not exist without the queen.

"Yes, and the abbess asks for you to meet her in the cloister."

"But it is time for vespers. Father will be displeased if I come to Mass late. Last year when I was delayed, he—"

"Sister Elspeth, *she* is here!"

Elspeth nodded as she rushed past her sister in the doorway. The queen's presence in the Abbey disrupted the customary round of days in every way.

She was stepping into the cloister yard before she remembered that she was not dressed to speak with the abbess. Her practice tunic was stained with sweat, and her hair, never compliant, surrounded her shoulders in a ruddy cloud of curls. She could not keep the abbess waiting, so she would apologize as she had before when her classes had lasted too late and she had come to the evening meal in her training clothes.

The yard was bare earth with a fountain in the middle. Around its base, spring flowers bobbed in the light breeze she had not noticed while teaching. She looked past them to see three women talking. The sisters hurrying to vespers were not walking too close, giving them privacy for their conversation.

"Ah, Sister Elspeth, come here!" called the abbess, who was more than a head shorter than the other women.

Nariko, who stood with the abbess, had traveled from her family's homeland beyond fabled Jerusalem and had been brought by the queen to England. Pale olive skin and long black hair edging a face with high cheekbones and eyes shaped like raindrops gave her an exotic beauty. She was also the master instructor, training the elite in the Abbey. From her father, she had learned ways of fighting unlike any seen in England. She taught the sisters how to defend themselves without a weapon other than their bodies.

The third woman turned as Elspeth walked around the fountain. With a gasp, Elspeth halted in midstep as she gazed at the queen. Eleanor of Aquitaine, onetime wife of the King of France, now Queen of England, was lauded for her quick wit and beauty. Elspeth could understand why. Even the passage of years could not dim the queen's loveliness.

Dropping to her knees, Elspeth bowed her head. What would her father and mother have thought if they had lived long enough to discover that their daughter had been brought into the company of England's queen? A Braybrooke woman, born of traveling minstrels, now was being presented to the queen.

"She is not as tall as I expected," the queen was saying when Elspeth's heart eased enough from its frantic thumping so she could hear.

"Do not let her size fool you." The abbess laughed as the queen motioned for Elspeth to come to her feet.

"I am told that you are the best in the Abbey with a quarterstaff." The queen appraised her coolly. "Is that true? Do not be modest, for I prefer the truth."

"I teach the other sisters how to wield a quarterstaff. I also know how to use other weapons, but I am most skilled with the quarterstaff. I know—" She silenced herself when the abbess gave her a warning frown. Talking too much was a habit she could not break, especially when she was nervous.

"Teaching others and being adept yourself can be two very different things." The queen smiled at Nariko. "I trust you will take no insult at my words, my friend."

"I take none, your majesty." She gave a rare smile in return. "I am pleased to have you meet one of my best students."

"That is still to be seen." The queen motioned toward the far corner of the cloister.

A brown-haired man stepped forward, and Elspeth flinched. She could not recall ever seeing a man, save for the priest, in this hallowed area. When he twirled a quarterstaff, she assessed him as candidly as the queen had her. He handled the staff with the ease of familiarity that came from long hours of training.

"Here," came a whisper from behind her.

She turned to see Sister Dominique holding out Elspeth's quarterstaff. It was not the one she taught with, but the one she used to give demonstrations. Iron tips were at either end, and the thick oak staff was smoothed from sliding her hands along it often.

Taking the staff, she glanced at the abbess, who motioned with her head toward the man. Many of the Abbey's sisters were gathered in the arched walkway surrounding the cloister's yard. Even when the chapel bell tolled, nobody moved except the man who was walking toward her with a smile.

"I will be careful not to hurt you, Sister," he said, his smile condescending.

"That is very kind of you. You do not need to be careful with me. I am ready to face the challenge you offer." She was babbling again, so she forced herself to add only, "I shall endeavor not to hurt you either."

His mouth twisted with fury that she dared to act as if she could even touch him with her staff, and his eyes narrowed. Giggles came from the walkway, but were quickly hushed. The abbess must have given them one of her stern looks.

Elspeth turned as the man circled her. She kept her staff at an angle across her body. When she bowed her head as Nariko had insisted at the beginning and end of each practice, the man swung his quarterstaff. Shocked that he had not returned her salutation, she toppled off her feet.

She groaned as she hit the hard-packed dirt. Her head

rang from the blow that resonated through her, and her eyes refused to focus. She heard warning shouts, so she knew nobody was going to stop the fight, even though the man had failed to follow honorable procedures.

Rolling out of the way, she heard his staff hit the ground where she had been seconds before. His vow not to hurt her was forgotten. Hers must be, too.

She scrambled to her feet and, grabbing her staff by one end, swung it. He held up his, but her blow sent him stumbling back several paces. Surprise widened his eyes once more. His mouth tightened when she smiled and bowed again, this time keeping her eyes on him.

With a bellow, he raced toward her. She paid no attention to the shouts around her as she halted each motion of his quarterstaff. He was taller than she was, and his staff was longer than hers, but she was quicker, so she was not at too much of a disadvantage.

Round and round they went, striking and feinting. She watched his hands closely, gauging his next change of position by how he held the staff. Yet, still he succeeded in knocking her off her feet when he whipped the staff against the back of her knees as she had Sister Dominique.

As he leaped forward to press the staff to her throat, she raised her staff and caught him in the belly. She pushed hard, forcing him and his staff to her left. Using one end, she swung the staff, striking him in the chest. He fell. She shifted her hands and slashed the quarterstaff against the back of his leg when he struggled to stand. She rolled away from him as he hit the ground with a thud.

Jumping up, she readied herself for his next attack. The man was lying on his back, his eyes closed. A trickle of blood curled down the side of his chin. As she inched toward him, wary of being tricked, she reached out with her staff and poked him. He did not move. She lifted his left hand with her staff. It fell back to the ground, lifeless.

Elspeth went to the fountain and leaned her staff against
it. She dipped her hands in the water. Carrying a handful
back, she dropped it on the man's face. He sputtered. She
grabbed her quarterstaff and put it against his chest as he
opened his eyes. Amazement filled them.

"I hope I did not hurt you too badly," she said.

He rolled away and took two attempts to get to his knees.
She held out her hand. He waved it away as he stood very
slowly. He wove when he tried to take a step. Picking up his
quarterstaff, he used it as a long cane to keep him on his
feet. He wiped blood from his broken lip and smiled. "Not
too badly."

She bowed to him and was surprised when he did the
same; then, hearing the soft rustle of silk, she turned to see
the queen standing behind her. The man was honoring the
queen, not the woman who had defeated him.

Elspeth started to bow as well, but the queen motioned
for her to remain where she was.

"You had a worthy adversary, Sir Bernard," Queen Eleanor
said with the gentle lilt from her homeland in Aquitaine.
"You are wise to concede the battle."

"I would like a rematch," Sir Bernard said as he raised
his head and shifted his grip on the quarterstaff.

"Perhaps another time." The queen looked at Elspeth,
her gaze cool and clearly evaluating Elspeth anew. "Lady
Elspeth has a task I wish her to do."

Lady Elspeth? Correcting the queen was inconceivable,
but Elspeth was not highborn and did not deserve such a
title.

As if Queen Eleanor was privy to her thoughts, she said,
"Every woman within St. Jude's Abbey who sets forth to do
my bidding is given the title of lady."

"Ask of me what you will. You know I am here to serve
you, and I will be happy . . ." Again she silenced herself, but
could not quell the thrill of anticipation rushing through

her. Until just over a year ago, none of the sisters within the Abbey had understood why they were receiving a warrior's training. Then, the queen had come to the Abbey for the first time since its founding and sought the assistance of one of the sisters.

It had been from the queen's foresight that St. Jude's Abbey was born. In perilous times, when one's allies could swiftly become one's enemies, a wise woman prepared for every battle. Not battles of faith, but battles that could topple the queen from power and weaken the English throne.

St. Jude . . . the patron saint of hopeless causes. The queen had chosen the Abbey's name well, for only when matters appeared truly hopeless had she come to call upon the women who lived within it. Then, with skills learned in its cloistered halls and gardens, the ladies of St. Jude's Abbey would go forth to serve Queen Eleanor.

"Walk with me," the queen ordered.

Elspeth obeyed and went with the queen toward the walkway. The other sisters stepped aside, giving Elspeth curious and sympathetic and even envious looks. Each of them wanted a chance to prove she was worthy of the queen's patronage, but each was aware, too, how desperate the situation must be if the queen had come to St. Jude's Abbey to seek help.

Queen Eleanor said nothing until they had emerged into the yard by the chapter house, a squat building beside the chapel. "The king is in Ireland, and he is to return soon. He will be traveling through Wales as he did on his way across the Irish Sea. From Wales, I have recently heard of a threat to his life."

Nodding, Elspeth remained silent. If she opened her mouth, she might talk and talk until she said the worst possible thing. Even in the Abbey, there were whispered rumors that the king and queen's marriage was foundering because of the king's infidelity, but no one spoke aloud what might be true or only gossip. She suspected the queen's concern for her husband's continued well-being was focused on making sure the throne one day would belong to her most beloved son, Richard. Henry had crowned his namesake as his heir almost two years ago, but the young king had not yet sired an heir of his own.

"Do you speak Welsh, milady?" the queen asked.

"I once knew some, because my family traveled through the Welsh Marches and north into Wales when I was a child, but I have forgotten what I learned."

"It will return to you, no doubt."

"No doubt," she replied, again not wanting to argue with the queen.

"Can you translate the words *Llech-lafar*?"

She searched her memory and was surprised that she knew part of the answer. "*Llech* is stone."

"Very good. *Llech-lafar* means speaking stone." The queen looked toward the west. "An old prophecy, reputedly belonging to the great magician Merlin of King Arthur's time, states that a man the Welsh consider an outlander king will, upon his return from conquering Ireland, step on *Llech-lafar* and die."

"Do you believe there is truth in such a story? There are many tales of Merlin throughout England and the Marches, and many of them have no truth in them." She had heard the myths during her childhood, and she had come to see that most were fables meant to teach lessons and to entertain.

Instead of answering her, Queen Eleanor said, "Lady Elspeth, I want you to go to Wales and find *Llech-lafar* and make sure that the king does not step on it."

"You want me to find a rock that may be just a legend?" she choked out. Sending someone on such an absurd quest seemed unlike rational Queen Eleanor.

"Yes."

"But if the king sails to England instead of Wales—"

"The sea currents and winds will carry him back to Wales. You ask many questions, but I need you to answer a single one. Are you willing to do as I ask, Lady Elspeth?"

She bowed. "It is my honor to do whatever you ask of me." The words were simple to say, but she had no idea how she would accomplish such a herculean task. How would she find a single rock among the crags and mountains in Wales? She did not ask that aloud.

"See that you do not fail." She held out a rolled scroll. "The future of England is in your hands."

Chapter 2

The sea was bloodred beneath the rays from the setting sun, which peeked from under a line of dark clouds just above the horizon.

"Isn't it wondrous?" asked a hushed voice. "I have never seen anything so beautiful."

"You certainly do not believe that, Vala." Tarran ap Llyr looked past the trees surrounding them to gaze out at the sea. He hated the color red. Once he had paid it no more mind than he had any other hue. That was before he saw liquid red spread across the floor of his home.

Pulling his gaze from the crimson sea, he heard a chirp from the goshawk riding on his left hand. He had raised Heliwr almost from the egg, and the bird seemed attuned to his strongest, darkest emotions. Maybe it was because the hawk's thoughts focused on the hunt and prey, too.

Tarran slowed his horse to match the pace of the old woman's. Her brows were nearly as white as her hair, and her moon-shaped face was lined with years of living upon the shores of the western sea. Although the afternoon was warm, she wore a voluminous cloak of black wool over her gown of the same color.

Vala laughed. She had not been able to hide her excitement with the passage of every mile they rode south and west. And why not? 'Twas not every woman of her many years who traveled the breadth of Cymru to find a home with her granddaughter. Even so, he could see how each passing mile weighed more heavily upon her.

"But I do believe it," she answered in her gentle voice. "I had heard of Cymru's beauty from those who have traveled before us. I want to savor every image of it, so I might enjoy the memories over and over."

His friend Seith ap Mil drew his horse up to ride beside them. Tarran nodded to Seith, who looked as garish as the flowers in the field with his bright red tunic and deep blue cloak. Even his stockings, which were as dusty as Tarran's from their days of riding, were still a grotesque green and looked like bulbs on his round legs.

"Do you think we can beg shelter from the lord in the castle that is supposed to be just past these trees?" Seith rubbed his hand on his generous expanse of stomach. "I would enjoy a meal not of my own cooking."

"I have not seen you turning up your nose at anything we have caught so far."

"We have had nothing but fish and bread for our Lenten meals. Heliwr has enjoyed hare and the occasional grouse."

"Are you envious of my hawk?"

"No, because we ate game too often before Ash Wednesday. Sometimes a man wishes for something more civilized, something like spitted chicken or a joint of mutton."

Vala laughed. "It would seem, Tarran, you are the only one among us who prefers the rough life."

Shaking his head, Tarran gave his horse a command while at the same time he tightened his hold on the hawk's jesses. His steed leaped to a trot.

Behind him, he heard Seith ask, "What did I say wrong now?"

Tarran owed his friend an apology. Later he would see Seith received it. Seith had been loyal even when Tarran

had been unworthy of such a friend. Yet, Seith did not understand how Tarran preferred the quiet of his own company and a few friends to a large household where someone
was certain to say something that brought forth the memories he was trying to submerge. So far, he had been unsuc-
cessful, for the red of the setting sun had sent a pain through
him that was as strong as if *he* had been the one stabbed.

Shadows beneath the trees held the dampness of the past
winter. His hand went to the knife he carried in his belt. He
fingered the dragon and leeks carved into the haft, ready to
draw it if needed. Such shadows welcomed thieves. Behind
him, the men and Vala grew silent as they rode through the
wood and crossed a wide, fast-flowing stream. In the far
west of Cymru, the laws of England were obeyed only by
those who believed they had something to gain from abid-
ing by the king's authority.

Tarran released the breath he had been holding when,
minutes later, they emerged again into the sunshine. Attack
now could not come without warning, and he doubted anyone would be bold enough to ambush them within view of
the castle. Robbers would fear retaliation from within the
walls surrounding the foursquare tower. The lord who held
the castle would be a fool to attack travelers within his
fief's boundaries, for that could focus the king's displeasure
on him.

The castle on the hill looked puny compared to the vast
mountains rising above its parapets. A darker gray than the
raw stone overlooking it, Castell Glyn Niwl sat in an area
cleared of trees. Upon closer examination, the walls were
edged with sharp rocks. No greenery softened the bases,
because those could be easily set ablaze or conceal invaders.

And a woman hung out of an arrow slit.

Tarran did not want to believe his eyes. It could not be—
It was! A woman hung from the narrow opening. Her slen-

der legs dangled against the wall, kicking wildly as she tried to find a toehold on the wall.

He exhorted his horse to a run up the hill while at the same time he gripped the jesses holding the hawk on his left hand. Heliwr chirped, preparing for the moment Tarran would send him aloft. He did not release the bird as he stopped below the woman. He saw three poles lying across the rocks and wondered what they were for, but quickly turned his attention back to dangling woman.

He stretched up his right hand. Her feet were beyond his fingers. Standing in the stirrups, he clamped his legs against the horse's sides. The horse shifted, and he growled a warning for it to stand still. Hoofbeats and raised voices came from behind him, but he did not glance back. He looked up at the woman.

"Let go!" he shouted.

She looked down at him and frowned. She shook her head, sending her russet hair swirling around her, and tried to dig her toes into a crevice between the stones.

Did she not understand Welsh? Maybe she was of a Marcher household.

"Let go!" he called in the Anglo-Norman language of the English lands east of Offa's Dyke. He had learned it as a child at the same time he had Welsh. "I will catch you!"

"Go away!" she ordered. "I have no need of your help!"

"Is she mad?" Seith grasped the reins of Tarran's horse to keep it from moving. He took the hawk, balancing the bird on his left arm, which was as fleshy as his thick legs.

"Probably, but even a madwoman does not deserve to fall to her death." Tarran clenched his teeth. By St. David, he never wanted to see another woman broken and bloody and dead. He pulled out his broadsword, and, stretching up, he tapped the woman on the buttocks with the flat side. "Let go!"

Instead of obeying, she kicked at him and clung like a

burr to the arrow slit. "Will you go away? I don't need your help. I don't want your help. I want you to go away. Will you go now?"

She must be mad!

He raised the sword again. This time, he struck her sharply on the right elbow.

She screamed as the fingers on her right hand lost their hold. For a second, she hung by her left hand as she grappled to get another hold with her right. Her fingers slipped, and she groaned. Then she was falling. He reached up, catching her before she could strike the rocks. Her legs hit his chest, and his breath exploded out in a gasp. He gathered her flailing limbs to him. Her hand smacked his chin. Pulling her tightly to him, he dropped back into the saddle. Pain raced along his thighs as they absorbed the force of her fall. The horse whinnied in fear. He murmured to it, but looked down at the woman in his arms.

Red hair framed her face and curled around the shoulders of the slate-gray gown she wore over a light blue undertunic. It was a simple gown without much embroidery, but the fabric was finer than anything a peasant could possess. Her body, pressing against him, was curvaceous, but as firm and trim as a well-trained warrior's. Her delicate face urged a man to look at it and then want to look again and again. Her lips, parted as she panted with her exertions, were soft and lush. No sign of madness dimmed her dazzling, green eyes. She closed them, and her body strained against his as she struggled to breathe.

"How does she fare?" asked Vala, dismay heightening the old woman's voice.

"She lives." Tarran took a deep breath and released it slowly as he looked at his men. In addition to Seith, there were three others, all sworn to help him gain his revenge.

Iau ap Mil was Seith's younger brother and had a girth

almost as large. On either side of him rode Kei ap Pebin and Kei's cousin Gryn ap Dwnn. None of them spoke.

"God clearly was watching out for her." Tarran tried to keep the bitterness out of his voice. His beloved Addfwyn had not had anyone coming to her rescue. She had been alone when she faced her murderer.

A horn blared within the castle. Knowing it meant someone had noted them by the wall, Tarran paid it no mind as he looked again at the woman in his arms. Had she lost consciousness? The familiar surge of rage rose through him. The woman might be the most impossible creature ever to walk the earth, but that was no reason for someone to shove her out the arrow slit. It could not have been an accident, because the opening in the wall was too narrow for anyone to slip through easily.

"She wakes!"

Tarran did not need Vala's warning, for a shuddering breath had raced through the woman. It brushed her against him, causing him to draw in a sharp breath of his own. He scowled and swore under his breath. He had banished any hint of passion, save for rage and the hunger for vengeance for Addfwyn's death. He did not want it to return.

"Slowly, slowly," he ordered. "Open your eyes slowly, so you do not faint again."

"I did not faint," the woman replied, but her voice quivered as vigorously as she did.

"Then you do an excellent imitation of a faint."

Her eyes opened, and she frowned at him so fiercely, he wondered if his words had been closer to the truth than she wished him to guess. Why would a woman who had been rescued from death pretend to collapse in the arms of the very man who had saved her?

"You fool!" she muttered.

That was the last thing he had expected to hear. Had he

misunderstood her? Frowning, he asked, "What did you say?"

She pushed herself away from his chest and sat straighter. Even so, her eyes were a handsbreadth below his. Good thing, for they were flashing with the devil's own fire.

"Let me go!" she ordered. "You have ruined everything. Do you have any idea how long I have been waiting for this opportunity? I was almost there, and you came along. Did you get satisfaction out of destroying everything?" She shoved against him again. "Let me go."

"After you tell me who—" His breath burst out in a curse as she drove her fist into his gut.

She slid from his grasp and off the horse. Putting her hands on her hips, she turned her back to him. Her gaze focused at a spot high on the wall, obviously dismissing him.

He was tempted to tell her that Tarran ap Llyr was a man to ignore at her own risk. He did not want to argue with the redhead. Red! Another reason to curse the color. He was tempted to ride away, but he had saved her life, and he now must protect that life. There was one way. He would find the man who had treated her basely and teach that cur how it felt to be suspended by his fingertips over jagged stones. Only she could give him the man's name.

Jumping to the ground, he grasped her arm. "The least you could do is say thank you."

"Thank you? Most certainly, thank you." She dipped in a swift curtsy. "I must be blessed, o wondrous hero, that you chose this very moment to pass this way." Her sarcastic smile became a frown. "Blessed with bad fortune. Will you go away and leave me alone?"

"Who are you?"

She rolled her eyes as she tried to push her hair back from her face, but the curls continued to tumble over her shoulders and down her breasts. As she reached for the topmost pole of the three on the ground, she said, "I have no time for your questions. Begone."

Tarran whirled her to face him. The pole she had been picking up dropped, and the small crosspiece near the top struck his shin above his boot. He swallowed his gasp at the sharp pain.

Pulling her toward him, he asked, "Are you completely mad? Tell me why you were hanging from the wall."

"Let me go!" She drew back her foot, and he clamped his arm around her waist, tugging her against his chest. Her foot swung, but missed his leg.

Over her head, he ordered, "Kei, ride to the gate and give the lord within our greetings along with a request for an audience with him at his earliest convenience."

The man, who was as gaunt as Seith was round, nodded and started toward the gate.

"Do not let me delay you if you wish to go to the gate yourself," the woman said. "I trust you will find that Lord de la Rochelle is an excellent host. He is well respected by both the English and the Welsh, so you should be welcomed within the walls. If you were to—"

Tarran had heard enough of her babble. "What is your name?"

"If I tell you, will you let me go?"

"Tell me, and I shall see." He wondered anew about the man who had tossed her from the castle. He could almost sympathize with him. The woman was irritating . . . and enticing. As she squirmed in his arms, he relished the caress of her soft curves.

He cursed. She was mad, and her insanity had infected him. He needed no part of emotions that made a man vulnerable.

"What is your name?" he asked a second time.

He thought she would fire back some sharp comment, but, after looking over her shoulder toward the gate where

Kei was speaking with the guards, she said, "I am Elspeth Braybrooke. Now you know my name, so release me."

"My name is—"

"Not of any interest to me. I have no plan to speak it, and you have delayed me from a very important task." She twisted her arm sharply and broke his hold on her. "Good day, sir."

He seized her arm again. With another quick motion, she freed herself with remarkable ease. She gave him a triumphant smile before reaching for the poles.

Maybe he should leave her to her fate. Maybe he should see her indifference as a boon, for he could continue on his journey and do as he had vowed over Addfwyn's corpse. But how had the woman broken his hold so easily? Even Seith, who had trained with him since they were both young, had not been able to escape that grip.

Tarran stepped around her and put one foot on the topmost pole. She tugged at it, but paused when the wood protested against the stone.

"What do you want?" she asked as she raised her eyes. "Why don't you leave me alone?"

He took her hand, not in a tight grip, but as if he were handing her down from a horse. "Because I want to know how it came to pass that you were hanging from an arrow slit."

She frowned. "I do not see what concern that is of yours. Because you were riding by and chose to intrude does not mean I have to reveal anything to you. If you would please leave—"

"Child," Vala said, her soothing voice tinged with fatigue, "Tarran ap Llyr wishes only to be certain you come to no harm."

Elspeth had not noticed the elderly woman before. Standing nose to nose with an arrogant Welshman was one thing; being rude to an old woman was something else entirely. She counted to ten in Latin, then in Norman and in English before she said, "The only harm done to me this day was by Tarran ap Llyr's sword against my arm."

Rubbing her elbow, which still stung from the blow, she looked at the man, whose boot remained on the staff. Not to anyone would she admit that she had lost her breath because she had fallen from the arrow slit . . . *and* because she had seen his face. She had never beheld such a coldly chiseled face. His eyes, as black as his hair, were piercing and icy. With a warrior's strong arms and a broad chest to match his shoulders, he was daunting.

But she would not be daunted. She had not traveled across England from St. Jude's Abbey to be rattled by a Welshman's ebony stare. She had heard much about their race during her childhood. Dreamy and fond of poetry and song and fable, they were not true warriors like the Normans. Even their leader, Lord Rhys, Prince of Deheubarth, acknowledged that, for he had paid a vassal's homage to King Henry before the king left to subdue his onetime allies in Ireland.

"Move your foot, sir," she ordered.

He did not lift it off the pole.

"Doesn't a Welshman have the common decency to grant a lady her wish?"

"Doesn't a lady who is stupid enough to denounce a Welshman to his face have the common decency to soothe her rescuer's curiosity by explaining how she came to be dangling from an arrow slit like linen bleaching in the sun?"

"Rescuer?" She laughed coldly as he rested one hand on his knee and held up his other covered with a leather gauntlet. A rotund man held a hawk out to him. Was he trying to frighten her? He was wasting his time. "Sir, I told you that I have no need of a rescuer." Looking at the poles, she said, "I have told you everything you need to know, so you might as well let me go."

"Not until you answer my question, Elspeth."

"I have answered it." She scowled at him. "Why should I tell you more when you ruined everything!"

"Ruined everything? I saved you. Who pushed you out? Whom did you rile enough, Elspeth, to send you falling to your death out that arrow slit?"

"Out?" She laughed without humor. "I was not trying to get out. I was trying to get in."

Chapter 3

As the dark-haired man's mouth widened into a circle of shock, Elspeth knew she had never been so frustrated in her whole life. If Tarran ap Llyr and his companions had stayed away, she could have slipped into the castle and out without anyone being the wiser. The questions she had asked about *Llech-lafar* at Lord Rhy's castle in Cardigan, trying not to reveal why she was interested in that specific stone, had raised too many suspicions. Although she guessed she could trust Lord Rhys, who as Prince of Deheubarth was a liege of the king, she had not been sure of anyone else. Finally, when the queries about why she wanted to know the stone had become interrogations, she had slipped out in the middle of the night, hoping nobody would notice her absence until it was too late to give chase.

The mission given to her by Queen Eleanor had seemed preposterous when they stood within the walls of St. Jude's Abbey in far-off southeastern England, but now she was wondering if it was, instead, impossible. Names of those who might help her had been written on the queen's scroll. Elspeth had sought out each one, and not one gave her a clue to find one rock out of the thousands scattered across the countryside. The problem was not that the accursed

stone was unknown in Wales. It was known too well. She
had been directed to dozens of stones supposedly set in
place by the magician Merlin. Each time, she had later
learned that it was not *Llech-lafar*, that the mythical rock
was elsewhere. No one seemed to know exactly where.

So she kept looking and asking questions. The time she
had to find the stone was growing short. In Cardigan, she
had heard that King Henry was being held up from returning to Wales only by storms in the Irish Sea. As soon as the
weather cleared, he would sail. She had to find *Llech-lafar*
before he stepped on it and invoked its curse.

She had been told that at Castell Glyn Niwl there was a
wisewoman who might know the true location of Merlin's
stone. Elspeth had planned to sneak in, find the woman, ask
her questions and leave without drawing any attention to
herself. She was unsure if the Welsh would allow her to
continue her search if they knew why she wanted to find
Llech-lafar. Castell Glyn Niwl was held by a Marcher lord,
a Norman lord who had carved a holding out of what once
belonged to the Welsh, but there were likely to be many
Welsh living in the household. Not all the natives had gone
to live in the Welsheries in the mountains.

All had been going well . . . until Tarran ap Llyr had
ruined everything.

"You wanted to get *into* the castle?" Tarran asked, intruding on her thoughts.

"I said that, didn't I?" Elspeth bent to pick up the topmost pole. When he did not shift his foot, she considered
yanking on it. She glanced at the hawk, not wanting to injure
it. Its glowing eyes, despite their lighter shade, matched its
master's frigid stare.

"Explain why. It is the very least you can do to repay the
man who saved your life."

Elspeth heard the sharp song of a sword being drawn.
Her fingers itched to use the pole, but she stood motionless.

Only her eyes shifted. The man who had handed the hawk to Tarran now held his sword. Would he slice into her? She looked back at Tarran as he motioned for his companion to lower the sword. The other man obeyed, chagrin lengthening his face.

More questions filled Elspeth's mind. Some message she had not been privy to had been exchanged by the men. The other man was ashamed of his action, but he had been right to be prepared for whatever she might do. She wanted to ask who they were and why they were traveling with an old woman. She did not have the time to satisfy her curiosity.

Folding her arms in front of her, she said, "You did not save me, Tarran ap Llyr. You sent me falling to what could have been my death."

"Do you honestly think you could have climbed through that opening?" He eyed her up and down. "You are slender, but you have womanly curves wider than an arrow slit."

"I would have been able to slip through." She had *hoped* she could, but she would not share her uncertainty. Would he laugh at her? She had not seen as much as a hint of a smile on his face.

"With the help of these long poles?" He tapped one with his toe.

"Yes."

His dark eyes narrowed, again giving him an expression as ferocious as his hawk's. "There are crosspieces near the top of two. Were you standing on whatever you call these sticks in an attempt to reach the opening?"

"They are called stilts."

"You did not answer my question."

"I saw no need when you have finally seen the obvious. As it also is obvious, if you had not come along—"

"How long, once you discovered you could not crawl through that slit, would you have hung there before you fell onto these rocks or the sentries took note of you?"

"That should not concern you."

He muttered something she suspected was a Welsh curse. "If you will not answer that question, then tell me where and why you learned to walk on stilts."

"That is simple to answer. One never can be certain when some skill might come in handy, so a wise person learns when granted the opportunity."

"That is not an answer."

"It is the only one I have." She was not going to tell a stranger about her life before she went to live at the Abbey.

When he took his foot off her stilts, she gathered them up along with the third pole. She was careful to keep the top stilt in front of it to conceal the iron capping each end. She did not want to explain why she carried a quarterstaff. She might need the element of surprise if he continued to foil her attempts to do what she must do.

The man he had sent to the gate came running back, grinning widely. Elspeth glanced from him to Tarran, whose lips remained in their straight line. What a dour man!

"Lord de la Rochelle bids us welcome," the man said.

"Thank you, Kei." Tarran nodded toward the others, and they fell in line behind him.

"You have them well trained, I see." Elspeth chided herself. How unthinking could she be? Prolonging the argument increased the chance of Tarran's discovering the truth.

"They understand discipline in the hope of achieving what we have set out to do."

"And what is that?"

"That should not concern you."

She stood the poles upright and regarded him with an expression as cool as his. He had every right to throw her words back in her face, but she had to be certain he would not do anything further to prevent her from fulfilling her vow to the queen.

Elspeth had no idea how long she and Tarran might have

stood there, glowering at each other, neither willing to be the first to look away. The squawk of the bird on his left hand shattered their furious connection.

Rain began falling as if the hawk had called for it. Not a gentle spring shower, but an abrupt deluge. The old woman pulled up her cloak's hood as Elspeth, still holding the poles, ran toward the rocks.

She heard shouts, but did not slow. Suddenly a horse cut her off, its front hoofs flailing at her. A warning came from behind her. Tarran's voice! In one motion, she dropped the stilts and swung the quarterstaff. The rider bellowed as she knocked him from the saddle. He landed with a heavy thump.

She grabbed the horse's reins before it could step on the groaning man. She knelt, still holding her weapon.

"Are you hurt?" she asked.

The heavy man, who had muddy brown hair, opened one eye and snarled something she could not understand. He clutched his right arm where his hand hung at a strange angle.

"Yes, he is hurt," Tarran said from behind her. He gave his hawk to the man who had held it before. The bird flapped its wings and screeched, obviously not happy to be handed off to another. "You hit him hard." He pushed her aside and squatted to run his hands along the man's sides. When the man moaned, he said, "Iau, she broke at least one of your ribs." He examined the man's right arm. "Along with your wrist."

"I did not strike his arm," she said.

"But you knocked him from his horse. If he broke it when he fell, it still is your fault."

He was right. Elspeth bit back an apology when Tarran came to his feet and scowled at her. Keeping her head high, even though rain splattered against her face, she gripped the quarterstaff with both hands. Not tightly, but loosely enough so she could react to whatever he did.

"You *are* mad!" he spat.

"Me? You shouted a warning."

"To Iau! His horse could have hurt you."

"Exactly," she returned. "Did you expect me to do nothing to defend myself when his mount's hoofs were inches from my face? I could have been struck by iron horseshoes. I could have been trampled. How could I know if he was able to handle the horse? He could have lost control and—"

"Enough! You can make a man lose control of whatever wits he possesses." He put one hand over hers on the quarterstaff.

Heat erupted where his fingers touched hers, so fierce she was astonished the rain did not turn to steam. She jerked back, shocked by the sensation she had never experienced.

He caught the quarterstaff before it could hit the stones. With a gasp, she realized he now held her weapon. She grabbed for it. He held it over his head, out of her reach. She was amazed when the quarterstaff did not sway, and she knew his broad shoulders were matched by other powerful muscles.

"I will have that back," she said, blinking as the rain fell even harder. She ignored the man who came forward and knelt beside Iau. He checked Iau as Tarran had.

"So you can damage another of my men?"

"I told you! I would not have swung the staff if I had not thought I needed to be concerned for my well-being."

He snorted. "If you are concerned about that, why were you hanging out of an arrow slit?"

A cold raindrop rolling down her spine halted her answer. She took a step to her right. Surprise widened his eyes

as he turned to face her. She edged another pace toward her
right and the rocks. He matched her motion.

His boot must have grazed Iau because a groan came
from the prone man. As Tarran glanced down at the man
wrapping Iau's right arm, Elspeth saw her chance. She
jumped onto the rocks. She yanked the staff from his hands
with one of the twists she had worked hard to master.

He stared at her, astounded. He shook his hands, which
must be stinging. As she ran along the rocks, taking care
because the sides were becoming slippery, he called for her
to stop.

She did and bent to pluck a sack from where she had hidden it amidst the boulders. Untying the top, she pulled out
her undyed wool cloak. She leaned the staff against the castle's wall and swung the cloak over her shoulders. As she
pulled up the hood, she grabbed both the bag and the staff.

Turning, she saw Tarran still beside his men. All of them
and the old woman were looking at her as if she were some
strange creature.

She stepped off the rocks. While the rain came down
ever harder, she walked to where Tarran stood. She stopped
in front of him and, without speaking, placed one end of her
staff on the ground. The silence was unbroken, save by the
rain's patter and a single groan from the man on the ground.

A roar of laughter was followed by, "You are welcome
to complete your disagreement within Castell Glyn Niwl."
A mounted man was at the head of a group of foot soldiers
coming from the gate. He rode forward a single pace. "Lord
de la Rochelle awaits you within his hall." He bowed his
head, but could not hide his grin.

Elspeth sighed. It would be impossible now to sneak into
the castle, find the old woman who might know where
Llech-lafar was and leave without alerting the castle's lord.
She could say that she must continue on her journey. She
then could try another way to steal into the castle, but Tar-

ran or any of his companions could make Lord de la Rochelle aware of what she had attempted. Her chance at surprise was gone.

She picked up the stilts and shouldered all three staffs before walking toward the open gate. Hearing Iau curse, she looked back to watch Tarran help his man slowly to his feet. Regret at injuring the man pulsed through her, and she thought of the many times the abbess had warned her to think every action through before embarking upon it. But if she had let herself be injured, the king could be doomed.

The soldiers edged aside. How much had they seen? When one winked, she averted her eyes. She had been warned how different the world was beyond the Abbey's walls, where men vied for the attention of women. That warning she had not needed. She had not understood when she, as a child, had watched her mother push aside men's eager hands during a performance. The images remained, and she could recall the disgust in her mother's eyes as fingers pulled at her gown to drag her down into a lap. Her mother's brittle laugh, so unlike her real ones, had never disappeared from Elspeth's memory.

She would never allow a man to treat her like that. No longer was she the daughter of traveling players. She was a lady of St. Jude's Abbey. *A lady!* No man would dare to treat a lady so.

As she crossed the drawbridge and beneath the portcullis, Elspeth was aware of the others following. She became the focus of every eye in the outer ward as both men and women halted what they were doing to watch.

A hand settled on her arm. That heated sensation she had felt when Tarran touched her fingers danced along her skin again.

"Do not go off on your own," he said in not much more than a whisper.

"I can take care of myself." She appreciated his kindness, but if she let him think—even for a moment—she was incapable of protecting herself, he might be even more determined to remain close to her. She could deal with his anger and his officious orders, but not with the way he made her feel with nothing more than a commonplace touch. The sensations erupting from his fingertips banished even thoughts of her task.

"That is yet to be seen. A lucky blow against an unprepared man proves very little." He held on to her arm. "Even Heliwr is vulnerable at times."

"Heliwr?"

He glanced at the bird on his left forearm, and his expression softened slightly. "It is Welsh for hunter." His voice and his face hardened again as he added, "Would you stay near Vala while I speak with our host?"

"I will be honored to watch over her."

His dark brows lowered as rain coursed down from his thick black hair. "Be careful you do not knock her from the saddle also."

Anything she said would only add to his anger, so she shoved through the men to where the old woman was dismounting with the help of one of Tarran's men. The man, who closely resembled the man named Kei, glowered at her, but the old woman motioned for her to come closer.

"The lady will keep me from danger," Vala said with a gentle but exhausted smile. "You may join the others, Gryn." She put her hand on Elspeth's arm. "I am grateful for your protection, milady."

"I hope you have no need of it." She could not keep from smiling back. There was something about Vala that reminded her of the abbess. Did Vala cover an iron will with genuine kindness, as the abbess did?

While they followed the men toward the gate into the inner ward, Vala said, "I am sure you are curious why an old woman is traveling with five warriors."

"I am."

They stepped out of the rain for a distance of three paces before emerging into the inner ward. Elspeth's drenched cloak clung to her on each step. The odor of wet wool filled every breath.

"We are bound for Tyddewi," Vala said. "The city you Normans call St. David's. My granddaughter lives there, and now that I have outlived my usefulness to anyone else, she is welcoming me into her home." She smiled as she looked toward where Tarran and his men were crossing the inner ward. "He is generous to escort me there."

"Is he part of your family, too?" Elspeth saw nothing out of the ordinary in the inner ward. Low wood buildings surrounded a round keep against the rear wall. Through a small gate to her left, she saw the gray finger of a stream that edged around the back of the castle, offering protection from intruders.

Vala shook her head, sending drops flying from her hood. "I was his wet nurse. As he grew older, his parents found other tasks for me in Castell Gwalch Glas."

"Castell?"

"Yes. His father was sired by King Henry I of England. His grandmother was Princess Nest, who was wed to Gerald of Windsor."

"*He* is a prince?"

As if he had heard her question, Tarran paused and, turning, locked gazes with her again. She could imagine him with glorious scarlet robes, presiding over a grand hall where both men and women competed for his favors. A hall like the ones where her parents had been invited to perform for a lord's entertainment.

His intense eyes would not miss anything that happened in his domain. They would make timid the bravest man who bowed before him. Did a Welsh prince wear a golden crown? On his ebony hair, it would glitter like sunlight.

"He is not a prince in Norman eyes," Vala said, and Elspeth tore her gaze from Tarran's to look at the old woman who drew off her hood as they entered the keep. "The Welsh acknowledge sons, whether they are legitimate or not, as the rightful heirs to their father."

Elspeth tossed back her own hood. Making sure the long poles did not strike the low stone ceiling in the entry corridor, she walked toward an arched doorway. She heard voices coming from beyond it.

As she was about to go through the arch, a man stepped in front of her. He was as bulky as the keep and had no more hair than its walls.

"No weapons in the hall," he growled.

Elspeth hesitated. The idea of going among strangers without her staff unsettled her. She would feel naked and susceptible to attack.

"Heed the man, Elspeth," said Tarran as he came to stand in the doorway. On his arm, the hawk wore a well-made leather hood covering its eyes. "He is making a reasonable request."

She handed the man all three poles. He set them against the wall with the indifference of having repeated the motions many times.

"I see," she said as she stepped around the man, "that your hawk is not considered a weapon."

"Anyone with any knowledge of hawks knows that they attack only when hungry and only small creatures." Tarran looked at her from toes to top again. "Smaller even than you, so you need not worry."

"If you hope to insult me, you are wasting your breath. I have never found not being tall a disadvantage." She gave him her coldest smile as she remembered Nariko's speaking of how, in some forms of unarmed combat, Elspeth's height could be an advantage. "Who would one expect to present more danger? A man with a bristling hawk on his arm or a woman holding a staff? Surprise can be the greatest weapon of all."

"I would be surprised if you replied to any remark with only a few words."

She laughed as they entered the high-roofed hall. Again eyes turned toward her. From tables clustered near a raised table, from the larger hearth of a pair set close to the walls, from a corner where children were receiving a sewing lesson, from where the servants placed fresh rushes on the stone floor that was the same gray as the walls . . . everyone looked at her.

The only ones who ignored her were two men sitting to the left of the doorway. They wore simple, off-white robes with hoods pulled up against the damp air. They huddled close together, and she heard them singing quietly. Neither man looked up, and she wondered if they were performers practicing or residents of the castle entertaining themselves.

Biting her lower lip to silence more laughter, she hoped the lord of the castle was not as dismal as Tarran. Did Tarran ap Llyr *ever* smile?

"Why don't you surprise me," Tarran asked, "and restrain yourself while I greet our host? You still could prove me mistaken about your having no good sense." He did not wait for her answer as he walked toward the raised table, pausing to set his goshawk on a narrow ledge beyond where the swirling smoke would smother the bird. To a simple perch made of a single branch, he lashed the bird's jesses. He drew something out of the pouch he wore on his belt and put it beside the hawk. It must have been meat because the bird began to tear into it.

She looked past Tarran to the man at the raised table. From his broad girth to his goblet to the woman sitting on his lap, Lord de la Rochelle had the appearance of a man who enjoyed life. His hair was graying, but his pudgy face was unlined. He motioned for them to come forward.

Elspeth held back. The old woman did the same, and Elspeth was astonished when Vala put her hand on Elspeth's.

"In spite of what Tarran believes," Vala said, "you clearly have wisdom, milady."

She wanted to tell Vala how mistaken she was in her assumption that Elspeth was wellborn. In the Abbey, nobody had paid attention to rank. All that mattered were the skills mastered. She wished it was the same outside the Abbey. Or did she? She loved having the title of lady connected to her name. She must take care not to let pride betray her.

Locking her hands behind her back because she felt odd without a staff in them, she watched Tarran greet Lord de la Rochelle. The Marcher baron smiled and called for ale for Tarran's companions while Iau was helped to the corner where the children had been sewing. A tankard of ale was shoved into her hand. She took a deep drink, letting the warming liquid slip down her throat.

A serving woman held out her hands. "I will take your cloak, milady, to where it can be dried."

"Thank you." Elspeth surrendered it gratefully, but leaned forward to ask, "Do you know where I can find an old wisewoman reputed to live in this castle?"

"Are you speaking of Rhan?"

"Yes," she said, even though she had no idea what the old woman's name might be.

"She is sick with a fever, milady." The serving woman's face was tight with sorrow. "No one can see her."

"But I must see her!"

The woman regarded her with dismay. "Milady, you could sicken, too. Nobody is allowed in her sickroom until she is cool to the touch again."

Elspeth sighed as the serving woman went to put the cloak by the smaller hearth. By St. Jude, every possible impediment was keeping her from finding that accursed rock!

Tarran was looking at her again. Not just him, but the

baron as well. It was obvious that they were discussing her. When the baron laughed and clapped Tarran on the shoulder, her fingers curled into frustrated fists. If they had any idea what she was trying to accomplish . . . She halted that thought. No one must know.

Tarran crooked a finger toward her. She looked away. She was no beast or bird to come at his command.

"A word of caution, if I may," Vala said, and Elspeth realized the old woman had been watching her and Tarran. Exhaustion weighed down Vala's shoulders, but her eyes were focused under heavy eyelids.

"Most certainly." She kept fury out of her voice. Tarran paid no attention to how tired Vala was. He should have seen she was seated before he went to seek Lord de la Rochelle's welcome.

"Tarran ap Llyr is a man of very powerful emotions. You would be wise not to arouse any of them while he is upon his quest."

"Quest? I thought he was escorting you to Tyddewi and your granddaughter."

Vala's face became as colorless as her hair. "You must forget I used that word."

"Why? There is nothing ignoble about a princeling setting out upon a quest." She wished she had kept the sarcasm from her voice when the old woman bleached even paler. More gently, for Vala was not the source of her frustration, she added, "Especially if the quest is for an honorable reason."

"It is," said Tarran from behind her.

She turned and discovered he was standing so close that she could not see anything but his drenched tunic. It clung to his chest, emphasizing each plane. Muscular ripples teased her fingers to trace them. She should step back, but she could not move. She could barely breathe, and she wondered if he heard her heart banging against her chest like a smith's hammer.

Knowing she must say something before he realized how he overwhelmed her with his raw strength, she asked, "What sort of honorable quest have you set upon?"

"We seek a murderer. His name is Bradwr ap Glew."

"Who was slain?"

His voice remained steady as he said, "My wife, Addfwyn."

Chapter 4

Tarran waited for Elspeth to ask the questions he had heard too many times. How was his wife murdered? Where? Why? And what was he going to do to avenge her death? He had been pelted with those questions so many times he could answer them in order without pausing for thought. They were always asked the same way.

How?

Where?

Why?

What are you going to do to avenge her death?

He gave terse answers to the first three and pretended not to hear the last. Those who were part of his quest knew the answer to that final question. No one else. His plans for vengeance must not reach the ears of Addfwyn's murderer before Tarran had his opportunity to spill the cur's blood as hers had spilled when she was stabbed and left to die.

"I am sorry," Elspeth said softly.

He waited. The questions always came next.

"You must have loved her deeply to set aside your obligations to seek the person who stole her life," she went on. "I hope amidst your grief you have memories that bring you comfort."

He waited. She would certainly ask the questions now.

"Your quest is an honorable one," she continued. "I wish you luck in achieving its end." She turned to Vala. "You look very tired. You should be sitting. Let me help you."

Tarran stared as Elspeth put her hand under Vala's elbow and guided her to a bench. Was that it? He watched her help Vala sit, amazed that the hands that had swung the staff with such strength were gentle. His eyes traced Elspeth's profile. Her nose had a slight upward tilt at its end, something his mother had always said was a sign of impishness worthy of the fairy folk. Her mouth had that same slant, and he guessed she smiled often and easily, in spite of the number of scowls she had aimed in his direction.

But his gaze was drawn again and again to the lush, red curls swarming over the shoulders of her dark green gown before cascading down to her slender waist. It was a sight guaranteed to excite any man with a bit of life in him.

He looked away. He had no life left within him. His life had ended with Addfwyn's. Within him was only the dark, dank cold of vengeance not yet fulfilled. It had taken him almost two years to learn what he needed in order to obtain his revenge, and he would not toss that aside, not even for a chance to discover if Elspeth Braybrooke was as luscious as she appeared.

Forgive me, Addfwyn. He should not be thinking of another woman while his beloved wife's murderer lived. During the long months since he had stood by Addfwyn's grave and watched the dirt shoveled into it, he had not given any woman more than a cursory glance . . . until he had seen Elspeth Braybrooke.

"What have you heard on your journey?" asked Lord de la Rochelle from behind him.

Thankful that he had an excuse to tear his gaze from Elsepth, Tarran turned to their host. The Marcher lords had ceased being enemies of the Welsh more than two generations ago, but most Welshmen harbored rancor at how the

Normans had carved parts of Cymru up among them. De la
Rochelle's family was reputed to have claimed these lands
when William of Normandy came to subjugate Cymru as he
had the Saxon lands to the east where he was proclaimed
William the Conqueror.

"Nothing out of the ordinary," he answered. "Why?"

"Rumor says the King Henry has defeated Strongbow in
Ireland, but did not put him to death." De la Rochelle wore
a pensive expression.

Had the Marcher lord hoped Richard, Earl of Clare—a
brave man who had earned the name Strongbow—would
renounce his loyalty to King Henry? That would have led to
more bloodshed between the king and his Norman lieges
while the barons tried to seize as much of Ireland as they
could before the law reasserted itself. Had de la Rochelle
hoped to win lands in Ireland to go along with what his
family claimed in Aquitaine and in Cymru?

"King Henry is a just man, but he has never had patience
with those who do not come to heel," Tarran said, tilting
back his tankard.

"Or with threats."

"Threats?"

De la Rochelle lowered his voice. "You are Welsh. You
know the story of *Llech-lafar.*"

Tarran stared in astonishment. "The child's tale of Merlin's talking stone?"

"It is said that an outlander king who subjugates Wales
and goes to Ireland to fight someone with blood on his
hands will upon his return to Wales step on the stone and
die. He defeated Strongbow, who has the blood of the
whole Irish army on his hands. Now King Henry returns. If
he steps on *Llech-lafar,* it could mean the death of our
king."

Your king, he wanted to say, but did not. The Welsh had
given their allegiance to the Norman king.

"It is a child's tale," he said again. "If there was any truth to the old legends, you Normans would have been cast out of Cymru long ago."

De la Rochelle laughed and slapped him on the shoulder. "Well said. Come and have something to eat with that ale."

"As soon as I check on my man," he replied.

"Difyr will see that he is comfortable." The baron chuckled again. "She has many skills to make a man forget his injuries. Let her tend him while we enjoy more amusing old tales."

He did not answer quickly. He might not believe the myths that had arisen out of the mountain mists, but he had no intentions of joking about them with a Marcher lord.

"We have the whole night to enjoy your fine ale." Tarran took a drink. "And spin lies."

"The whole night? Don't you want to be with your lovely woman?"

He almost shouted, "Yes!"; then he realized de la Rochelle must be speaking about Elspeth Braybrooke. She was a beauty, but he was unsure if she was deranged or simply naïve.

Hearing a bellow, he looked over his shoulder to discover Kei and his cousin Gryn each holding one of Elspeth's arms. They were dragging her away from Iau. Did they think she would try to do him harm in de la Rochelle's hall? He saw her fury at being treated with such discourtesy.

He started to shout to the cousins to release her, but the baron laughed. "Your men are quite friendly with your woman, ap Llyr. It is said your Welsh women are eager to share their charms with many men."

He ignored the insult. It was meaningless. Elspeth was as Norman as de la Rochelle.

Before Tarran could order his men to release Elspeth, Gryn stumbled against Kei and both men fell against a

bench. It rocked before rising up toward Kei. He jumped
out of the way, but Gryn was not fast enough. The bench hit
him in the middle, and he reeled toward Elspeth. She
stepped out of the way, and he struck the wall before sliding down to the floor. She glanced at him and Kei with disdain and walked back to where Iau was being tended.

"Amazing woman," murmured de la Rochelle. "To be
pulled about like that would have left most of them screech-
ing like a soul being ripped from a body."

His stomach curdled like rotten milk. Why did even the
simplest, most common phrases remind him of Addfwyn's
death and his yet unsated hunger for revenge?

"You are lucky to have such a woman," the baron added.

"She is not my woman."

"No? Does she belong to one of your men?"

"No." He glanced at Kei who was helping his cousin to
his feet. Gryn was wobbling. The two of them looked half
drunk. Impossible, because they had not had time to drink
more than a tankard of ale. Was Elspeth's madness conta-
gious? "She has only recently joined us."

"Is that so?" De la Rochelle's eyes began to glisten with
undisguised lust. "Where did you meet her?"

Tarran cursed under his breath. *He* was not naïve, and he
should have guessed where the baron's questions were
headed. Saving Elspeth's life meant he had assumed the obligation of protecting her. He had failed to protect
Addfwyn. He would not fail again.

"I met her beyond your walls," he said, not wanting to
reveal more. De la Rochelle might claim that a woman discovered hanging from an arrow slit on his castle belonged
to him.

Tarran walked across the great hall to where Iau was
propped against a wall. He could see only Iau's outstretched
legs because Seith's girth blocked his view. Seith's back
was as stiff as if he were hefting a great burden. Stiff with

what? Anger? He heard a grumble and looked to his left to see Gryn leaning against the wall, his mouth twisted with rage. His men did not trust Elspeth. Why else would they have drawn her away from Iau? But they clearly had too much honor to do her injury, for they had released her.

Putting his hand on Seith's rigid shoulder, he edged forward to stand beside his friend. He raised a hand to halt Seith's question. He doubted he could have answered because his breath caught when he saw Elspeth kneeling next to Iau.

"You handled the staff well, milady," Iau said, admiration filling his voice.

"Thank you." Elspeth was checking the tight wrap around his wrist with a serenity that suggested she knew what she was doing. Balancing Iau's wrist on one palm, she said, "Difyr, when the strips of leather are dry, spread egg white over the bandaging. That will harden and protect his wrist while it heals."

"I have never heard of such a thing, milady." The young brunette was trying to hide her disbelief.

"It is a practice used in the Holy Land." Elspeth smiled. "I learned it from one who has traveled from there." Not giving Difyr a chance to ask another question, she went on. "I apologize for causing you damage, Iau ap Mil."

"You wished only to defend yourself. I would have done the same." Iau looked at Difyr, who was hovering close to him, a candid invitation in every motion as she let her breast brush against his arm too often to be accidental. "I cannot say I mind staying here while I heal, Difyr."

The brunette gave him a smile that was both shy and coy at the same time.

"You intend to remain here?" asked Elspeth. She drew her hand carefully from beneath his wrist as Difyr balanced it on a sling, which she tied around his shoulder.

Iau chuckled as he tickled the brunette beneath the chin.

"I would be a liability when I cannot draw my sword. It would be better if I stayed here instead of continuing on with Prince Tarran."

"You address him as prince?"

"He is one." Iau's brow rutted as he scowled. Because she questioned him, or because answering her required him to look away from Difyr, who was making no secret of how she would be happy to distract him from his pain? "We Welsh know the wisdom of having an heir when the sons born within marriage do not survive their sire. A very logical system. Don't you agree?" He smiled when his gaze shifted to Tarran. "Thank you for bringing me some ale to ease my anguish, milord."

Tarran held out the tankard to his man. He hid his irritation that Iau had taken that very moment to take note of him. Hearing Elspeth's reaction to Iau's pointed question would have been very interesting . . . and enlightening.

"It seems you are suffering very little pain with such attentive caretakers." The words he had intended to be a jest fell flat.

His men stared in astonishment. Since Addfwyn's death, he had not attempted even a weak joke. Why had he now? He wished he had left his mouth closed when his men looked away, embarrassed on his behalf.

There was no need, because the serving wench Difyr still looked only at Iau. He could not guess what Elspeth's expression was because she had her back to him. She came to her feet with the same grace he had seen her exhibit while using her quarterstaff.

"May I speak with you?" he asked.

She faced him, and he wondered if someone had struck him in the gut. He could not breathe as he met her gaze. Her eyes were the deep green of an evergreen tree, a rich color that suggested something hid in their shadows. Her wild, red curls hinted that she belonged in the wood when the leaves donned their brightest hues with the coming of winter.

"Most certainly, Prince Tarran," she answered with a coolness he had not heard her use before.

"Alone?"

If she was surprised by his question, he saw no sign on her face. "Shall we go to that empty table? There is something I wish to speak with you about as well."

"Really?" He offered his hand to her.

When she put her fingers on the top of his hand, he almost drew it back. Lightning seemed to erupt from where her fingers touched his. Not even his leather gloves could insulate him from the heat. Her fingers clenched on his much broader ones, and he was astonished by the strength of her grip. He was more amazed when she just as quickly released his hand and walked toward the table, then paused. She did not look back, although she clearly was waiting for him to catch up.

Curiosity riveted him as sharply as the lightning-fire had. She was hiding her face. Why? Did she want to keep him from discovering her response to his touch? He was tempted to tell her that she was trying to conceal what she had already divulged. Was she leading him toward an empty corner in hopes of seducing him as the wench was attempting to do with Iau?

Tarran swore silently. Had Elspeth struck him in the head with one of her flailing feet? That would be the easiest explanation why he seemed to be losing his mind. For two years, every thought had been of finding Bradwr ap Glew and making him rue killing Addfwyn. Now that he had set upon a course to do exactly that, his thoughts were being waylaid by this redheaded woman.

Red! How he hated that color! He needed to remember that each time he looked at Elspeth Braybrooke.

As soon as he had matched his steps to hers, she asked

with barely restrained ire, "How could you—a prince—allow Vala to ride for such a distance without rest?"

"She did not complain," he blurted, surprised at her question. He had assumed she wished to complain about his men.

"I am sure she did not, but *you* are the prince, not she. *You* are the one who should be solicitous of your retainers, whether healthy young warriors or an aged woman who has served you all your life. She is exhausted."

He started to answer, then realized he did not have one. She was right. Again he had become so focused on his own concerns that he had failed in his duty. He was obligated to protect Vala from the rigors of their journey. Instead of answering, he motioned for Elspeth to sit on the bench.

She did, and her eyes widened when he sat beside her.

"What do you have to say to me," she asked, "that you wish nobody else to be privy to?"

"Why do you ask that?"

"I can think of no other reason why you brought me here and now are sitting so close."

He could think of several. Those thoughts must have been on his face because she looked away as swiftly as his men had when he attempted that feeble jest. By St. David! What was wrong with him? Until he had seen her hanging from the arrow slit, his thoughts had not wavered. Now he had to struggle to keep them focused.

No, that was not true. They focused too well on this red-haired sprite. It was an effort not to stare at her lips as they formed each word. How would they taste beneath his? Was a Norman woman's kiss different from a Welshwoman's? He shoved aside those thoughts before he gave in to the yearning to find out.

"Why are you traveling alone?" he asked.

"I have found no one who wishes to go in the same direction I am."

"You are not witless. You know how many dangers await any traveler, especially a lone woman."

"I know." She smiled, but there was nothing warm about her expression. It reminded him of Heliwr's intense stare in the moment before he was cast off from Tarran's hand and sought his prey.

"But you are not frightened?"

"I am vigilant, Prince Tarran. There is a huge difference." She raised a single eyebrow. "As your men have come to see."

He had no interest in listening to her complain about his men. He would deal with them later. For now . . . "Even vigilance is no shield against attack."

"You are telling me what I already know. As you can see, I have reached Castell Glyn Niwl safely."

"From where?"

Her eyes lowered. She had faced him boldly until now. Why was she reluctant to say where she had journeyed from? Someone might be pursuing her, and she wanted to leave no hint of where she had traveled. She might have run away from whatever Norman estate had been her home. She might be insane.

No, he could not believe the last. She reacted with a clear confidence that could not belong to a clouded mind.

"Where are you going?" she asked.

"We travel south toward Tyddewi. If you are traveling in that direction too, I could use your help."

She looked past him, then back to him. He wanted to turn around to find out what she had been looking at. He did not. His men were gathered in the great hall, and de la Rochelle was no enemy.

Neither had been Bradwr ap Glew.

"Why do you ask my help when your men have made it clear they wish I were anywhere but where they are?" she asked.

"I am thinking of Vala. I know she would be glad for another woman's company on our journey."

"You are kind to consider her needs."

"I owe her a great debt. If you wish to travel with us, we leave at sunrise."

She frowned. "I thought you wished to put Vala's needs before your own."

"I do, but—"

She wagged a finger at him as if he were a stripling. "You speak of caring about her with one breath, then speak of an early start with your next. She needs to rest. Not just tonight, but for a day or two. Can you grant her that?"

He glanced at where Vala had her head propped on her palm as she leaned her elbow on the table. She swayed, fighting sleep. She would not ask him to linger at the castle.

"Yes, I can grant her that," he said quietly.

Elspeth smiled, and he fought back the thrill coursing through him. Her smile could make a man feel like a hero, even when he was unworthy. "Thank you for considering my words," she replied. "I will consider your offer and let you know what I have decided before you take your leave, Prince Tarran."

He wanted to hear why she was delaying giving him her answer, but he had no chance.

De la Rochelle strode up to them, saying, "Ah, here you are."

Tarran thought he heard a relieved sigh from Elspeth, but he could not be certain because the baron was greeting her warmly again. De la Rochelle held out his hand to her. If she hesitated putting hers on it, Tarran saw no sign.

The baron bowed over it. "Do come and join me at my table. It is too seldom that I have such a charming guest."

Tarran stood as Elspeth did. She smiled as their host led her toward the raised table. There was excitement in her steps. Had she decided she would rather be with the

Marcher lord than with Tarran? De la Rochelle was a Norman as she was, so maybe she was more comfortable with him.

The baron's single glance at Elspeth as he sat her beside his magnificently carved chair told Tarran that comfort was not what de la Rochelle planned for her. Hearing her long-winded answer to some question the baron must have asked, Tarran climbed the steps to the raised table. He swung one leg, then the other, over the bench to her left. He watched as the baron laughed heartily at something that had been scarcely amusing. The covetous look in de la Rochelle's eyes was unmistakable, but Elspeth seemed either unaware of it or welcomed it.

He realized he was again mistaken because, when the baron put his hand on her arm, she drew away as quickly as she had when her fingers were on his own hand. Her smile remained, but became brittle like cliffs pounded too long by the sea. He wondered how long before it cracked.

"You should save your praise for Vala, milord," Elspeth said. "I doubt many women of her years would be brave enough to ride such a distance to help her granddaughter during the birth of her first child."

Vala's granddaughter was with child? Tarran had heard nothing about that. Vala seldom spoke of feminine matters, but a great-grandchild was something quite different. His brow lowered. Was Elspeth spinning a tale for the Marcher lord?

He looked toward the old woman who was watching them. Her head's slight motion toward Elspeth and de la Rochelle might as well have been a shouted order because he recognized Vala's expression. It was the one she had worn when she had scolded him during his childhood for neglecting his duty. He had not seen it since Addfwyn's death.

He swore silently again. He did not need Vala's admonition to know de la Rochelle's intentions toward Elspeth.

"Vala has never shrunk from her obligations," he said.

De la Rochelle shot him a furious look for intruding, but he pretended not to see it.

"The women of my family's line have shown they are worthy of being lauded in song." Tarran hated babbling, and for the first time since she had opened her eyes while lying in his arms, he wished Elspeth would say something.

As if he had spoken his thoughts, Elspeth added, "It seems every family in Wales has stories of valor. I have heard a few put to music by skilled minstrels, and they are splendid." She gave a laugh that suggested she had not a single worthwhile thought in her head, something Tarran knew only a fool would believe. "And there are many wondrous legends that seem connected to the world around us." She smiled at Tarran, and again he felt as if someone had knocked his breath out of him with a single blow. "Which is your favorite, Prince Tarran?"

"The story of Prince Pwyll pretending for a year that he was Death, so he could defeat's Death's greatest enemy."

"I have not heard that story," she said, turning slightly from the baron.

De la Rochelle's voice became a low rumble. "I would be glad to tell it to you while we eat."

"While we eat?"

"Elspeth," Tarran said, "I believe you mentioned you wanted to be certain Vala eats as she should after our long day of traveling."

The baron frowned. "A servant can—"

"Thank you for reminding me, Prince Tarran." Her voice was tranquil. "If you will excuse me, I shall check on Vala. You will excuse me, won't you, milord?"

"Yes," the baron replied in a tone that suggested he had

no idea why she would wish to exchange his company for that of an old woman.

She stood and bent down as if to check her shoe. So softly Tarran knew only his ears could catch her words, she whispered, "Thank you."

"My pleasure," he replied as quietly.

Elspeth almost laughed at Prince Tarran's wry answer. She squeezed Tarran's arm with a motion as simple as when she congratulated one of her students on a well-placed blow. But there was nothing simple about the sensation that rushed through her, as powerful as a storm wind and as frothy as the foam on beaten eggs. It made her want to shiver and giggle at the same time.

When his brow lowered, she released his arm and went to where Vala sat at an otherwise empty table. Many of the hall's residents were already stretching out by the hearths to sleep until the sun rose.

She should not have touched Prince Tarran. Hadn't she discovered how unsettling his touch was? He was no friend. He was a powerful man who never smiled. Even so, the brush of his fingers against hers—or hers against him—exploded a thunderous pulse inside her.

It might be simpler to deal with her reaction to *his* fingers if she was not trying to keep Lord de la Rochelle's away from her. The baron had acted as if his life depended on touching her. She had avoided his eyes because they suggested their conversation should be far more private. Did he treat every woman who entered Castell Glyn Niwl that way?

By St. Jude! If Prince Tarran had not interfered, she could have slipped into the castle and out without encountering the lecherous baron. And why had he failed to tell her he was a prince? Was he ashamed of being the son of a bastard? That made no sense, for he was acknowledged as a prince by his countrymen.

Elspeth's hope that she had herself under control was banished when, as she sat next to Vala, the old woman said, "You are shivering, child. Is something amiss?"

"I am fine." She was glad she could turn her back on the raised table. Watching her mother suffer a lord's lecherous hands had been horrible. Having the baron paw her with the same eagerness sickened her even more. How had her mother endured it?

Vala shook her head. "You are ashen. Even when you were lying in Prince Tarran's arms by the wall, you had more color."

"I was furious then!"

"You are furious now. You are shaking as you did when you were on your feet and confronting Prince Tarran."

Elspeth smiled sadly. "Thank you for your concern, Vala, but I am fine. Or, to be more honest, I will be once I leave Castell Glyn Niwl."

"A lovely girl like you will draw attention everywhere you go."

Not when I return to St. Jude's Abbey, she wanted to reply. She had always loved her life there, but, until she had left, she had not appreciated how much freedom she had within its walls.

When Elspeth did not answer, Vala pushed a wooden trencher toward her. On it were large pieces of bread and fragments of overcooked fish.

"I learned many years ago that any problem seems less insurmountable when one has food in one's stomach," the old woman said with a gentle smile.

Elspeth picked up a chunk of bread. Breaking off a handful, she nibbled at it. The bread was fresh and delicious. She took care not to wolf it down. Until her first bite, she had not realized how hungry she was. The food she had taken from Cardigan had run out yesterday.

"May I give you a warning, child?" Vala asked.

She nodded, her mouth filled with the heavy bread.

"Iau ap Mil is an even-tempered man, as is his brother Seith. However, neither Kei ap Pebin nor his cousin Gryn ap Dwnn could be described that way. They are displeased with the injuries you caused their comrade."

"I know." She reached for a tankard and washed the bread down with ale. "Prince Tarran has already told me as much."

Vala smiled, obviously satisfied.

"Were you," Elspeth asked in astonishment, "telling me that to find out what he had said?"

"I knew what he would say, but it is good to have words confirm it." She paused, then asked, "What does he have to say about how you sent two of his best men crashing into that bench?"

Elspeth tore off another handful of bread. "Nothing."

"Nothing?"

"He did not mention it." She released the bread when she saw it squeezing between the fingers of her clenched fist. When Prince Tarran had asked to speak to her alone, she had been certain he wished to discover how she had freed herself from his two men with such alacrity. Had he failed to notice, while talking with Lord de la Rochelle, that she had used the skills Nariko had taught her? With a quick snap against one man's hand and a twist, she had sent one into the other. In their efforts to keep from falling, they had bumped the bench, sending it up toward them. She had not laughed because she had been too vexed by their assumption that they could drag her about the hall.

"Odd," murmured Vala.

"I did not expect him to apologize for their crude behavior."

"The prince must not have seen how you came to be free of Gryn and Kei's grips."

"Oh." She was unsure, for once, what else to say.

"Have you accepted his offer to travel with us?"

Elspeth stared at the old woman. "How do you know that he asked me to go with you?"

Vala picked up some fish and sniffed it. "I am familiar enough with his expressions to know what he is thinking." She nibbled on the fish.

"Does he ever smile?"

The old woman lowered the food to the trencher, her face falling into sorrow. "He used to smile often and easily." She sighed. "I wish he would again. Maybe you can convince him to, because the rest of us have failed since Lady Addfwyn's death."

She did not answer. She could not take on that duty, because it might get in the way of the obligation she had to the queen. Prince Tarran's invitation to travel with his men and Vala would not matter if the wisewoman Rhan's information sent her in another direction to find *Llech-lafar*. It would be simpler if her path was not the same as his, so she did not have to spend more time with Prince Tarran and his quick-tempered men. Yet, she could not dampen the hope that they could journey together. Then she could relish the flush of warmth coming from his fingertips.

What was she thinking? Her enjoyment of Prince Tarran's intriguing caresses could not outweigh her responsibility to Queen Eleanor. She needed to find that accursed stone and return to St. Jude's Abbey before she did something completely witless.

Chapter 5

Elspeth stepped through the chilly shadows by the arched gate into the long, narrow courtyard. It was not far from the gatehouse. The ground was bare, and she could see where many feet had crossed it during the muddy season.

On the other side of the wall, two men were talking. She could not discern their words, and she did not strain her ears. She had seen the guards walking down the tower stairs from the upper room of the gatehouse where the portcullis was raised and lowered. Unless one of them knew where *Llech-lafar* could be found, nothing they had to say would interest her.

Odors from the garderobe drifted from beyond the keep. The kitchen offered more appetizing smells, and she guessed breakfast would soon be served.

That was why she had chosen the early hour for practice. She did not want to pretend not to be bothered by their host's hands, which seemed to multiply whenever he came close. If her reflexes had not been honed at the Abbey, she doubted she could have parried each bold finger.

Leaning the stilts against the wall, she carried her quarterstaff to the center of the courtyard. The morning sun, just rising above the mountains to the east, had barely warmed the air. She shivered, although it was not as cold as it had been several weeks ago when she crossed Offa's Dyke into Wales. The sun soon would disappear again into the clouds that crouched across the sky like a beast about to pounce; she needed to practice before it began raining. She removed the metal tip from each end. She hated having them on her staff, but the abbess had been insistent. No sister went beyond the Abbey's walls without a way to defend herself.

"Even to the death?" Elspeth had asked.

The abbess had nodded, shocking her.

"But I can halt any enemy by knocking him senseless or disabling him in some other way. I do not need to kill him."

"That is true if you face a single enemy. If you face more than one, you may find that a wounding blow is not enough."

Elspeth had argued until the abbess reminded her about the vow of obedience she had taken upon her arrival at the Abbey. The abbess would not change her mind. Elspeth, who knew exactly how much force she needed to render a man unconscious, must be willing to kill in order to save the king's life.

As she had left that meeting with the abbess, nausea twisted through her stomach. The feeling returned as she tossed the metal tips next to the stilts.

She would not be fooled as she had been by the queen's man. Even so, it seemed strange not to bow to acknowledge her opponent. It had become a habit as comfortable as well-worn shoes, even when her opponent would be a pole used by Lord de la Rochelle's men while training with lances. Atop the pole, a sack served as a head. Someone had drawn two eyes on it. Although it was taller than most men, it offered her a focus for her practice.

She gripped the quarterstaff, one hand over and one under, and balanced lightly on her feet. The most important skill she had learned was gauging her opponent, watching for strengths and taking advantage of weaknesses.

Feeling foolish, but needing the solace of habit, she bowed from the waist to her opponent. The round eyes on the sack stared sightlessly back at her.

"You are taller than me," she said as she circled the pole, talking aloud as if her students watched. "Your staff would be much longer than mine, but I can jab my staff beneath yours."

She lunged forward, shoving one end of the stick toward the pole.

"But you would counter before I could strike your knees." She twisted her staff upward at a sharp angle. "I must keep your staff from coming down on my head or shoulders. I must be quick. Otherwise, your longer reach and greater height will tip the balance of our battle against me."

Sliding her hands along the staff, she swung it up and stepped forward. The staff struck the stuffed head just below its chin. The fabric tore, and feathers exploded out.

She whirled away. Spinning her staff over her head and down in front of her, she halted when she saw two men by the low gate. A trio of other men were trying to peer past them.

"Impressive," Lord de la Rochelle said as he and Prince Tarran walked toward her. "Don't you think so, ap Llyr?"

She was not surprised that the baron did not address Prince Tarran by his royal title. No Marcher lord would accept that Welsh tradition, for to do so could question their right to rule in Wales. She saw the glances exchanged by the baron's own servants, clearly bothered by how Lord de la Rochelle spoke to him.

"Yes, very impressive," Prince Tarran replied. "She is quite skilled against a pole."

"As she was against your man."

"A lucky hit." He turned his back on her, dismissing her. "Iau's injuries came when he tried to dodge her wild swing and fell from his saddle."

"So she did not strike him?"

"No."

Elspeth's nails dug into the staff. Prince Tarran was lying. She silenced her retort. He must have some reason for concocting the story for the baron. So far, neither man had done anything to keep her from accomplishing her task. She must not become embroiled in any alliances or disputes between them.

Lord de la Rochelle walked past Prince Tarran and smiled broadly. "It is a unique sight to discover a woman wielding a staff with skill."

"I have practiced long, milord," she replied coolly. If he came any closer, she could . . . Her fingers tightened on the staff. She forced them to relax. She could not strike the baron when her only provocation was his lack of chivalry.

"So it would appear." He reached for her staff. "Maybe you would show me that last move you made."

She leaned her staff on the ground, keeping him from touching it. She smiled as Prince Tarran faced her, his hands clasped behind his back.

"You would find my quarterstaff useless, milord," she said, "because it is too short for a man of your stature. I am sure, when you are in the company of a woman, you are accustomed to having the use of a much longer staff."

The baron laughed heartily. "You need to watch yourself with this one, ap Llyr. She is accurate when she takes the measure of a man." Bowing his head, he said, "When you are finished here, I would enjoy sharing breakfast with you. Come to the great hall, and someone will bring you to me."

Elspeth nodded, even though she did not intend to share breakfast—or anything else—with him. Once the men had departed, she could continue her practice until everyone was eating. Then she would sneak into Rhan's chamber.

Prince Tarran did not follow as the baron walked away.

He stood in silence, his hands locked behind him. She could almost believe he had no more life than the sack at the top of the pole.

If he was going to say nothing, she would speak. "Why did you lie to Lord de la Rochelle?"

He tapped her staff. "You fool! You really have no idea, do you?"

"If it gives you and your men solace to believe my skills did not best Iau ap Mil, then believe the tales you have created. I know the Welsh love storytelling, but I did not guess that included lying about what both of us know to be the truth. I—"

He grabbed the staff on either side of her hands. He raised it with one quick motion beneath her chin. Putting his face close to hers, he growled, "Be silent, woman!"

She tried to shove the staff down, but he was too strong. She took a step back. He matched it. She edged away again. He kept the distance between them the same. She yelped when she bumped the pole. He did not let her slide either to the right or left.

She lifted her chin and met his stare that was no longer cool. It was on fire with frustration.

"You asked *me* a question," she said, forcing out each word past her clenched teeth.

"A question that required nothing more than a yes or no."

"I gave you the answer I thought was appropriate. If you don't agree, you can—" She choked as he pressed the staff against her throat in a silent warning.

He put his nose almost against hers so she could see nothing but the intensity in his eyes. "Heed me well, Elspeth Braybrooke, when I tell you to guard yourself with our host. He has been asking questions."

"About what?"

"You."

"I guessed that." She suspected her own eyes were now ablaze with frustration. Maybe she did chatter too much, but Prince Tarran's answers were too terse, always leaving her with more questions. "What does he ask about me?"

He lowered the staff a hand's breadth below her vulnerable throat. "He wants to know if we are lovers."

She laughed. Even as she did and he drew back, scowling, she was certain she would come to regret it, but she could not halt herself. If anyone else suggested that Elspeth Braybrooke, the daughter of itinerant performers and now a lady of St. Jude's Abbey, might share the bed of a Welsh prince, she would have called that person mad.

"Forgive me, Prince Tarran. I should not have laughed, but the very idea—"

His brow lowered farther.

She needed to try something else. "*You* must admit that such an idea is ridiculous."

He leaned toward her again. "Is it?"

"Yes! We met only yesterday, and you have been unable to hide your contempt for everything I do and say. At every opportunity, you turn your back on me, brushing me aside as you would a pest. You may have asked me to travel with you, but only because you are concerned about Vala. Not because you care—"

"Be silent!" He stepped closer, and she pressed back against the pole once more.

She hardly dared to breathe. Any motion would brush his hard chest. His strong legs were against her skirt, and she was abruptly aware of every male angle along him. "But you asked me—"

His mouth clamped over hers, driving her head back against the pole. There was nothing gentle about his kiss. She tried to turn her head away, not wanting to be overwhelmed by his anger. He jerked the staff out of her hands and tossed it aside.

Her hands free, she shoved against his chest and kicked his shin. When he roared out a curse, his hold on her lessened enough for her to slide from between him and the pole. She ran toward her staff. He followed and grabbed her arm. He spun her to face him.

Her motion was instinctive. Bending her knees, she pulled her arm sharply against his thumb. He stared in disbelief as she broke his hold and grabbed his shoulders. She gave a half turn. He flipped over her hip and hit the ground. He groaned, closed his eyes and did not move.

Shock struck her at the same moment. She had just sent a prince flying. Already she had hurt one of his men. Had she injured him, too?

"Prince Tarran?" she asked, kneeling beside him.

He opened his eyes.

"Are you all right?"

"How did you learn to do that?" he murmured.

"The thumb is far weaker than the other fingers. Putting pressure against it helps break a stronger hold, so one can escape."

He shook his head and winced. "Can you have some sympathy for my aching skull and answer my questions simply?"

"Yes."

"Good." He paused, then rose on one elbow. "Why did you attack me? Have I done something to infuriate you?"

"You have done everything possible to infuriate me."

"By trying to help you ward off de la Rochelle's advances." He sagged to the ground, shutting his eyes. "Maybe you welcome his attentions."

"No, you were right about the baron. What you are wrong about is that I need you to protect me."

"So you think you can stand alone against any foe."

"I have thus far."

He opened one eye and somehow managed to glare at

her. "What enemies have you faced? Have you battled only with your own good sense that tells you not to try to climb into a castle through an arrow slit?"

"I am not going to argue about *that* again. Are you hurt?"

He closed his eyes again. "If this is the way you treat your allies, I will make every effort not to become one of your enemies. Why did you attack me?"

She sat back on her heels. "I did not want you to kiss me."

"You could have told me."

"You did not give me a chance to say more than two words."

"It takes only one word to say no."

"But you kept interrupting me."

"I did?"

"Are you sure you are all right?" She put her hand on his forehead to tilt his face toward her. If his eyes were unfocused, he could be suffering from a concussion.

He pushed her hand away and stood. "I am fine." He pulled her to her feet, but did not release her. "De la Rochelle will not be so forgiving if you toss him to the ground." He winced as if even speaking pained him.

She guessed it did, because she had taken such falls herself while training. Had his head been worse than bruised? She reached up to run her fingers along the back of his scalp.

He grasped her hand, forcing it away. "What are you doing now?"

"I am only trying to examine your hard head." She gave him a scowl as fearsome as his own. "Maybe I should be more concerned about the ground being broken by your head."

"Maybe you should be more concerned about de la Rochelle."

"Stop worrying. I can take care of myself."

"Can you?" He twisted her wrist gently and bent toward it. His breath was warm, but sent shivers up her skin, as he asked, "Can you take care of yourself if he does this?"

He pressed his mouth to the inside of her wrist. The sensitive skin simmered beneath his lips. Her other hand clenched onto her skirt as she tried to dampen the quivers surging through her.

Raising his head slightly, he whispered, "Can you?"

"Take care of myself?" Her voice shook, but she added, "Yes."

"Even if he does this?"

Her answer vanished into a soft moan when he ran the tip of his tongue along her neck, burying his face in her hair. She gripped fabric more tightly and felt his firm chest beneath her fingers. She was no longer clutching her skirt. She was holding on to the front of his tunic as powerful sensations battered her.

His breath burned against her ear, and she shut her eyes, savoring its heat.

"Can you?" he whispered.

"Yes." Her voice was no louder than his. "Yes, I can take care of myself."

"Are you sure?"

"I think I am."

"Doubt?" There was a hint of amusement in his voice that she had never heard. "So tell me, can you take care of yourself if he does this?"

He captured her lips, but this time his mouth was gentle. It overwhelmed her, sending every sense reeling as if she had been knocked off her feet. His fingers splayed across her cheeks, combing up into her hair. He tilted her head back as he deepened the kiss until she was gasping against his mouth. When his tongue brushed across her lips, she could not imagine denying him the inner secrets of her mouth or anything else he wanted. It slipped into her mouth, and she curved her hand around his nape.

He drew back, but she did not. If she moved even an eyelash, the splendor might vanish. Beneath her fingertips, fine hairs teased her to explore farther. His breathing was slow and deep as his chest brushed her, but hers was as rapid as if she had carried *Llech-lafar* the length of Wales.

Llech-lafar! Elspeth lowered her arms and stepped away, turning to look at the pole where torn fabric fluttered. From the corner of her eye, she saw his hand reach toward her, then draw back.

"Thank you for your concern, Prince Tarran." She almost choked on his title. He was a prince. She should not be kissing a prince, for so many reasons that she could not begin to count them. The most important was that her only claim on the title of lady came from her connection to St. Jude's Abbey. "I assure you that I am quite capable of taking care of myself with Lord de la Rochelle." *It is you I am not sure I am capable of taking care of myself with.*

"If you are certain . . . "

"I am."

"Then it appears that I have intruded on your practice long enough." He bowed his head and walked through the arch.

She reached for her staff, then froze when she saw how her fingers trembled. After scooping up her staff, she grabbed the stilts. She held the three staffs to her chest, but even her years of training could not slow her frantic heartbeat as she fought to keep from calling Prince Tarran back.

Chapter 6

Tarran was pulling on his left boot when Seith ap Mil stamped into the room where they had slept last night. De la Rochelle had been a generous host to offer them a private chamber instead of having them sleep in the great hall. The room was the best they had used since leaving Castel Gwalch Glas. In addition to a bed with a canopy to keep away any mice and bugs falling from the ceiling, there had been several freshly filled straw pallets for his men. The aroma of dried grass and herbs sweetened the room and drifted about on the breeze blowing in along with rain at the sole window. The sill was so deep the rain puddled there instead of falling to the floor.

If he had been traveling only with Heliwr, he would have found a way to protect the hawk from the storm and ridden south at dawn. He did not like any delay, but they were not far from Tyddewi. It would not take long to go from the cathedral city to the southern shore where they could obtain a boat to Lundy Island. There they would meet the new fleet preparing to sail west, and he might discover exactly where Bradwr ap Glew was.

As his friend walked toward him, drawing Tarran's attention back to him, Seith's boots woke more scents from the rushes scattered on the floor. He was so indignant that both his chins were bouncing on each step.

Girding himself for an outburst, because Seith never attempted to hide his feelings, Tarran put his foot on the floor. He tried to jam his toes into the boot past where the buckle had rusted closed.

"Have you lost the rest of your mind?" Seith demanded.

"I was not aware that I had lost any of it." He stood and tried to wiggle his toes forward a bit more.

"By St. David's front tooth, Tarran! You know you have not been yourself since Addfwyn died. We have understood your grief. We have pledged to help you find Bradwr ap Glew, even if we have to sail beyond the edges of the horizon where no man may return again."

"I know what you have vowed! I remember it every hour of every day, whether I am awake or I suffer from yet another of the nightmares that stalk me."

"Forgive me." Some of Seith's bluster fell away.

Tarran finally got his foot situated in the boot. "I hope you are here to tell me that your brother is doing well."

"Yes, the wrappings around his arm seem to be offering much protection. He tells me the lass put egg whites on the leather to make it stiffer."

"Elspeth Braybrooke suggested—"

Seith spat a curse. "She is not as she seems. She has many unexpected skills and odd bits of knowledge."

"True, and we should be grateful she could help your brother."

"After injuring him."

"The broken wrist was his fault for not staying atop his horse."

Seith nodded. "Whatever else Elspeth Braybrooke is, she is deadly serious about something she never mentions."

"True," he said again. "But what?"

"*That* is the question, isn't it?" He lowered his voice,

even though there was nobody else in the room. "Milord, she is a *Sais*. Like other outlanders, so she must be here for a reason. Why has she said nothing of it?"

"Seith, spit it out. You are not disturbed by one Norman woman traveling through Cymru. What is really bothering you?"

His friend walked toward the window and leaned on the deep sill. "I would not have believed it if I had not seen it with my own eyes."

"What?"

"How she sent both Kei and Gryn to their knees with no weapon other than her hands."

"You are jesting."

"I am not. She escaped their holds on her with ease." As Seith explained, flinging his hands about while he tried to show what Elspeth had done, Tarran listened. What Seith was saying sounded unbelievable, but Tarran knew every word was true. His friend's voice faded into silence as he crossed the room to where Tarran sat.

"You do not act surprised," Seith said.

"I am familiar with her ability to throw a man off his feet." He rubbed the back of his head.

"She did the same to you?"

"Yes, and it was quite a shock."

Seith choked on an obscenity, then demanded, "How could that be? You are Prince Tarran. You are a great warrior." His face crumpled. "Milord, forgive me for not telling you earlier about what happened. I had not realized you had not seen what she did."

"There is no need for apologies. If I had been prepared for what she could do, I might have injured her while attempting to halt her. And she will not be able to astound us with her tricks again." He stood. "And who knows? We may need her skills on our way to Tyddewi."

Seith's hand grasped the hilt of his sword. "By the vow

I swore to you, I pledge that I will die before I allow a woman to defend us."

"I am not asking for you to step aside."

"Good," came an answer from beside the door.

Tarran recognized Kei's voice. Looking toward the door, he saw Kei's cousin there as well. The two seldom were separated, save for when one or the other found a woman to entertain him. Kei had been fostered at his cousin's keep, and Gryn depended on him as he would an older brother.

"Maybe," Kei went on as he came into the room, "she is a sign that our luck is changing."

"An odd statement from a man she bested with such ease," Seith grumbled.

"I can set aside my shame in order to see Bradwr ap Glew pay for his." Kei raised his chin, looking far older than his seventeen years. "Can you, Seith ap Mil?"

"It is not your brother she maimed. You are bemused by her because she is pretty."

Gryn slapped both men on the shoulder. "So we all have noticed."

"Pretty women cause trouble." Seith's tone became even grimmer.

"That is true," Tarran said.

"She has already hurt my brother and you."

Kei and Gryn began asking questions about how Elspeth had injured him and arguing over which one would have the honor of teaching the wench that doing damage to a prince had vile consequences. Tarran waved them both to silence.

They obeyed, but Seith did not. "Yet, you asked her to travel with us."

"Vala will be glad to have another woman with us," Tarran said.

"You could leave her here."

Kei muttered, "She was willing to climb in. She will be just as ready to risk her neck climbing out."

"And I will not," Tarran said sternly, "have another innocent woman die because I was not willing to assume the duty of watching over her."

"She is not Lady Addfwyn, and—"

"Seith, there will be no more discussion on this matter."

His man nodded reluctantly. When Tarran glanced at the cousins, they also nodded. He considered asking them to swear to help him keep Elspeth safe, but they would see that request as an affront to their honor. The three men had pledged to follow him and do whatever they must to help him slay Bradwr ap Glew in retribution for Addfwyn's death. If that now included helping him watch over Elspeth, they would agree.

While his men began to talk about gossip they had heard in the castle, Tarran walked to the room's window. He looked through the rain to discover he had a view of the courtyard where Elspeth had been practicing. He should have left at sunrise. Had he delayed because of Vala or because he had not received an answer from Elspeth about traveling with them? He despised the pleasure that erupted within him each time he saw her. She looked nothing like his beloved Addfwyn, and she was prickly and sharp spoken. Addfwyn had been calm and possessed a quiet humor. Yet, Elspeth was the first woman to stir him since he had wed Addfwyn, for she had the same understanding of duty and obligation as he did.

As rain swept in, striking his face, he told himself that he had been stupid to kiss her, even to stop her babbling. That one sample had honed his need for more. Another woman might have been frightened by his strong emotions or by his warnings about de la Rochelle. She had held her own . . . and then she had held on to him, reminding him of what he had set aside by Addfwyn's grave.

Forgetting what it was like to have a woman in his arms had made everything simpler. He wished he could forget again. As the image of Elspeth's face, softened with desire, formed in his mind, he hid his own in his hands. How could he forget *that*?

Chapter 7

The great hall was brightly lit with lamps in every niche along the walls. Such displays seemed out of place during Lent, but nobody acted as if anything was amiss. The stone floor was slick where water had been tracked into the large chamber. Smoke clung, close and smothering, held within the hall by the storm.

At the raised table, Elspeth sat between Lord de la Rochelle and Prince Tarran. She would have preferred to join Vala at one of the tables below, but the baron had been insistent. She did not want to infuriate him by refusing. Keeping strong emotions at bay seemed the sanest course.

Prince Tarran must have come to the same conclusion. Nothing he said or did suggested anything had happened in the courtyard, but when she had glanced at him, she had seen unbanked fires in his eyes. Could he have been moved too, by their kisses?

She had not looked at him again. If she saw those powerful passions, she doubted she could maintain her fragile hold on her composure. She had been thwarted during the afternoon to get into the chamber where Rhan the wise-woman was recovering. She could have slipped into the room on her first attempt if she had not let thoughts of the Welsh prince's kisses distract her, causing her to fail to no-

tice a woman standing along the corridor. That woman had
ordered her from the tower.

She wished she had reason to be kept away from Lord de
la Rochelle, who continued his attempts to seduce her. Each
time she pushed his hands aside, he seemed to see that as a
dare to touch her again. She fingered the haft of her knife,
then drew her hand away before she could be tempted to
drive it into the baron. Lord de la Rochelle's fingers groped
along her leg. She slapped them, and he grinned. Maybe she
should mention she was a sister at St. Jude's Abbey. She
was unsure if even that fact would halt him.

Wishing she had an excuse to leave the table, she
watched the three entertainers. Hardly anyone else was paying attention to them, she realized, when the juggler, the
older of the two men, dropped a ball, and nobody groaned
or even cheered or laughed. Had her parents' hard work
been ignored like this? She never had watched people who
came to their performances. She always had been fascinated, enjoying the moments when her father or mother
presented a new trick after months of practice. The magic
of what they could do, even when she learned the skill herself, never dimmed.

"You are quiet this evening," Lord de la Rochelle said. "I
trust nothing is amiss."

Yes, she wanted to shout. *There is a person within your
walls who might know the answer to where I can find*
Llech-lafar, *and I am being prevented from speaking with
her.* She smiled as she had all evening, even as bile burned
bitterly in her throat.

"No." She grimaced when the juggler dropped another
ball and ran to retrieve it.

"If their ineptitude annoys you, say so, and I will send
them from the hall." He put his hand on her knee as he had
several times since the meal had begun.

She lifted his hand away as she had several times already, each time hoping he would tire of the disgusting sport.

"No, sending them away is not necessary." She could not imagine being the reason that the entertainers were thrown out into the stormy night. She guessed the older man and woman were husband and wife while the younger man was their son. If her parents were alive and she still traveled with them, it could have been her family performing at the castle.

"Maybe you would prefer a story," the baron said.

"Do you have a bard here?"

Lord de la Rochelle whistled. In a far corner, a hooded man stood. He was one of the men who had been singing when she had first entered the hall. The other man was not to be seen. Maybe one waited upon the baron's favor while the other slept or ate. The lights from the many lamps glittered off the metal on the man's belt and from a pendant that dropped down his robe the color of porridge. For a moment she thought it was a crucifix, and she wondered if he was a wandering friar. Then she realized it was a round stone or bauble. The man stuffed it beneath his cassock as he came forward and bowed.

"We wish a story," the baron said.

"Which one?" The hooded man's voice was even and pleasurable, just as a poet's should be.

Lord de la Rochelle picked up a fish from the trencher and tore it in half. With a smile, he asked, "Ap Llyr, can you think of a better story than the one of *Llech-lafar*?"

Elspeth swallowed her gasp as she clutched the table. Why was the baron mentioning the legendary stone? She forced herself to take a deep breath. Had her face lost all color? It felt icy cold.

She must not surrender to panic. She should expect the name of the accursed rock to be on many lips in Wales. Anyone who knew the tale could not mistake that the prophesied time of Merlin's curse on an outlander king seemed to be their own.

She released her stale breath and raised her head to discover the hooded man looking at her. Or she assumed he was, because he had not lowered his hood. Knowing she must say something, she asked, "What about the tale of Pwyll who took Death's place to slay his enemy?"

"Not his enemy." With a single deep drink, Tarran emptied his tankard. "He slew Death's greatest enemy."

Lord de la Rochelle shook his head. "A dreary tale, as too many Welsh myths are." He waved away the storyteller. "I would rather watch these incompetent performers than listen to a dismal tale. Do you believe there is more to *Llech-lafar* than legend? You called it a child's tale, but do you believe its curse can come true?"

She started to reply, then realized the baron was addressing Prince Tarran. She hoped the two men would pay her no further attention during the meal. She had been warned. As word spread that King Henry was planning to return to Wales from Ireland, the tale of *Llech-lafar* would be repeated often. Nobody must connect her quest with that story.

Looking past the three entertainers who were preparing for the next part of their performance, she saw Prince Tarran's companions sitting near one of the hearths. Vala's face was long with fatigue and worry. Elspeth had hoped Vala would find some sleep during the rainy afternoon, but when Elspeth returned from her foiled attempts to reach the castle's wisewoman, Vala had engaged her in conversation. No hints from Elspeth had encouraged the old woman to rest.

"And now," Lord de la Rochelle said with a roar of laughter as his hand slid up her thigh, "other fools are planning to join the ships sailing west from Lundy Island to the colonies that may not even exist."

She pushed his hand away, and he laughed again.

Prince Tarran replied, "There are many who believe Prince Madoc reached a distant land far out in the ocean."

"Another Welsh legend." The baron motioned for both his and Prince Tarran's tankards to be refilled. "There is nothing beyond Ireland except a few islands where outlawed Norsemen settled after being cast out of their own lands."

"Who is Prince Madoc?" Elspeth asked.

She had expected Prince Tarran to answer, but the baron said, "He is the newest Welsh myth. It is said he sailed the western sea until he found a land inhabited by a gentle race. That is the story he told in an effort to persuade fools to follow him on another voyage west last year. Now others gather on Lundy Island. They will sail into oblivion at the edge of the sea. Prince Madoc was probably killed by his half brothers to keep him from claiming his father's lands." He took a deep drink before adding as he squeezed her knee, "Let us enjoy some better entertainment." His fingers slithered up her leg again.

Putting her own hand over his to halt him, she realized he was not going to be sensible. She looked at the pitcher of ale on the table. It had been emptied and filled again several times. The baron must be close to intoxication. If she could disconcert him long enough for him to drink himself into a stupor, she might escape without resorting to knocking him senseless.

How did you endure so many years of being pawed, Mother? She knew the answer, for her mother and her father had said often that one must do whatever was necessary to provide for their family. That lesson had been repeated at St. Jude's Abbey, for each lesson was instilled with a reminder that service to the Abbey—and the queen—was paramount.

"Yes, let us," she said, hoping what had worked when

her mother fought off salacious lords would serve her as well.

Prince Tarran shifted on the bench, but said nothing. Maybe he was beginning to trust her.

The baron came to his feet and held out his hand. "If you will come with me . . ."

"Where? Why not enjoy our entertainment here?"

"Here?" His eyes grew round; then he chuckled. "You make an interesting suggestion."

"I thought we could make it interesting for everyone if we remained here." She folded her arms on the table and smiled at the entertainers. She needed to use *all* the lessons she had been taught. Not just the ones she had learned at the Abbey. "Don't you think so, milord?"

He sputtered before he answered, "It is not as I imagined."

"No? Then if I may be so bold as to say so, you need more imagination, milord." Coming to her feet, she said, "Wait here."

"Wait? For what?"

"For some very interesting entertainment."

When she stepped past him, Prince Tarran reached out a hand as he had in the courtyard, then drew it back again. Her own fingers longed to smooth the anxious lines from his brow. He stood and pushed in the bench as if she needed the space to go past him.

"Be careful," he murmured beneath the wooden legs scraping against the uneven stone floor.

She gave him the slightest nod, not wanting to risk the baron overhearing. Keeping her smile in place, she went down the steps and across the hall to where the entertainers stood. She was aware of everyone watching, curious what she had planned. One man reached out toward her skirts as she walked by, but the man beside him slapped away his hand with a terse whisper that was loud enough for Elspeth to hear.

"She is *his*!"

The words added speed to her feet. Even though she had to be grateful that Lord de la Rochelle's apparent claim on her protected her from his lascivious men, she still had to keep the baron away until she could discover what information Rhan could give her.

As she neared them, the performers appraised her uneasily. The older man, his sandy brown hair glued to his forehead with sweat, stepped protectively in front of the dark-haired woman and the younger man.

"Milady." He put his hand to his forehead and gave a half bow.

"Good evening." Wanting to put them at ease, she hurried to add, "I have enjoyed your performance."

"It has not been our best," he said.

"That happens when your audience is not the best."

"You understand much, milady."

She smiled. "Will you tell me your names?"

"My name is Cors ap Fflam. My wife and my son."

"I am Elspeth." She hesitated, then said, "Elspeth Braybrooke, daughter of Mercer Braybrooke."

The entertainers exchanged an excited glance before Cors asked, "Do you speak of Mercer Braybrooke who could juggle as many as five items at once?"

"Yes. You honor my father's memory by recalling his amazing abilities."

"We are pleased to meet his daughter. No wonder you understand our situation." Cors faltered as he looked at the high table where she had been sitting.

Elspeth wished she had the time to explain to Cors and his family, but smiled as she pointed at a staff twice the length of her quarterstaff. "May I borrow that pole?"

"With the daughter of Mercer Braybrooke, we would

gladly share anything." He motioned for his son to bring the
long staff. "How can we help?"

"Come with me and pray that I know what I am doing."

Again the family appeared baffled but followed her toward the raised table. Her plan was simple, but she must
take care. If she humiliated the baron, his lust might become rage.

As she paused in front of the table, Lord de la Rochelle
asked, "What is the staff for?"

"A challenge, milord."

"I thought—"

"Your interesting suggestion of different entertainment
gave me an idea." She tapped the bottom of her chin as she
assumed the contemplative pose the abbess did each time
she pondered a problem. "I thought to myself: what sort of
different entertainment would Lord de la Rochelle enjoy?"

"An easily answered question," the baron said, stretching
across the table to finger the hair draped over her breast.

She ignored his men's snickers as she edged away. She
turned so the baron would not see her repulsion and took
the staff from Cors's son. When she saw Tarran's face
harden into a frown, she found it more difficult to pretend
not to notice. So far, he had trusted her as she had asked.

"I told myself," she continued as if the baron had remained silent, "that Lord de la Rochelle comes from a long
line of brave warriors. I knew that Lord de la Rochelle
would enjoy a challenge. The prize would then be sweeter.
Was I wrong, milord?"

"No."

She wanted to smile. He had to give that answer, or he
would shame himself before his men and his guests.

"Then let me set the challenge." She turned to Cors and
his son. "Each of you take one end of the staff and hold it
out between you." Looking at the raised table, she said,
"Milord, please take note of the hurdle set between these

men. My challenge is that I can pass any height you can jump over this staff."

He put his hands over his stomach and laughed. "I am more than a head and a half taller than you. Your legs cannot be as long as my arm from fingertips to elbow, or so I assume."

"That is something you must only assume . . . for now." Resting one elbow on the table, she smiled at him. "And, if you do not accept my challenge, then *I* may assume that you are not interested in any other entertainments tonight."

As the baron gave a roar and rushed toward the steps, Prince Tarran bounded over the top of the table. He landed inches from her.

She stepped back, startled. "What are you doing? You are going to injure yourself!"

"I have had enough of your nonsense." Prince Tarran's gaze drilled her.

"Then leave!"

"And let you remain with him?" He hooked a thumb toward where the baron was reeling down the steps.

"I can handle the baron."

"Are you sure of that, Elspeth?" He gripped her shoulders. "If you have miscalculated, you may need my help."

As if on cue, Lord de la Rochelle growled, "Ap Llyr, you have no part in this."

"I wish only to give the lady some advice. You would not want her to break her neck tonight, would you?" He gave the baron an icy smile.

Elspeth shivered. She had been curious about Prince Tarran's smile, but when he wore such a cold one, she wished she had never seen it.

The baron muttered something, then cleared his throat before ordering Cors and his son to set the pole at a height that pleased him. Several of the baron's men gathered to debate the height and flatter the baron with how easy his victory would be.

"Elspeth, you are toying with fire," Prince Tarran said quietly, "and you could find yourself in a situation even you cannot talk yourself out of. De la Rochelle will not appreciate being made to look like a fool."

"I know what I am doing."

"That is what you said this morning in the courtyard."

She looked hastily away. "But tonight I *do* know what I am doing."

He put his hand on her arm and glanced at where the baron's men were pouring him more ale, already beginning the celebration. "He expects to win, and he expects you to be his prize."

"Please understand." She faced him. "If I do not do something, he will force me into his bed tonight."

"Not while I—"

She shook her head. "I don't need your help with this."

"It is what a man does for a woman whom he has taken under his protection."

"Protection?" Her eyes widened. "I have no need for you to protect me. I can take care of myself, Prince Tarran." She turned away to watch Lord de la Rochelle consider the height of the bar.

"Tarran," came a whisper from behind her. The name rustled against her hair and swirled across her skin, enticing and mysterious and with an aura of danger that eclipsed any the baron could devise. "You don't have to call me 'prince.'"

"You are a prince." She did not move as she relished that ethereal caress. "I should address you thusly, as the others do."

His fingers on her shoulder brought her to face him again. The flames within his eyes were blazing with the potent emotions he was, for once, making no attempt to hide.

"The others are of this land. You are not. You are a *Sais*." He paused, then said, "That means outsider."

"I know what it means. You are not the first to use it."

"We are ready!" announced the baron.

"Elspeth—"

"Say nothing, Tarran," she ordered. "It is too late to turn back."

Tarran's hand remained on her shoulder as they walked to where the baron was about to make his jump. She hid her shock that the pole was almost even with the tabletops. The baron was tall, but she had not expected him to set such a goal for himself.

"He would rather fail," Tarran murmured as if she had spoken her thoughts aloud, "than have you better him. But, Elspeth, he does not intend to fail. He intends to win you."

"I know."

"And what you will do if he wins your challenge?"

She shivered but said nothing. Lord de la Rochelle could not win, if everything went according to her plan. But if he did . . . No, she could not let that happen.

The baron downed another tankard of ale. To his men's cheers, he raced forward and leaped. His foot caught on the pole. He crashed to his knees, but Cors and his son held the pole, not letting it fall.

The baron was brought to his feet and handed another tankard. He limped as he walked to her and bowed. "Your turn."

"Yes, it is." She motioned for everyone to step aside. Walking up to the pole that was almost as high as her waist, she pretended to examine it and gave Cors and his son an encouraging smile. She could have asked them to release the staff if the baron touched it, but to lose a patron like Lord de la Rochelle could mean their starvation.

Calling, "Ready!", she gathered her skirt up enough so she could run. She gasped when her arm was seized. She tried to shake it off; then she twisted her arm to break the hold on her. It tightened as Tarran stepped in front of her.

"Milord," he said to the baron, "I have one more suggestion for her before she takes her jump."

"You have said enough to her." Lord de la Rochelle stamped his foot like a child. "Let her learn how foolish she was to make such a wager."

"You would not deny the lady a fair chance to meet the challenge she has set up, would you?"

Lord de la Rochelle hesitated, then said, "No, tell her what you must." He strode toward where his men were emptying their tankards.

"Release me," she ordered as soon as the baron had turned his back.

"Why? So you can end up hobbling like de la Rochelle?" Tarran tugged her arm, bringing her closer. "If that is what you are thinking, Elspeth, then you need to think again. He's not going to give you a chance to reconsider. He only did so this time because a blooded warrior must give his opponent every opportunity to match his feat."

"Let me go," she whispered. "I know what I am doing, and our host is growing impatient."

"I would guess so, because he is eager to get you into his bed."

She raised her chin. "Which is no concern of yours."

"Sadly, it is."

"It is?" Her heart banged against her breastbone. Had the kiss in the courtyard stirred something in him, too?

"I know you think you can stand alone, and maybe there are times when you can, but not tonight."

Her heart deflated with a sad thump. "Would you stop acting as if you are my heaven-sent guardian angel simply because you caught me when *you* knocked me from the wall?"

He cupped her chin in his other palm. "Elspeth, you became my responsibility the moment you showed you needed someone with common sense to watch over you."

"I have common sense!" She struggled not to soften against him as his fingers splayed across her jaw. So easily she could forget about Lord de la Rochelle, the absurd challenge and even common sense itself while she slipped her hands up into his hair to draw his mouth down to hers.

"I have seen no proof of that."

Fury burst through her anew. Not just at his cool words, but because he seemed impervious to the yearning rising through her like a fierce storm.

Grabbing his arm, she drew his hand away as she lifted her chin out of his palm. "My plan is to duck beneath the staff."

"Beneath it?"

"I told him I would pass the height he jumped. I did not say I would go over. I will pass under it."

He uttered something in Welsh, something she was certain was a curse. "And how do you think he will act when you show him to be a fool?"

"He has tried to make a fool of me by pawing me." She wanted to add more, but her plan was falling apart around her.

"A different matter." Without a pause, he raised his voice. "De la Rochelle, she has retracted her challenge."

"What?" cried Elspeth at the same time as the baron.

"You would not wish the lady to be hurt, I know," Tarran said.

Lord de la Rochelle limped toward them. He slammed his tankard on a table. "A challenge is a challenge."

"Yes," Elspeth added, "he is—"

Tarran squeezed her arm in a silent warning. She considered grasping his other arm and flinging him to the floor, but had to admit her frustration with the baron had led her to make a foolish wager.

"If you will not retract it," Tarran said, "then you must change it to prevent grave injury to the lady."

The baron's smile returned. "I will agree to a change as long as the challenge is for the same prize."

Tarran released her and stepped toward Lord de la Rochelle, halting when a thicket of bare daggers surrounded him. Across the room, Tarran's men were also held at bay by daggers and swords. Lord de la Rochelle's orders that weapons remain outside the great hall had not been enforced for his men. A sickening cramp twisted Elspeth's stomach as she realized the baron had manipulated her into the ever-increasingly volatile situation.

"Be an honorable man and put an end to this nonsense," Tarran said so calmly she could have guessed they sat at the table enjoying the meal. "She was drunk on excitement, and she should not be held responsible."

"Drunk, is she?" The baron laughed. "Let's see how intoxicated the lady is." He pointed to the staff the two men held. "My challenge is for the lady to walk across that."

"She could fall and hurt herself."

He slapped the table beside him. "The distance to the floor is less than what I jumped over." He waved a hand, and his men parted to let him pass. With an elbow, he shoved past Tarran. His men swarmed forward to pen Tarran in again with their blades.

Elspeth straightened her shoulders as she met the baron's gaze. A hint of a victorious smile tipped his lips. Like a hound, he believed he had run his prey into a trap. She hoped he was wrong.

"Will you accept," he asked, "or will you submit?"

She forced a smile. "I will accept if you will."

"Me? I jumped over the staff."

"But you struck it with your foot. If I can cross between two tables without falling, that is a show of perfection. You must show the same, milord."

"There will be no need if you cannot cross without tumbling off." He laughed. "Then I win, and I *tumble* you, milady."

Elspeth nodded, hiding her disgust. Walking to where Cors and his son were steadying the pole between two tables by sitting on either end, she kept from glancing toward Tarran. The baron's men shouted wagers as she climbed on a bench and onto the table where Cors's son sat. Nobody was betting she would succeed. They were gambling on how few steps she would take before she fell.

When Tarran moved toward her, she thought the baron's men would halt him. They did nothing as Tarran stopped near the middle of the pole with his arms outstretched to catch her. She wanted to reassure him, but she could not. She had to concentrate on the task ahead.

Not a sound could be heard save for the fires snapping on the hearths as she slid her foot onto the pole. She looked from Cors to his son. Both were watching her feet, and she knew she could trust them to keep the pole from rolling.

Her heartbeat resonated in her ears. What the baron asked was not impossible. Before sickening, her mother had given her the most basic lesson in how to dance across a pole. Elspeth had tried to practice at St. Jude's Abbey, but had put aside that half-learned skill when she became immersed in studying the quarterstaff and other arts available at the Abbey. The last time she had tried to walk across a pole had been at least five years ago. She had not been able to cross the full length because she had been giggling. There was nothing to laugh at now.

The distance between the two men was about the length of her quarterstaff. Maintaining her balance and rushing across with a couple of quick steps before she could fall would not work as it had when she was a child.

You know it is not impossible. Just because it appears so to others does not mean that you cannot do it.

Her shoulders stiffened as her father's voice emerged from her memories, patient as he had been when he taught her a trick they had hoped she would someday use. She had not thought of those words for so long. She was astonished his voice could still echo within her mind.

Keeping her eyes focused on the lintel above the arched door on the far side of the hall, she edged one foot, then the other, onto the pole. She heard someone draw in a sharp breath. Tarran? Cors or his son? Someone else? She did not dare to look.

She held out her hands as if gripping her staff. She had to keep her balance when wielding it, just as she did now. She shifted her weight to let her slide her left foot forward again. The pole sagged slightly and vibrated as if pulling in a deep breath, too. She tried to ignore that motion as she eased her right foot forward.

She wobbled and desperately fought for her balance. Lord de la Rochelle's men cheered, and she could imagine the lusty grin he was wearing. Her stomach ached with loathing. She would not lose. She quickly stepped forward. Any second could be her last on the pole. She almost ran toward Cors.

Then she was on the opposite table, and the hall became silent.

Beside her, Cors whispered, "Well done. Just as I would expect from the daughter of Mercer Braybrooke."

"Thank you." She could not say more because arms scooped her from the table and against a hard chest.

Tarran! She leaned her head against his shoulder, enjoying his strength. She did not need his protection, but she could imagine nowhere else she would rather be than in his powerful arms. Closing her eyes, she drank in his musky maleness that was foreign to her life at the Abbey. It was more intoxicating than the baron's ale.

"If you are waiting for me," he murmured, "to say you

were right that you could handle de la Rochelle alone, you will be waiting a long time."

"I am not waiting for you to say anything."

"Good." His fingers stroked her knee as he whispered against her hair. "But I must say that you were magnificent."

He set her on her feet, She wanted to plead with him to hold her again, but said to their host, "Your turn, milord."

"I doubt the pole would hold me." Lord de la Rochelle limped away. As he reached the steps to the raised table, a blond serving lass came forward to offer him consolation on his double defeat. He draped his arm over her and bent to whisper in her ear. She giggled.

Tarran released the sour breath he had been holding since . . . when? Since Elspeth foolishly challenged their host? Since de la Rochelle had challenged her in return and she stepped out on the narrow staff? No, he had been able to breathe then. His breath had failed him when he took her into his arms after her amazing performance.

"I am lucky that I am easily forgotten," Elspeth said.

Easily forgotten? He doubted he could ever forget her sparkling eyes or her welcoming lips. He doubted he would ever want to forget them.

The thought shocked him more than her ability to walk on a pole. Even if she traveled with them to Tyddewi, she would be gone from his life within days. Surely then she would fade from his mind. She was not like the memory of Addfwyn's death, which would never leave him.

"You are lucky," he said in lieu of his troubling thoughts, "that de la Rochelle is still sober enough to know he risked more than a bruised knee if he tried to follow you across the pole. Why must you act silly when you possess rare insight and intelligence? There were other ways of persuading de la Rochelle you were not interested in his offers."

"Tell me how! I tried being polite. I tried humor. I did

everything I could to halt him short of driving my knife into his hand. I even risked breaking my neck."

"Enough!" He grasped her hand. He knew he should not touch her, but he could not halt himself.

"If you do not wish to hear my answers, then do not ask me questions." She eyed him up and down as boldly as the baron had her. "Or are you hoping to instigate another fight as you did this morning?"

Tarran forced his face to remain blank, but every other part of him reacted to the memory of what they had shared in the empty courtyard. The craving for her lips pierced him as fiercely as if she had stabbed him. No matter how he tried, he could not force away his yearning for them, eager and soft, beneath his. There had been an innocence in them, but she had quickly mastered how to return his kiss, thrilling him.

When he did not answer, she turned on her heel and walked to where Vala sat. His men rose and went to another table, but Vala welcomed her with warmth. He saw tension ease from Elspeth's shoulders as she sat next to Vala. She looked as if she belonged with the old woman.

Tarran strode out of the great hall, then went back in. Seeing a serving wench with a pitcher of ale, he signaled to her. She hurried to him. He said nothing as he took the pitcher. She gave him an expectant smile, but he left her standing there as he rushed away from the laughter and the conversation and the men and women who were vying for each other's attentions.

He wanted silence and a chance to think. If he had been thinking clearly that morning, he would not have kissed Elspeth.

Forgive me, Addfwyn. You know I gave you my heart, and you took it with you when you died.

He waited for an answer, but none came. None ever came. The only way he could hear his wife's soft laugh or her warm voice was to draw a scene from his memories. Yet, each of those memories was a separate torment.

He tilted back the pitcher and drank. Some of the ale coursed down the front of his tunic, but he let little escape. When it was empty, he set the pitcher in a niche along the passage.

He kept walking and emerged into the cool night. The honed winds of winter had vanished, but the night air held a spring chill from the western sea. Looking up, he saw the rain clouds were gone. Thousands of stars twinkled. The moon had not yet risen.

The lights blurred together, and he wondered how much ale he had downed tonight. He was amazed that he had no idea. It was not like him to overindulge in ale, but neither was it like him to taste with such eagerness lips other than his wife's.

He put his elbows on a parapet and leaned his forehead against his palms. He had not even looked with lust at another woman since Addfwyn died. How could any other woman give him what she had? Why would he want to share with any other woman what he had with his beloved wife?

Most especially, why would he want Elspeth Braybrooke in his bed? She had laughed at the suggestion that they were lovers. He should have let her amusement insult him, and he should have walked away.

Yet, tightness swelled along him as he recalled the flavor of her sun-washed skin and the eager puffs of her breath against him. That reaction was a reminder that he was still alive. He did not want to be alive. He wanted to be with Addfwyn, but that was impossible. In death, he could not gain the vengeance he had vowed he would exact on her killer.

And he could not kiss Elspeth again.

He cursed and slammed his fist against the parapet. Pain

resonated up his arm. He waited for it to clear his head, so he could toss aside the appealing image of Elspeth's face just below his. The pain only made his eyes unfocus more.

He was drunk.

By St. David, he knew better than to surrender his self-control to ale. With his back against the parapet, he slid down to let his legs dangle over the edge of the wall. He leaned his head back against the stones and looked up at the sky.

On the morrow, he must find a way to tell Elspeth that she had delayed too long in her answer, that he was leaving without her, that she needed to find someone else to plague with her constant chatter. No matter how she pleaded, he would tell her no. Even if she offered a kiss and more . . .

His mind lingered on that thought, and he closed his eyes. He should shove the thought aside, but he took it with him as he fell asleep.

Chapter 8

He was dreaming. Tarran knew he was, because he could hear his heart beating within him, and his lungs rose and fell with each breath.

Yet he stood within the hall of King Arawn, the lord of Annwfn, the land where ancient Welsh warriors' souls were taken after the king in his guise as Death claimed them. In the world of men, the king was feared, but within his own lands, legend said that he was revered. His hall was set in a great valley where crops grew to many times the size of the plants found in the fields of men. In his hall gathered the bravest warriors and the most beautiful women, many of whom once had walked among men. Others were of a race older than man, the race that King Arawn called his own.

At the great table, the king sat. The face of Death in Annwfn was handsome. It was the perfect match for the exquisite lady who sat at his side, finding the choicest bits of food for him to feast upon while he listened to music so magnificent that a living human could not hear it without weeping.

Tarran's cheeks were dry, and he lived, for he had not engaged in battle with an enemy during his quest to find Addfwyn's murderer.

Addfwyn! She must be among the favored company

within the great hall, for only Arawn's lady could be fairer than Tarran's beloved wife.

He scanned the hall. To walk its length would be a journey as long as circling the base of *Yr Wyddfa*, the great mountain to the north. Among the glittering gathering, finding Addfwyn might be a task worthy of a great hero like Pwyll, who, the old stories said, had fought a great demon in Death's stead.

What about the tale of Pwyll who took Death's place to slay his enemy?

He ignored the question posed by a soft voice that lingered in the corners of his mind. The question had been asked among the world of the living. He was not there any longer. He was in Annwfn, the world of the dead, where he could seek his wife.

Then he saw Addfwyn. With her dark hair loose around her shoulders, it draped over her like a cloak. He ached for that silken cape to cover his bare skin again.

Her gaze touched his, and he was beside her. The long hall had been vanquished by the touching of two souls that had been apart too long. Sitting beside her, he reached to draw her into his arms.

Addfwyn slipped farther away on the bench. He started to follow, but the thought of Elspeth doing the same as she avoided de la Rochelle burst into his mind, freezing him to that spot. He pushed that image from his head.

What about the tale of Pwyll who took Death's place to slay his enemy?

No, he did not want to hear Elspeth's voice. He was with his beloved Addfwyn. He should be thinking solely of her, not of an impossible woman who exasperated him.

"Addfwyn," he said softly. So much he had wanted to tell her, but he could not recall a single word.

"You should not be here," she whispered.

"I vowed to spend the rest of my days by your side. If you are here, I should be as well."

"Your time is not yet come."

"If I were to appeal to King Arawn, maybe he would grant me the chance to join you here as soon as I have avenged your death."

She raised her hand to stroke his face as she had so often before her death. She drew it back before she touched him. "Even Death himself cannot change what is and what is to come."

"There must be a way." He reached for her hand. His fingers closed on nothing even though he could see her arm in front of him. "Addfwyn, why can't I touch you?"

"Because you do not belong here. You still walk in the world of men. There you will stay until it is time for you to cross the veil to this land."

"Let me find a way to come and be with you."

She shook her head. "You who were my husband must live your life as it is deemed you should. Go back to your world. There is much undone for you there. You must finish it before you can rightfully come here."

He wanted to argue, but the words disappeared from his mouth. The beautiful scene faded like the last light at twilight.

He woke, once more alone.

Chapter 9

When Elspeth entered the great hall the next morning, it seemed oddly deserted. Maybe it was because the lamps had gone out and nobody sat at the raised table. She went toward where Vala was breaking her fast. One of Tarran's men was with her, Kei ap Pebin, if she recalled his name correctly. He was one of the men who had tried to drag her away from Iau. She thought he would leave when she approached the table, but he did not move. He watched her closely.

Vala looked over her shoulder and gave Elspeth a welcoming smile. "Come and join us."

If there was any emphasis on the last word, Elspeth did not hear it. Kei ap Pebin must have because his scowl deepened.

"Good morning," she said as she sat beside Vala.

The old woman pushed a bowl of barely warm porridge toward her. Elspeth took a few bites before putting her spoon on the table. Throughout the night, her stomach had been doing leaps and rolls. Sleep had been impossible. Even when she slipped out of the keep to practice with her staff in the moonlight, hoping to exhaust herself, she had failed to find her way into the forgiving arms of slumber.

"Where is Tarran?" she asked.

Kei scowled at her. "Why do you address him so infor-mally?" He gave a taut laugh. "Or is that your way of re-minding us that you are Norman?"

"You need no reminder of that," she retorted.

Vala held up her hands. "Starting a new day with an old quarrel wastes that day."

Elspeth murmured an apology. She knew how to be courteous, even if he did not. "To answer your question, Kei, Tarran requested that I use his given name."

"There," Vala said with a smile. "A perfectly reasonable answer. If you have further questions, my boy, you should pose them to Prince Tarran."

"I do have one question." He folded his arms on the table, the fingers of his right hand hovering just above his knife beside a half-eaten loaf of bread. "Why did you en-danger us with your pranks last night?"

She folded her arms on the table to mirror his pose. "I was the only one in danger last night. If you think, Kei ap Pebin, I will share some man's bed so you can enjoy an-other meal and a comfortable bed within his walls, you are mistaken." Turning to Vala, whose face was once again long with dismay, she asked in a gentler tone, "Do you know where Tarran is?"

Before the old woman could answer, a deeper voice said from behind her, "Prince Tarran did not return to our cham-ber last night."

Seith ap Mil was a wall of flesh that moved with the ease of a man half his size. He was not fat, but thickly muscled, the sinews along his lower arms resembled ropes holding to-gether that mass of muscle. His clothes were eye-searingly bright at such an early hour.

She came to her feet so her neck did not ache as she looked up at him. "Is that usual for him?" She tried to pay no attention to the cramp deep in her stomach. Lord de la Rochelle had quickly turned to another woman last night.

Had Tarran done the same? The ache in her neck settled once more in her stomach.

"It has become so." Seith sighed.

Vala sighed.

Kei sighed.

"Will someone explain?" she asked, unnerved.

Vala glanced at the men, then said, "Sleep has eluded him since his wife was murdered. When he can sleep, nightmares leave him as weary as if he had not slept at all."

"I understand that."

"You have nightmares?" Vala's sympathy was as warm as an embrace. "I am sorry to hear that."

Before Elspeth could correct the old woman's wrong assumption, a man pushed past Seith. He wore a badge on his shoulder that identified him as Lord de la Rochelle's steward. He held a rolled scroll in one hand.

"Tarran ap Llyr?" he asked, although anyone with eyes could see Tarran was not at the table. "Which one of you speaks for ap Llyr in his absence?"

"I do," said Seith.

The steward slapped the scroll in his hand and walked away.

"What is it?" asked Gryn, who must have come to the table after the steward because Elspeth had not noticed him before now.

Seith broke the wax seal and unrolled the scroll. He glanced it, then at her. "Can you read?"

"Yes."

"It is written in Norman instead of Latin, so I cannot read it." He held out the parchment, his lips tight at the insult from the baron. "Will you?"

"Yes." She took the crinkly scroll with care and unrolled it on the table. The few words on it had not needed to be presented in such a formal fashion, but she guessed Lord de la Rochelle had no intention of making an appearance in the great hall. Whether he was suffering from too much ale or loitering in his private chambers with the serving wench or ashamed to stand before his men when she was there, she could not guess.

"What does it say?" asked Kei.

She let the scroll snap closed. "Just what you would expect it to say. Except for Iau, who may remain to heal, you are to leave the castle before the sun reaches its apex. To remain condemns you to a much longer stay, but in a cell." Picking up the scroll, she handed it to Seith. "You must find Tarran immediately and let him know."

When she began to walk away, Seith called after her, "Are you leaving with us?"

She did not pause as she called back over her shoulder, "I will let you know before the sun reaches its apex. Tell Tarran not to leave until I give him my answer."

"But if he insists . . ."

"Don't let him go until I give him my answer!" She ran from the great hall, knowing she had no time to waste. She must speak with Rhan the wisewoman. Nor did she have time to think about what would happen if the old woman's words sent her in a different direction from the one Tarran intended to take . . . or if they sent her in the same direction.

Elspeth looked both ways along the corridor. It had a barrel roof, but was so narrow that she wondered how a man of Seith's size could navigate it. She had never seen its like. It was a brilliant design because it kept any attackers who might enter the castle from going more than one at a time along the corridor. She saw small hatches in the roof. Like the ones in the gatehouse below, they could be opened to send boiling sand down upon invaders. Doors so low that she would have to duck to enter the chambers beyond were set at regular intervals along one side. If two doors were open at once, an enemy would be trapped between them, unable to swing his sword.

She wondered whom Lord de la Rochelle feared so much that he had devised such a corridor above the great hall. It might be the Welsh or a personal adversary. Either way, the baron was well prepared.

As she needed to be.

Within the hour, Tarran—she still found it difficult to address a *prince* by his given name—would expect an answer from her about joining his men and Vala on their journey south. Difyr, the brunette serving woman who had helped bandage Iau, had revealed where the old woman Rhan had been moved. She would have told Elspeth anything to get her to leave so she could lavish more attention on the wounded man.

Elspeth counted doors. The fifth should be the room where Rhan was quarantined. Her steps faltered. If she became ill, she could fail to find *Llech-lafar* in time. Yet, she must take the risk.

Leather hinges creaked as she opened the door. They screeched even more loudly as she closed it after her. The room was small, not more than a few paces in each direction. A single lamp was lit and placed in a corner. No window allowed in air, and the scents of illness and body waste tainted every breath. The room was empty save for a pallet covered by a blanket.

As she inched closer, she could see a form beneath the blanket. It was so emaciated that there seemed to be no more than a finger's breadth between the blanket and the pallet.

"Who are you, child?" came a surprisingly strong voice from the pallet.

"I am Elspeth."

"There is no Elspeth in this castle."

"I am a traveler who has been granted a haven here."

A bony finger rose and motioned for Elspeth to approach. "Why have you entered my chamber?"

"Are you Rhan, the wisewoman?" She knelt by the pallet and stared down at a lined face that reminded her of the raw, striated rocks in the mountains. Surprisingly thick white hair spread across the stained pallet. Someone must have recently brushed it because it had the sheen of freshly fallen snow.

"I am," said the old woman on the pallet.

"Do you possess knowledge of more than the stillroom?"

Rhan laughed, a low, husky sound that reminded Elspeth of a knife being whetted on a stone. "I have seen many things in my life, child. Each thing I have seen has taught me a lesson, so I know many things that have nothing to do with the stillroom I once oversaw." She raised one tremulous finger. "But if you come to seek a potion to turn a young man's heart in your favor, you have come in vain. I do not mix such potions anymore, and I will not pass along the secrets to you."

"I do not seek a love potion."

"No? You look like a young woman dealing with questions of the heart."

"I do not seek a love potion." She was glad she could not be tempted. At the Abbey, it was taught that such potions were worthless, but at night after vespers the sisters had gathered to talk. More than one had asked in a whisper if it was possible for a magical combination of herbs to warm a man's heart.

"Then why have you come to speak with old Rhan?"

"I wish to learn more about *Llech-lafar*."

"I know the rock you speak of," the old woman murmured.

"Do you know where it is?"

"Along the River Alun."

"Where is that?"

The old woman frowned. "Who are you that you do not know of the River Alun?"

"Is it the river near Pembroke Castle?"

The king had left for Ireland from Pembroke, so he might return there. He could have stood on the rock on his way to Ireland, because the curse would be called forth only when he returned.

"No." Rhan's scowl deepened. "It runs out to sea not far from where St. David's Cathedral stood before it was consumed by fire. Why do you wish to know about *Llech-lafar*?"

She fisted her hands on her lap. Near St. David's Cathedral? That meant she needed to travel in the same direction as Tarran and his companions. Joy, irrational and wiping every other thought from her head, danced through her. She tried to dampen it, but a phantom wisp remained to send waves of quivers along her skin.

With every bit of her strength, she kept her voice even. "I am asking because I am curious."

Rhan shook her head, then winced as if that simple motion hurt. "You are a *Sais*. Your people cross Offa's Dyke for only two reasons: conquest and hope of wealth."

Elspeth smiled. "I do not come for either reason. I am here to find out more about *Llech-lafar* because I am curious if the legend has any basis in truth."

"And to ensure your Norman king does not step on it?"

She hoped her flinch was not visible. The old woman was indeed wise. "I have no say in what King Henry does. He is a man with a fiery temperament, and he does as he wishes, paying no attention to any counsel offered to him."

Rhan reached out and took Elspeth's hand. Her hold was fragile, and Elspeth did not dare to pull her hand away. The old woman might be injured. Turning Elspeth's hand over,

Rhan drew it close to her eyes. She mumbled something and then released Elspeth's hand.

"Go back, child," the old woman said. "Go back to your homeland before you bring forth the very curse you wish to halt."

"If you are trying to frighten me, I am not easily sent running. I wish to find out the truth about *Llech-lafar*, and I intend to remain in Wales until I do."

"The truth is in your hand."

"What truth? Why would my hand reveal the truth about *Llech-lafar*?"

Elspeth held up her hand and stared at it. She could see calluses left from her work with the staff. There was the small scar where, as a child, she had been bitten by a dog, but that had almost vanished. The side was scraped from her attempt to climb into the castle. She was tempted to shake that torn skin in front of the old woman and say that someone who risked her neck to sneak through an arrow slit would not be deterred by baffling words.

"It says nothing more of the stone, but it shows much about the truth that you risk everything you hold dear if you continue upon the path you are walking. Go back and admit defeat. It is the only way to ensure you do not lose all you keep in your heart."

The door opened with its ear-aching squeak. A woman peered in and cried, "What are you doing in here? Begone! Now!"

The woman's face blanched when Elspeth stood. Was the serving woman fearful of scolding a lady her lord wished to seduce?

Bending again, Elspeth said, "Thank you, Rhan, for your information."

"Heed my warning, child! I beg of you!" She moaned.

The woman by the door hurried forward, pushing Elspeth aside, her concern for her patient overcoming her dismay.

Elspeth left the room, closing the door behind her. The shriek from the hinges seemed to stab her. She had the information to find *Llech-lafar*. Was the rock within sight of the remains of St. David's Cathedral? She would search from one end of the river to the other to discover the exact location of the stone. As she got closer to it, someone was sure to have further information to assist her. She would find the rock, make sure the king did not step on it and complete her task for the queen. Then the king would not die as a result of the curse. All would come about as Queen Eleanor hoped, and Elspeth . . .

She trembled. She did not want to believe that by doing as she had vowed, she doomed all she loved. No sister in the Abbey would hesitate to sacrifice herself to do the queen's bidding. None of them would expect Elspeth to falter in completing her task because of a risk to the Abbey. She believed that wholeheartedly, but she did not want to imagine being without a home . . . again. The Abbey had offered her a haven after her parents' deaths. The idea of losing that and having no place else to go was horrifying. She did not want to think of that.

But what if the old woman was right?

Chapter 10

Are you certain she did not say where she was going?" Tarran paused his pacing in the castle's outer ward. He looked at Seith, who held the reins of the horse where Iau sat in obvious discomfort.

His friend gave a helpless shrug. "Elspeth said only that she would let you know her answer before the sun reached its apex, and she asked that we do not leave until she gave it to you."

"She said nothing about *us* leaving." Gryn was standing next to Kei by their horses in the narrowing shadow of the gatehouse. The ward was almost deserted, a bad sign. "Only you, Prince Tarran. Why don't you bed the lass as she wants and be done with the matter?"

"And with her," his cousin added.

"Enough!" He grimaced, hoping none of his men guessed he had not meant to use the word he had spoken to Elspeth so often. On his arm, his hawk flapped its wings, clearly shocked by Tarran's vehemence. "I asked a question. I would like an answer."

"Seith told you all we know. She said that she would let you know her decision about traveling with us." Vala, as always, was trying to bring peace among them.

He usually appreciated her calm demeanor as much as

he did the feisty opinions of his men. He would not surround himself with men who agreed with whatever he said. Such men did not challenge him.

Challenge!

That they were being banished from Castell Glyn Niwl could be blamed on Elspeth. Even so, he would never fault her for trying to protect herself. Just as he could not fault Addfwyn for saying, in his nightmare, that his time had not yet come to join her in Annfwn. He continued to ache with the emptiness left in the wake of the disturbing dream.

"The sun is almost to its apex," Seith said. "If we remain . . ."

He nodded. He could not risk Vala being subjected to de la Rochelle's wrath. Nor could he ask his men to face a foe of far greater numbers because he had delayed.

"Go ahead," he ordered.

"Without you?" Seith shook his head. "We will not leave you."

"Go. I will follow soon." He glanced at the sky. "I have a few minutes before the sun is at its peak, and I promise you that I will be beyond the gatehouse before de la Rochelle can accuse me of loitering."

Vala put a hand on his arm. "Be careful."

"I will."

"For both yourself and the lady."

He nodded, patting her hand. "I will."

He walked to his horse as the others mounted. He watched while they rode under the gatehouse's arch and out onto the road at the best speed Iau could maintain. He was not surprised that his man had not wanted to remain behind, in spite of flirting with de la Rochelle's serving woman. None of them would give up their quest. Tarran would not deny Iau the chance, even though they would have to travel more slowly.

The sun was climbing too swiftly. Tarran took his

horse's reins and walked toward the gate to the inner ward. There were a score of rooms on the keep's four floors, and Elspeth could be in any one.

His lips tightened. She would not be in de la Rochelle's chamber. But if he left without her . . . No, leaving her within the baron's walls was unimaginable.

Yet, if he stayed too long, he could face de la Rochelle's delight as he was thrown into a cell beneath the great hall. That would mean Addfwyn's death left unavenged.

He should go.

He had to stay.

As he crossed the empty ward, he saw a motion to his left. A servant must be coming out of the stillroom. Not a servant, he realized when sunlight flashed off a whetted blade, but a man-at-arms. He saw the silhouettes of others moving along the upper wall. Another man stepped from the inner ward along with the sound of a sword slipping out of its sheath. From behind him, he heard an answering echo.

He was surrounded. De la Rochelle intended for him to pay dearly for failing to follow the order to leave Castell Glyn Niwl. Any other time, Tarran would have been glad to risk his life to show the baron that he did not bend his knee to a Marcher lord without a battle. His life was not his own to gamble now. Vows he had taken must be kept.

Releasing the horse's reins, he drew his sword. His horse whinnied softly and backed away a few steps. It knew to stay away from a naked sword.

"Go!" he ordered softly to Heliwr, sending the hawk up into the air. He would rather chance losing the bird than to see it captured and having to answer to the baron.

The bird rose, landing on the top of a tower, obviously unsure what prey Tarran wanted it to hunt.

De la Rochelle came out onto the steps leading to the wall. He was dressed for battle with mail over his tunic. His sword belt strained to reach around his stomach. It cinched him in so tightly that Tarran was surprised he could breathe. How long had it been since the baron had readied himself for combat?

But it would not be de la Rochelle he must fight. The baron's men wanted the honor of capturing him. Stroking the hilt of his sword with his thumb, he waited. The next move belonged to de la Rochelle.

The baron did not wait long. "I told you to be gone!" he roared. "Now you shall pay the price of not obeying my orders." He raised his hand, and something clattered from the direction of the gatehouse.

Tarran swore. The portcullis was being lowered, trapping him within the castle like a beast caught in a snare. If he did not turn and run, he would be tossed in the dungeon, fulfilling his vow neither to Addfwyn nor Elspeth.

He clenched his jaw. He would not suffer in a cell for de la Rochelle's entertainment. Raising his sword, he shouted his family's battle cry.

Even as his shout resonated through the outer ward, another sound battered it down. It came from his right. He saw the baron's men's heads turn.

A cart burst out of the stableyard. De la Rochelle's men jumped aside before it ran over them. Shock strained the baron's face. If this was not de la Rochelle's idea of a jest, then . . .

The cart raced toward him. He raised his sword to defend himself, then saw bright red hair flying out behind the driver.

Elspeth!

"Jump aboard!" she called as she sped past him.

He whirled and stared after her, wondering how she expected him to catch a cart going at such a speed. She slashed out with her quarterstaff, striking his horse to send it racing away. The cart matched its pace until the steed fled under the gatehouse and beneath the lowering portcullis.

She pulled on the reins, and the cart turned in an unbelievable arc. On one side, its wheels left the ground. It tilted wildly. She did not slow. De la Rochelle's men scattered.

With a crash, the wheels hit the ground. The cart was heading for him again. The baron bellowed orders. His men rushed forward, but they would never halt the cart. Others positioned themselves between the cart and the slowly lowering portcullis.

With a shout, Elspeth slapped the reins on the horse, and the cart gathered even more speed. Did she expect him to jump between the wheels and clamber aboard? No, for he saw something flapping on the back. She had lowered the back of the cart, giving him a way to get into it. Even so, he had only one chance, and he needed to judge it accurately. A single misstep, and he could be crushed by the wheels.

She called something, but he could not hear her over the shouts from the baron and his men. He ignored them as he focused on the wagon.

Closer.

A bit closer.

A bit closer.

Now!

He threw himself into the cart. He slammed against three staffs leaning against one side and groaned. He bit back a curse as he struggled to sit.

"Stay down!" she shouted.

"What?"

"Stay down!" Holding the reins, she crouched beside him.

"You cannot see where we are going!"

"The horse knows because it saw yours find the sole escape route." She slapped the reins, then hunched against the cart's floor. "Stay down!"

He heard men shrieking as the cart dispersed them again. Looking back, he saw them pointing in the direction the cart was going and laughing. Realization why was a blow in his gut.

"Turn!" he shouted. "The portcullis is coming down."

"I know."

He grasped her arm. "Turn before we hit it and are broken into as many pieces as the cart will be."

"Let go! I know what I am doing."

He did not have a chance to argue. The sunlight dimmed. They were beneath the gatehouse. He released her, knowing it was too late to turn. He had to give her whatever slim chance there was.

"Down!" she cried.

He flattened himself on the cart. The honed tips of the portcullis were only inches above him. One struck the side of the cart. It rocked, but she kept them from tipping over. With another shout, she somehow made the horse go faster. One of her staffs bounced out of the cart. She glanced back, but slapped the reins again. The hanging board on the back of the cart was pierced by the portcullis. With his sword, he slashed the hinge holding the board to the cart. It cut through, and the board splintered beneath the portcullis.

But they were back in the sunshine and careening at the horse's top speed along the road toward the south. In front of them, his horse was galloping but at a less frantic speed, so they passed it.

Tarran sat. Raising his left arm, he whistled. Heliwr came spiraling down to settle on it. The bird squawked to scold him for sending it up without prey in sight. He whistled a different note, and his horse's ears twitched before it began to follow.

"Are they giving chase?" Elspeth asked.

He looked back. "No. It will take them a few minutes to get the portcullis back up high enough for anyone to get out. De la Rochelle knows it will be too late by then." He leaned his elbow on the side of the cart as she sat back on her heels and slowed the horse.

"Are you all right?"

"I am fine, save for a few bruises." He looped the horse's reins around a ring on the side of the cart. "I have far fewer bruises than de la Rochelle would have been glad to give me."

Elspeth took her gaze from the narrow strip of road that followed the headland out toward the sea. "You should not have stayed."

"I did not count on de la Rochelle being too impatient to wait for the sun to reach its greatest height. And you did ask that I stay until you gave me an answer about traveling with us."

"That was before."

"Before what?"

"Before I discovered you would be stupid enough to remain once the sun was near its peak."

"I could not leave. I am responsible for you."

She tightened her hold on the reins. "How many times must I tell you that I do not need you to protect me?"

"I might believe it, if it were true."

"I saved *you*."

"So you did, and I am grateful." He patted the side of the cart. "What inspired you to take a wagon from de la Rochelle's stable?"

"It was not part of a plan to save you because I figured you had enough good sense to leave before midday." She scowled. "I got it for Vala. Riding on horseback is too much for a woman of her years."

"Tyddewi is not far."

"So having a cart should not slow you much. You asked me to watch over her, and that is what I am doing. She is exhausted from your journey, and she is sad because she cannot make you smile as you used to. She—"

He held up his hand. "You have made your point. Was getting the cart what delayed you?"

Elspeth was tempted to say yes to avoid more questions from Tarran, but she would not lie unless she must. "I had someone I needed to speak with. That was the reason I came to Castell Glyn Niwl. I was finally able to talk with her. It was a fascinating conversation, and I am afraid the time rushed past swiftly. I realized it was almost midday and—"

"Do you ever answer a simple question with a simple answer?"

"I thought I was. You asked me where I had gone, and I was telling you."

"You were telling me far more than I wished to know."

"If you did not wish to know, then you should have asked your question in another way."

He leaned toward her, a pose that emphasized the breadth of his chest. His tunic pulled back across it, flattening against the sharply defined muscles she had discovered when he pulled her close. Her heart thumped wildly, startling her, for he was not touching her. Every breath was becoming harder to draw than the one before it. The air seemed to vanish around her.

"Very well," he said with a patience she had not guessed he possessed. "I shall pose my question in a different way. I shall make it a statement. Do not wander away when it is time for us to leave."

"That is no statement. That, *Prince* Tarran, is an order."

"It is." He frowned vehemently. "Will you obey it?"

"I always obey reasonable orders. But I must ask you to make those orders clear because I cannot guess your plans. If you will—"

"If you will be silent, I might have a chance to let you know what I planned."

"And what do you have planned?"

Setting Heliwr on the side of the cart and lashing the hawk's jesses to keep it from flying away, he reached in front of her and drew back on the reins. They slowed to a stop.

"We need to catch up with the others," she said. "Why are we halting? Have you lost your mind?"

"Most likely."

He framed her face with his hands, tilting it toward him. As his mouth slanted across hers, she shifted to rest against him. Slowly, yet with an eagerness she understood so well, he explored her lips. When her fingers rose up his arms and around his shoulders, he leaned her back onto the cart's bed. His arm was beneath her and he was above her. She was surrounded by his virile strength, and she did not want to escape.

His tongue darted into her mouth as she gasped for breath. At the same time, his fingers crept up over her breast, seeking along it as his lips had her mouth, leaving no part untouched. Her mind was awash with unfamiliar craving as a sea of engrossing sensations swelled through her.

She wanted to touch him. She wanted to offer him a share of the pleasure he was giving her. When her tongue stroked his before sliding into his mouth, she quivered beneath him. There was as much bliss in discovering him as there was in him touching her.

When he toyed with the tip of her breast, she clenched her fingers on the back of his tunic. Nothing, not even rapture, must sweep her from him. Her ragged breath was loud in her ears when his mouth left hers to shower kisses across her cheek and along her jaw. She whispered his name as his tongue laved her ear, tracing the whorls in slow journey to release every pleasure waiting there.

"You are delicious," he whispered against her ear. "And outrageous."

She opened her eyes to gaze up at him. "There is nothing outrageous about wanting to keep you out of Lord de la Rochelle's dungeon."

"I would have liked to see de la Rochelle's expression when we escaped his trap." He smiled, shocking her, for his face was transformed as if a lamp had been lit behind it. She touched his cheek where his eyes crinkled with lines dug deeply enough to show her Vala had been correct. He used to smile often.

She traced those lines from his cheek to his temple. Her fingers combed through his black hair, letting it slip between them in a hundred separate caresses. With a sigh, she whispered, "We should find the others. They will be worried about us."

"Yes, we should." He brushed her lips with his.

With another groan, she steered his mouth back to hers. A teasing kiss was not enough. She wondered if her craving for him ever could be sated. Or if it should. No, she would not think of that. As he pressed her against the boards in the wagon bed, she surrendered herself to his touch.

Laughter struck Tarran's ears as if someone had boxed them. The wagon shifted, and he looked up to see the familiar faces of his men. Rising to his knees, he watched Elspeth's face lose its softness as she realized they were no longer alone.

"We helped in your rescue, too, Elspeth. You can show us your gratitude as well." Kei slapped his thigh and laughed again.

Only his cousin joined him, and Gryn halted when he realized nobody else was laughing.

Elspeth's color rose when Kei leaned over the side of the

wagon and winked. He reached toward her hair, but she slapped at him. She missed, because Tarran grasped the front of Kei's tunic and jerked him up against the wagon. He raised his fist. Kei's eyes grew round with astonishment.

"No, Tarran," Elspeth pleaded. "He is your friend."

Her fingertips on his arm brought him to his senses. He pushed Kei back as he released him. He had been ready to drive his fist into the face of a trusted friend. He had been about to imperil their fellowship . . . because he was furious that his seduction of Elspeth had been interrupted. Instead of being angry, he should be grateful to Kei for intruding.

Vala aimed a frown at both of them, and Kei and his cousin edged toward Iau, who was hunched over on his horse. Tarran jumped down from the wagon.

"We are glad you are alive and free," Seith said as he handed Elspeth out of the cart.

"So are we." Tarran clasped his friend's arm in a warrior's salute. Did Seith realize he had won Tarran's gratitude for assisting Elspeth? If Tarran touched her again, he wondered if he could stop from making love with her, no matter who else stood nearby.

When Elspeth lifted out the two staffs remaining in the cart, no one spoke. Both, he noticed, had crosspieces on them.

"Iau needs to ride in the wagon," she said without looking at anyone. She leaned one staff against the wagon. Tipping the other, she broke off the crossbar. Tossing it into the cart, she gripped the stilt as she had held her quarterstaff.

He heard Vala and his men's quick intakes of breath as she went through a series of motions with the staff. She was testing it, he surmised, to discover if the balance was right. She twirled it, jabbed it into an invisible foe, swung it in smooth motions that suggested each one was simple. He knew they were not and that she was incredibly skilled. Tossing the staff back into the cart, she hefted the other stilt.

She put her foot on the crosspiece and snapped it off. Again she threw the shorter chunk of wood into the cart. Again she went through the same motions. Only when she paused, a relieved smile easing the lines on her face, did she seem to notice the others watching her.

She set one end of the staff on the ground and asked as if nothing out of the ordinary had happened, "Did anyone remember to bring any food from the castle?"

Elspeth pushed at a boulder with her staff, then kicked at it. Her only reward was a sore toe. During the past hour, while Tarran and his men fished for their meal, she had walked a half mile along the riverbank on both sides and seen dozens of rocks big enough for the king to step on. How was she to know which one was *Llech-lafar*?

"You will break a toe that way," Tarran said as he pushed past the brush edging the river. The basket he carried had freshly caught fish in it.

She wondered if everyone else was as sick of eating fish as she was. Easter was coming soon, and they would be able to return to eating fowl and meat.

"Is this the River Alun?" she asked.

"No. That is farther south and west. Why do you ask?"

"All the talk of *Llech-lafar* has made me curious about where it might be." By St. Jude! She had been walking along the *wrong* river.

He set the basket of still flapping fish on the ground. "Why are you fascinated by that old Welsh legend?"

"The tales of King Arthur and Merlin belong to those on both sides of Offa's Dyke."

"The Saxons maybe, but you are Norman. Those stories do not belong to you."

She squatted and tapped her fingers against a rock. How was she going to find one rock among the myriad in Wales?

And once she found it, what would she do? The rock she had kicked was solidly set in the ground.

Coming to her feet, she said, "The Normans and the Saxons have become one nation. Only the Welsh deny the inevitability of Wales's joining that union."

"Along with the Irish and the Scots."

She shivered. "The Scots are wild men, and the king would be wise to leave them alone."

"Maybe we Welsh should be a bit more savage." He pulled her into his arms.

"Maybe you should be." She laughed as she dropped her staff. She guided his mouth to hers.

His tongue seared her lips before slipping between them. Her lips parted in a soft sigh when his arm cradled around her shoulders, tilting her back against its iron strength. He drew back, and she opened her eyes to see him searching her face.

"What?" she whispered.

"Hush. I want to look at how the sunshine glows on your face."

She brushed her fingertips against his cheek. Glorious sensations leaped along them, luring her closer. As his mouth recaptured hers, she wondered if the sun's heat had consumed her.

Something struck her foot, then struck it again.

With a yelp, Elspeth pulled back. She looked down at a fish flipping from side to side on the ground. It must have jumped out of the basket. Bending, she picked it up. She drew her knife and put it out of its misery. She wiped the knife on the grass before putting it back in its sheath.

She picked up the basket and held it out to him. "Next time, kill them as you catch them."

"I will do that." He put his hands over hers on the basket and drew her toward him. His nose wrinkled. "The smell of fish is not the sweetest perfume, is it?"

She slid her hands out from beneath his and bent to pick up her staff. As she straightened, she saw him watching her.

"You should not be out here with only your staff to protect you," he said.

"It is all I need."

"Really?" He arched a single brow.

She laughed. "It is all I need to protect me, I should have said. If you are worried, I would be glad to show you."

"I have seen you practice with it, but that is not the same as battling a real foe. If you are suddenly attacked, you might not have time to get to your staff."

"I know a few other tricks than the ones you have seen."

"Such as?"

She motioned along the riverbank. "Go ten paces in that direction. I will go an equal number in the opposite direction."

Tarran was puzzled, but did as Elspeth asked without more questions. She had called it a trick, but what did she intend to do? He set the basket of fish on the bank beside him. He wanted both hands free . . . for whatever she planned.

She shouted, "If we are attacked and you are closer to my staff than I am, you could help me this way." She lifted the staff and sent it arcing toward him.

"You should have thrown it harder!" he called as one end of the staff struck the rock she had kicked. "It will not reach me."

"Watch!"

The staff bounced, arcing toward him at the same height she had sent it flying. He caught it with one hand, astonished that it was once more upright.

"Toss it back to me!" she yelled.

"How?"

"Hold it up as if it were a spear and throw it at the stone."

"It may break."

"It will be fine. Trust me, Tarran."

Trust her? Could she really have no idea how much he trusted her? She had saved his life with her quick thinking. She had at the same time obtained a vehicle to carry Vala and Iau to Tyddewi.

He trusted her to be brave and resourceful . . . and beautiful and breathtaking.

It was himself he could not trust. To let himself become enmeshed in her life would chance his being hurt as he had when he cradled Addfwyn's head and saw no signs of life on her gray face.

He lowered the staff. Picking up the basket of fish, he carried them toward where she stood. He held out her quarterstaff. She took it, baffled.

Bending, he kissed her cheek. His lips lingered, basking in the warmth of her living flesh. He wanted to explore all her warm skin to expunge the memory of how cold Addfwyn had been in his arms. But he must never—not even for a moment—forget why he was on his quest.

"Tarran?" she asked. In her voice, he heard the same entreaty that pounded through him with every beat of his heart.

No sweet touch and bright eyes filled with life must distract him, so without answering, he walked away.

Chapter 11

Elspeth wanted nothing more than to get out of the cart and walk. Her body ached from hours of traveling on bumpy roads. Even singing quietly had not relieved her boredom and discomfort. Each melody had taken on the tempo of the wagon's rocking. She held the reins with her left hand and stared at the curves in the road ahead. She paid no attention to the hills between the track and the land sloping toward the sea. The salty air was no temptation to explore the shore, and the sea breeze teasing her hair could not pierce her fatigue. She was chilled and her clothes damp against her skin.

She looked through the misty rain at the swaying backs of the oxen pulling the wagon. Trading the horse for oxen had been a good idea, because they had more stamina. But Elspeth wondered if the slow-moving beasts were any improvement. The yoked oxen seemed to find the worst section of the road. All attempts to steer them had been for naught. They moved forward when Tarran's horse did and stopped when his mount halted.

She shifted, and her foot struck one end of her makeshift staff. She grabbed it before it could strike Vala, who was napping in the back. Iau had his eyes closed, but she was unsure if he was asleep or lost in pain.

What a mess everything had become! She *had* obtained information about *Llech-lafar*'s whereabouts at Castell Glyn Niwl, but lost her good staff. Rhan's warning rang in her ears. Was losing that staff part of what the old woman had foreseen? But even knowing that misfortune awaited in the future was not the worst aspect of their stay at Lord de la Rochelle's castle. Her vagrant thoughts constantly wandered to Tarran and how he had looked when he smiled.

She wanted him to smile again . . . when he was holding her. There was no chance of seeing another unexpected smile when his back was to her as he led the way along the road.

Maybe on the morrow, she would switch places with one of his men. That man could be bored in the wagon, and she could enjoy riding beside Tarran whenever the road was wide enough.

But riding would present new problems. Her staff was not meant to be carried while riding. She could untie her fabric belt and lash one end of the staff to her horse's saddle. The other end she would be able to balance across her lap. That would work as long as they traveled through open fields. When they came to a forest, she might have no choice but to walk. She had no idea how she would keep up with the riders. At the moment, walking sounded like an excellent idea, but she had agreed to watch over Vala. She could not renege on that vow.

She glanced at Vala, who, even asleep, wore an unsettled expression. The old woman had been unable to hide her disquiet since they fled from Lord de la Rochelle's castle. Each mile seemed to make Vala shrink farther into her cloak.

Or, Elspeth wondered, was the old woman unnerved by whatever kept Tarran's men's heads swiveling from one side to the other? She had no idea what they sought. Shelter or a sign of an enemy? She had seen Tarran and his men

conferring as they began traveling at dawn, but she had not
been invited to participate.

If she cooed and swayed her hips like the dark-haired
wench who had gained Iau's attention, would she be able to
persuade one of the men to divulge what they had discussed? She stiffened at the thought of using such ploys,
and one ox lowed.

Tarran glanced over his shoulder and scowled. Why did
he always use *that* expression? He seemed to reserve his
fiercest glowers for her. Not even Kei, who had wisely kept
the wagon between himself and Tarran since they had left
the castle, earned such a frown.

"What is wrong?" he called back.

"Nothing."

"Then keep the beasts quiet. We have no idea who might
be among the shadows."

"The oxen did not make as much noise as you are now."

"I would not have to shout if you kept them quiet."

He looked ahead again before she could think of a suit-
ably scathing reply. Those were the most words he had spoken to her since yesterday afternoon. He acted as if she had
no more life than the stones in the walls edging the fields.
His conversation with her since he had walked away from
the river had consisted only of "Good morning" and "Good
night."

It would be easier if that did not change. Then she could
think of finding *Llech-lafar* instead of having her mind drift
back to the exciting moment when Tarran had drawn her
beneath him in the wagon.

She was startled when Tarran drew in his mount so the
cart could catch up with him. She waited for him to speak,
but he did not. When the oxen slowed, he motioned for her
to keep going.

She did with a sharp order to the oxen. She looked back.
He rode beside Vala, who was opening her eyes. His con-

cern for the elderly woman revealed there was more to him than the ice prince.

She sighed. She already knew there was more to him than his cold exterior. What she could not understand was why his moods shifted more quickly than the Welsh weather.

"We shall be going only a mile or so more before it becomes too dark to travel," Tarran said with the kindness he always showed Vala.

"I am glad," she answered in a monotone.

"How do you fare, Iau?"

The younger man struggled to sit. Elspeth put a hand under his elbow to help him, then clasped it tightly when the wagon's front right wheel fell into a large hole.

Something cracked. Pulling back on the reins, she jumped out before the cart had come to a halt. She shook her head as she looked at the wooden wheel. One of the spokes had shattered, and two others were cracked.

"Is the wheel broken?" asked Tarran, swinging down off his horse.

"Not completely." She pointed to the damage as his men crowded around.

"Then we can continue as long as we are careful and the road is smooth."

"No. It will be dark soon. The oxen could pull the cart into a bigger hole, and it could be damaged so I cannot fix it."

Seith gasped. "Are you saying you know how to fix it?"

"Yes."

"You have a multitude of unexpected skills, Elspeth," Tarran said. "Tell me: where did you learn to fix a broken wheel?"

"I learned from my father." She bent again to check the wheel before he could ask more questions. If she told him the truth, she suspected nothing would change. Tarran had been imperious and had ordered her about since he first shouted to her on the castle wall. She simply did not want to be pummeled with more questions. "How far are we from Tyddewi?"

"Four days. No more."

"Good." Standing, she wiped her hands on her gown, which was covered with dust and dirt. "If we spend the night here, I can repair the wheel on the morrow."

Tarran nodded. His men helped Vala and Iau from the cart. They started a small fire and spred their cloaks on the ground around it. Tarran vanished for a short time and returned with his hawk on his arm. He also carried a string of fish and a single dead rabbit. Soon the fish were gutted and cooking over the fire. He cut up the rabbit and gave pieces of it to his hawk.

Elspeth listened as the men spoke of the route ahead. They were careful, she noted, not to speak of any plans beyond delivering Vala to her granddaughter's house. Gryn started with, "After we leave Tyddewi," but said no more because his cousin's elbow jabbed him hard in the ribs. She told herself it was just as well because if they spoke of their plans, they might also ask about hers.

When the meal was done, Seith and the cousins went to make sure their horses were secure for the night. Vala sat beside Iau and gave him something to drink. Elspeth guessed it was to help him sleep.

Only she and Tarran remained by the fire. Rising, she said, "I should take care of the oxen."

"Seith offered to check on them." He did not look away from the flames.

"Thank you."

"Thank *him*. He said you probably were tired of looking at the rear ends of the beasts."

"Then I will thank him." With a laugh, she gathered up the remnants of their meal and tossed them onto the fire as she sang her favorite song. She was glad to be out of the bouncing cart. With her foot, she brushed the crumbs into the embers.

"Do you have to sing all the time?"

"Sing?" she asked, puzzled. "Why does it bother you? I sing when I am happy and when I am doing chores and—"

"You are babbling. Do you ever close your mouth?"

Elspeth clamped her lips shut and did not answer.

"Very amusing." He held his cup over the fire to warm the ale in it.

"Sarcasm?"

"It is a potent weapon at times."

"Do you believe you need a weapon against me, Tarran?"

"You mistake my meaning."

"Do I?"

"Not about sarcasm, but you may have mistaken my meaning in . . . other things." He leaned back against a rock. His face was hidden in the deepening shadows. Even so, his voice betrayed his tension. "I still love my wife."

"I know."

"I have no interest in falling in love with anyone else."

"I know." She hoped he could not see her face either, because it might divulge how difficult those two words had been to say. Swallowing hard, she went on. "I have no interest in falling in love with anyone either. Once I reach my journey's end in Wales, I must return to England and my obligations there."

"You never explained why you are here."

"I thought I had."

"No. Why don't you tell me?"

Elspeth was saved from answering when the fire snapped and dimmed. "We need more wood."

"Stay here while I get it."

She bristled, vexed with his assumption that she was incapable of doing anything but following his orders. And

even that he seemed to believe she could not do well. She
was exasperated, as well, with his being icy cold one moment and then drawing her to him for a heated kiss the next.

"I do not need your help, Tarran," she said coolly. "Nor
do I need your clumsy attempts to seduce me."

"Clumsy?"

"Why are you taking offense when you do not care?"
She put her hands on her hips. "Or do you need to believe
that every woman you kiss without caring about fairly
faints at your attention?"

"I did not say I did not care about—"

"Your prowess? Do you want me to tell you how honored I am to be kissed by a prince?" She shook her head and
sighed. "Why do you try to infuriate me? Is it because you
fear too much laughter and too many good spirits will un-
dermine the grief you wear wrapped around you like a hair
shirt? Do you believe if your grief lessens, you will find
your resolve to slay Bradwr ap Glew faltering?"

"That will never falter. I will never forget that men I trust
told me how they saw him covered with blood."

"And now you let him triumph over you every day by allowing him to steal even the hint of joy from your life." She
went to the cart, drew out her staff and walked away.

In spite of herself, she strained her ears to hear if he
called to her to come back. He did not.

Elspeth bent her head into the thickening mist. She
should be happy that he had been honest with her. If he had
not held her with such fervor after their escape from Castell
Glyn Niwl, she would be offering him sympathy now for
the grief he refused to relinquish. She would have cheered
his efforts to obtain his vengeance. She would have been
tempted to help him.

Instead she wished he would take a walk in the dark and
plunge headfirst off a cliff.

She climbed a short way up the steep hillside. Matted

grass left from the previous summer tried to trip her, but she pushed through it. Her shoes became soaked within a few steps, and briars, green and supple, snagged her gown. If she had any wits left, she would return to the fire and let Tarran wander about on the hillside looking for wood.

She was not going to find any, for the only trees on the wind-scored hillside were at the top far above her. Pausing, not wanting to admit defeat to herself—or to Tarran—she gazed at the line of trees. They stood like guardians, protecting Wales from the sea. Or maybe, if Tarran was typical of Welshmen, they had grown to protect the rest of the world from the Welsh. She looked toward the sea and thought of Lord de la Rochelle's story about Prince Madoc.

Could a Welsh prince have been witless enough to sail beyond the horizon? She almost laughed. If Tarran thought he would find the man who had murdered Addfwyn, he would not be stopped by the known limits of the world.

She turned to go back down the hill. The rain was falling more heavily, but each drop was still as fine as a spider's web. They tickled her skin, and she remembered her father holding her high and turning her about in a similar shower. He had laughed. She had always loved when he laughed, because his lips would crease his cheeks, and his eyes would become deep slits. The sound was like friendly thunder.

Her steps faltered. So many memories of her family were bursting forth. She had seldom thought of them at the Abbey. Caught up in her life there, she had used the walls to keep her grief at bay. Along with the pain of losing her parents within hours of each other, she had locked away memories of the joy. She did not want to lose those memories again.

Elspeth took another step, and her foot slid from beneath her. She dug the staff into the ground to keep from falling. As she fought for her balance, she was amazed to see stacks of rocks in front of her. What was left of low walls marked off a square, flat area. Had an ancient fort once stood here? To the left, a knob on the hill with raw stone ledges would be difficult to climb, but she could imagine ancient soldiers standing at its top, scanning the fields for danger. Had the fort's residents fought legionnaires or enemies who had threatened Wales before the Roman empire claimed these hills as its frontier?

A flash caught her eye. She leaned on the staff and looked up the hill. Who was there? The lantern probably belonged to a farmer seeking a lost cow or sheep. The flicker was now almost directly above her.

Sheets of rain rippled on the wind like a cloak being shaken out. Suddenly someone appeared to her right, parting the curtain of rain with the light from another lantern. It shimmered off the wet stones and blinded her. She raised her staff to defend herself.

"Put that down, Elspeth."

Tarran! She was about to ask him what he was doing on the hillside, but he halted her by asking the same question. He carefully climbed across the rock shelf.

"I told you I was going to look for some wood," she replied.

"You will not find any here. There are no trees growing out of bare rock."

She was irritated that his voice was steady. She was breathing heavily from the climb. Sitting on the rock wall, she balanced her staff on her knees.

"Tarran, do you want us to keep snarling at each other? We will if you continue to use that tone. I am quite aware there are no trees here. I was coming back down, but halted when I saw a light on the hill's top."

Raising his lantern, he scanned the area above them. "Where did you see the light?"

"At the very top." A distant bleat and a man's shout told

her that she had guessed correctly. Someone was seeking an animal.

"Whatever was lost is now found," Tarran said as if she had spoken aloud. "You are lucky *you* did not get lost when she is casting rain."

"What? Who is doing what to the rain?"

He gave her the cool smile she was learning to despise. "It is our way of speaking about rain. 'She is casting rain.' The saying comes from the old times when people believed rain was a gift from one of the goddesses ruling over earth and sky."

"Goddess?" Her smile was as icy as his . . . and the drop of rain slithering down her back. She did not let him see her discomfort. "I had not guessed any Welshman allowed himself to be ruled by a woman."

"Not a woman, a goddess."

She shook her head. "You have too many old stories here."

"True. Every tree and every rock has a tale to tell."

"*Every* rock?" she asked before she could halt the question.

"Why are you so curious about rocks?" He stepped closer. "What nonsense are you involved in, Elspeth?"

She intended to give him an answer. She had one ready. What it was she could not recall as she gazed into his eyes. They glistened in the lantern light like two rain-washed stones. Hard, but containing a hidden warmth that was shadowed by the night. Her fingers were reaching to stroke his cheek before she could halt them. She jerked them back.

"Elspeth . . ." His voice could have been the night wind, soft and mysterious. It lured her to risk everything to discover what else might be hidden in his eyes. It dared her to throw caution aside and cede herself to the pleasure she had found in his arms.

She looked away. Was *this* what Rhan had meant when

she gave her dire warnings? If Elspeth continued on her quest to find *Lech-lafar*, she would have to forsake any chance to explore the passions Tarran let her see so seldom. No, that made no sense. She did not love Tarran ap Llyr. Even if she had been stupid enough to, he had told her by the fire that he had buried his heart with his wife.

"Elspeth . . ."

She ignored the entreaty he put into her name. "I have told you that I am interested in the old stories of Wales. You keep talking about magic rocks and magicians and a prince who fought in Death's stead. I am curious if there is anything magical about this hill." *Other than you and the way you make me feel*, she added silently.

With a snort, he clamped his hands on her shoulders.

"You are lying!"

"Me? I am not the one who hides every emotion behind a mask."

"Is that what you think I am doing?"

"Yes!" Twisting her shoulders, she broke his hold on her.

He rocked backward. The lantern flew out of his hand. He shouted as he teetered on a rock. In horror, she saw he was close to the edge of a sharp drop. She grasped a handful of his tunic and jammed her staff between two stones. She heard it creak. She tried to plant her feet, but could not on the wet rocks. Risking a glance down, she saw a larger boulder in front of them. She took a deep breath and drew out her staff. They slid downward toward the cliff.

She turned her foot to the side and winced as it struck the stone. Pain flew up her leg, but she ignored it. Hoping the staff would not break, she forced it between another pair of rocks. It caught. She slammed into him and heard him grunt as they came to a stop against a large boulder. She tried to push herself back, but her shoes were as slick as the stones beneath them. The staff slipped through her wet fingers and rolled down into her ankle. It bounced away. She peered through the darkness to see where it had gone.

Putting her hands up, she tried to edge away from Tarran. She had to find her staff. Without it, she felt too vulnerable.

"Help me!" she cried, sweeping out one foot in an attempt to discover where the staff was.

"You are safe, Elspeth. You are not going to fall." He pulled her to him.

Her reply went unspoken as her breasts brushed his chest. His firm thighs pressed against her legs.

"Don't do this again," she whispered, her quarterstaff forgotten. "Don't hold me like this if you plan to tell me later that you do not care about me."

"I never said I do not care about you. You assumed that from my words."

"Which were a warning that you were interested in sharing my bed but nothing else."

"That is partly true."

"Which part?"

"You guess." His mouth covered hers.

She stiffened, wanting to shove him away but fearful that he might fall over the cliff. As a wondrously sweet heat coursed through her, she softened. She should halt him from splaying his hands across her back as he drew her so near she was aware of every angle along him.

A woman screamed.

Elspeth jumped down from the slippery rock and ran in the direction her staff had gone. She scooped it up and raced, half sliding, down the hill. Tarran passed her as she reached its base.

Someone leaped out of the darkness. She sensed rather than saw a sword slashing toward them. She brought the staff down on it.

Tarran pushed her aside. She started to protest, then heard his sword strike the other one.

"Protect those who cannot protect themselves!" he shouted.

Knowing he meant Vala and Iau, she looked at the cart parked by the fire. The oxen were still yoked to it. She called Vala and Iau's names. When they answered from beside the cart, she sped toward them, whirling the staff on one side of her and then the other. She hoped that would give any other attacker pause. From behind her and to her right, she could hear striking swords. Shadows shifted through the darkness, but she could not tell which belonged to a friend and which to an enemy.

"Let me help!" she cried as she saw Vala trying to assist Iau into the wagon.

The wounded man moaned as they lifted him awkwardly into the cart. Elspeth squatted to give the old woman a knee to climb up next to him.

"Next time, give Iau a sleeping potion *after* we are ambushed," Elspeth said with a strained smile.

"Tarran?" whispered Vala.

"He is fighting over there." She pointed into the darkness.

"The others?"

"I heard them fighting."

"Oh, dear heavens!"

"Stay down. I will do what I can to protect you."

Edging around the cart, Elspeth held her staff at the ready. Her right hand beneath it, her left hand over it, she could quickly turn it in any direction. Hearing Kei shouting a warning, she whirled to her left. She slashed the staff up beneath the arm of a man holding a dagger. He shouted in shock. That sound became a groan when the other end of her staff slammed his shoulder, knocking him backward. He tripped on his hooded robe and fell.

"Watch behind you, Kei!" She swung the staff around to

strike another hooded man's arm before his sword could slice into Kei.

Tarran shouted to his men, and they ran to surround the cart. As he rushed to join them, he called, "Elspeth, get into the wagon!"

She ignored the order. In the cart, she would be at a severe disadvantage because she would not have enough room to swing her staff.

"I am guarding Vala and Iau!" she yelled, motioning with her staff toward where more men were pouring out of the dark. "*Perygl!*"

Even in the faint light, she saw Tarran's amazement when she used the Welsh word for danger. He raised his sword and yelled words she could not understand. His men raced after him to meet the new attackers.

"Milady!" cried Vala.

Elspeth spun and saw a man sneaking toward the cart. When he stepped into the light from the dying fire, she saw he was taller than Tarran. He wore a hooded robe as the others did, but the sleeves were too short, revealing beefy arms. In one hand, he held a bare sword.

She faltered, then steeled herself. She was the most skilled staff-fighter at St. Jude's Abbey. She had proved that by defeating the queen's champion. Queen Eleanor had selected her because the queen trusted Elspeth's skills would be triumphant beyond the Abbey's walls. She would not fail the queen. She *could* not.

The man laughed when she took her stance, her staff ready to counter whatever move he made. She would not let him unsettle her. He snarled something that she guessed was an insult by the way his lips curled.

"I don't speak Welsh, so your words are wasted on me!" She tried to laugh, but the sound snagged in her tight throat.

When he raised his sword, she blocked his swing by striking his arm. Amusement vanished from his face as he slashed at her again, this time with more power. Again she halted him by knocking aside the blade.

He twisted it, and suddenly the sword pressed down on her staff. She fought to keep it at a height where she could best wield it. He pushed down. She was not strong enough to battle him that way. Again he chuckled. Again he spat the word she could not understand as he pushed her backward toward the cart. His breath burned, thick and fetid, in her face. She could not look away. Any wavering could mean his overwhelming her.

Vala shrieked, but Elspeth focused on the man. Sliding her hands along the staff, she grasped it at one end. She yanked on the staff, and his sword popped up.

He bellowed in anger, then choked when she drove the staff into his midsection. He reeled back several steps and fell to his knees, grasping his stomach. She swung the staff and struck him in the head hard enough to knock him unconscious.

She whirled to see another man clambering into the cart. With a shout, she leaped forward and swung the staff again. The man fell back with a groan.

"Thank heavens!" Vala called when Elspeth looked toward her.

Before Elspeth could reply, an arrow hit the wagon. She gasped and jumped in. Grabbing Vala's arm, she pulled down sharply. The old woman moaned as she fell to the wagon bed beside Iau. Not in pain, but in fear as several more arrows struck the wagon while others flew overhead.

"Wait here," Elspeth ordered.

"Where are you going?" Vala clutched her arm.

Easing her arm away, Elspeth said, "Tarran and his men need cover, too." She stretched a hand toward the front of the wagon. She pulled it back when more arrows arched toward them.

"Stay down!" Vala began to weep.

That was advice Elspeth knew she had to take. She knew as well that the men needed her help.

She lifted the staff over the front of the wagon, fishing for the reins. An arrow bounced off it. The impact almost forced the staff out of her grip. She bit her lower lip as she heard the sharp clash of swords from where Tarran and his men fought. She tried again.

"I have them!" She grinned at Vala and slapped the reins on the oxen.

The cart rocked, and she looked back. A man was trying to climb aboard.

Pressing the reins into Vala's hands, she shouted, "Go!" She picked up her staff and turned to face the man.

She froze when his sword tip touched the center of her chest. He smiled broadly. He did not need to say anything. She lowered the staff. If he gave her the chance, she would knock him from the cart.

He would not give her the chance, for he drew back the sword to thrust it through her.

"Stop!" came a shout as a hooded man stepped into the light from the fire and raised his hands. "Stop! Now!"

The man in the cart froze with the sword tip once more against her breast. She swung her staff up, striking his sword. It spiraled out of his hands. She raised the staff to propel him from the cart, but the lower end of it was caught. She tugged on it, then saw a hooded man was holding it.

"I said, 'Stop.'" His voice was calm, but she could not see his face beneath his hood. "And that is what I meant, milady."

"Who are you?"

"The one who, tonight, has saved your life."

"Why?"

"Obey my command, milady, and you will learn."

She frowned. "I will not let you or anyone else hurt these people."

"My order is for all who are fighting. Are you ready to stop, or do you wish for your companions to die?"

The answer was simple. She lowered the staff to the wagon bed and wished she could shove aside the feeling that nothing else would be simple from this point forward.

Chapter 12

Elspeth stood next to Tarran. Vala sat on his other side. Behind them, his men were gathered in a semicircle. Gryn had his right hand pressed over a thick bandage on his left arm. The sword had almost missed him, but the scratch was deep enough for Vala to be concerned. Kei and Seith were unhurt. Tarran had an incision above his right wrist, long rather than deep. He had insisted that it be tended to later. Elspeth had agreed, because they were outnumbered, and a bandage on an arm would do little good if a blade pierced a beating heart.

Across the now brightly burning fire, the hooded man was alone. She was not fooled. His men were waiting just beyond the firelight. Several were barely conscious. Others had been bleeding when she saw them taken away by their comrades. There had been more attackers than she had realized. She was amazed to be alive.

The hooded man took a single step forward. The golden staff he carried seemed to capture the fire's power. Kei uttered a curse. It was bitten off in midword, and she guessed Tarran had motioned him to silence. She said nothing as she watched the hooded man. He was followed by a slightly shorter man whose hood was so wide it drooped nearly to the front of his collar.

The robes reminded her of a friar's. She bit her lower lip. Their robes were like the ones worn by the bards at Lord de la Rochelle's castle. Did these men belong to the baron? Impossible! The baron would not send warriors after them disguised as friars.

Who could these men be? Neither minstrels nor friars ambushed travelers.

The taller man, who had ordered the fighting to cease, handed his staff to the shorter man before drawing back his hood. He settled it onto his shoulders as if he usually wore it that way. His motion revealed a tonsure, but his head could be shaven or balding. No friar would command a small army. Friars were men of peace, begging for what they needed while teaching God's lessons.

Her eyes were caught by a pendant over his cassock. On it were round beads that appeared to be made of glass. Their color was impossible to discern in the darkness. Unlike the man at Lord de la Rochelle's castle, he did not seem concerned that others saw the beads. He wore a similar bead on a ring on his left hand. Again she could not see its color, but the ring glinted with silver. Elusive memory teased her. She had seen something like it before, but she could not recall where or when.

As the man came closer, he glanced at her and paused in midstep so abruptly the shorter man stumbled into him. He eyed her from head to foot, then bowed his head. When he straightened, curiosity blossomed in his eyes that were so pale they looked colorless.

Tarran must have seen it, too, because he edged between her and the two men. "I am Tarran ap Llyr. My traveling companions are members of my family and retainers. Why have you attacked us?"

"You travel in my lands without my permission."

"These lands belong to Lord Rhys, Prince of Deheubarth."

The man's lips twisted. "He holds them for the Norman king, for he has yielded his birthright to an outlander."

"A mistake, I agree."

Elspeth choked back a gasp. Why had she failed to consider the possibility that Tarran and his men would be happy to see King Henry gone from Wales? That his men called him "prince" was a clear sign that they did not accept Norman ways.

Tarran, if you knew of my quest, would you try to halt my attempts to save King Henry? Would you be happy to see the Normans banished with his death from Wales?

"Not that it matters," the man continued, "for those who live within these hills and along the shore know that these lands are mine."

"By what right do you claim these lands?"

"I claim them because I am Druce."

Tarran's face registered no sign of recognition of the name or title or whatever it might be. His men appeared as baffled as she was.

Druce motioned to the hooded man standing behind him. "This is Orwig, my assistant. He is learned too in the ways of Cymru when it was not subject to a foreign king."

The shorter man did not lift his hood.

"Who are you?" the man named Druce continued, pointing to her.

"I am Elspeth Braybrooke," she said, stepping forward, "and—"

Tarran grasped her arm, shoving her behind him. She yelped when his fingers dug into her skin. His glower warned her to silence, but she would have retorted if Vala had not put her fingers on Elspeth's arm gently and shook her head.

"I have given you my name," Tarran said. "We are travelers on the way to Tyddewi. You may believe you have a claim to this land, but you have yet to explain why you at-

tacked us on lands belonging to King Henry and Lord
Rhys, Prince of Deheubarth."

Druce chuckled, the sound as icy as sleet striking frozen
grass. "Neither the king nor his vassals guard these hills.
We do."

"You are not the king's servants?"

Elspeth tightened her grip on her staff when she heard
Tarran's companions draw their swords. She watched
Druce's men, but they did not move from the shadows.
Were they always so obedient?

"We serve no man," Druce said.

"Then which god do you serve?"

Druce laughed again. "If you hope to pry for answers
you believe I am keeping from you, let me warn you that
you are wasting your time. We are who we are."

"I wish the answer to only one question," Tarran replied.
"I wish to know why you attacked us."

"Because you travel without my permission on my road
and among my hills."

"What must one do to obtain your permission? We go to
Tyddewi to take an old woman to her granddaughter. We
are traveling in peace."

He watched as the hooded man named Orwig leaned
forward and whispered to Druce. How had these people escaped the notice of the authorities? King Henry would be
merciless to anyone attempting to usurp his power. The
foray into Ireland to force Strongbow to kneel showed that.

The taller man listened to Orwig, then strode around the
fire to stand in front of Tarran. Druce stared at him, then
said something that was neither Norman nor Welsh. From
the shadows, his men gave an answer. A single word that
sounded like nonsense to Tarran.

"What are they saying?" Elspeth whispered behind him.

He motioned her to silence. He sensed her frustration.

Because it matched his own or because he had come to know her well in the past few days?

"You have my permission to travel through my lands," Druce said with the magnanimity of a high king speaking to his lowest subject. The ring on his left hand flashed in the firelight as he gave a broad gesture. "Orwig and I will escort you."

"That is not necessary."

"It is. Within my land, there are dangers even a prince may not be prepared for."

If Druce and his men expected him to react to the fact that the hooded men knew he could claim the title of prince, Tarran hoped they were not disappointed when he continued to regard them with the same serene expression. He would give them no chance to surprise him again.

"Then we should welcome your assistance," Tarran said.

"Yes, you should."

The man's arrogance was an affront, but Tarran did not have the luxury of taking insult. He had seen the number of men Druce commanded. There must be a double score loitering in the shadows. If Druce gave the order to attack, Tarran's men would be overwhelmed. Elspeth might be able to defend herself, but neither Vala nor Iau could. Even if she were able to get them into the cart, Druce's archers would slay the oxen before they had gone far. And the cart's wheel . . .

Tarran recognized defeat. The taste was acidic in his mouth. He must keep himself and his men alive to get his revenge against Bradwr ap Glew. Furthermore, he could not risk those he had vowed to protect.

"Good." Druce motioned, and his men came closer to the fire. Their bows were unstrung and their swords sheathed, but each weapon was a reminder that Tarran had made the only possible choice. "We will stay here tonight. Tomorrow—"

"The cart's front right wheel needs to be repaired before we can go far."

Again Druce was the benevolent despot. "I have men with the skills to fix it. You will be on your way before the sun reaches its midday peak."

Elspeth muttered, "Can't anyone in Wales pick a different time for a deadline?"

Tarran was astonished to feel his lips twitch as an unexpected bubble rose in his throat. Laughter? He had not laughed with honest amusement since Addfwyn's death. Why did he want to laugh now while facing a dangerous foe? Again he gestured to Elspeth to be silent.

"On the morrow," he said.

Druce walked back to where his men were gathered. The man who had not shown his face trotted behind him like an obedient cur.

"We need to rest," Tarran said to his companions. "Vala, if you have more of that pain potion, give some to Gryn as well as another dose to Iau."

"And you?" she asked.

"I am fine."

"He is lying," Elspeth said quietly. "He needs the potion as well. If he let Druce see so much emotion, he must be weaker than he wishes us to know."

Not wanting to reveal how insightful her appraisal was, Tarran stirred the fire higher before sitting among his men. Elspeth helped Vala, but let the old woman tend his wound. Was she unwilling to come close to him again? He could have used her warmth. The sparse heat from the flames barely sliced through the damp night.

How easy it would be to banish the night's chill when he sought the sweetest heat deep within her! His palms itched to cup her firm breasts again before his mouth explored them, sliding up each mound and down into the valley between them as her heart pounded out her craving for him. As she had pressed close to him on the hillside, he had relished her strong, lithe lines. She had a warrior's body, honed by long hours of practice, but it was also a woman's body, pliable and waiting for him to become part of her. He thought of her practicing with her quarterstaff and how those same motions would move her with him, slow and then faster until they were melded together by ecstasy.

He moaned.

"Did I hurt you?" Vala asked with concern.

"I am fine."

"If you will turn so I can bandage—"

The only movement he could make now would be within that red-haired temptress. The pulsing ache for her had hardened him until he found any other motion painful.

"Just do what you can," Tarran retorted.

Vala looked at the bandage she was putting on his arm.

He regretted his sharp words. Vala was not the one consuming him with fantasies that weakened him at the very worst time.

"I am sorry," he said. "I need to keep watch on those men."

"Is that what you truly need?" The old woman gave him a grin. "*She* would relieve your pain better than any potion would."

He did not pretend to misunderstand. "She would not be willing to be a single dose." He looked past Vala to where Elspeth sat cross-legged with her quarterstaff on her knees. The flames flickering on her face accented her cheekbones and the determined line of her jaw. The recalcitrant curls were a fiery cloud around her, emphasizing her slender curves.

"There is no reason she must be only a single dose."

He looked at the old woman who had been as a mother

to him. "Vala, she is worthy of more than a few quick tumbles on a hidden hummock."

The old woman tied off the ends of the bandage and smiled. She said nothing more, but he knew she was pleased to have persuaded him to reveal that truth. He wanted to warn her not to speak of their conversation, but that was unnecessary. Vala knew the value of being tight-lipped . . . unlike Elspeth who chattered like a songbird. But, he was coming to realize, Elspeth did not talk for the sake of spewing out words. Her comments, long-winded though they might be, held the wisdom of an accomplished warrior.

When Vala went to check on Iau, whose snores were competing with those from the far side of the fire, Tarran shifted across the wet grass to where Elspeth sat. Her gaze was focused across the flames. She was as ready to fight for those she considered allies as one of the women of ancient legend. Her strength was as alluring as her soft lips. He fought his need to push her beneath him so he could find release for his craving with her.

She did not look at him as she whispered, "Why did you agree for Druce to travel with us?"

"You know the answer." He struggled to make his voice even. "You see the number of his men."

"We defeated Lord de la Rochelle's men when they tried to stop us."

"We did not have Vala and a wounded man with us then."

Her shoulders sagged slightly. "I should have considered that."

"The daylight will offer opportunities to put an end to our strange alliance." He picked up a strand of her hair and twirled it around his finger. "Don't worry, Elspeth. I allowed *you* to travel with us, didn't I?"

"That is different."

"How?"

"I did not set my allies upon you with bare swords."

"No, you did not. Yet Iau will not ride with us beyond Tyddewi because of you."

"There is no need to discuss that again."

"True, but it is something *you* should recall." It was something he needed to remember as well. She was enticing, but his duty first was to his quest and his men. If he were to bed her once, maybe he would be satisfied and be able to think of something else.

As she looked at him, her eyes glistening in the firelight, he knew he was fooling himself. Her passions were as strong as wine, and having once enjoyed their intoxication, he knew he would be even more eager for another chance to savor them.

"If you wish to speak of something else," he said sharply, wanting to escape his thoughts, "then tell me why you decided to travel with us."

"I told you. I want to go in the same direction you are traveling."

"Why?"

"Are you hoping I will say it is because of you?"

He held her chin between his thumb and forefinger. "Be careful of your teasing, Elspeth Braybrooke. Someone might take you seriously, and you shall find yourself in more danger than you were when a man held a sword to your heart."

"More danger? What could be more dangerous than that?"

She was being honest, he realized, rather than coy. She did not perceive what thoughts her smile or her wide eyes or her wild hair created in a man. Whoever had trained her as a warrior had failed to explain the other weapons a woman possessed that could defeat any man. Her inno-

cence sent another throb pounding through him, driving all
sanity before it.

He was kissing her before his next thought formed. She
was willing and he was able. He tugged her closer. She was—

He yelped as her quarterstaff tipped up on her lap and
struck him in the head. Releasing her, he considered thank-
ing her for the knock on the skull. It was a painful reminder
of what he should be doing. What he had vowed to do.

"I am sorry, Tarran," she whispered. "Are you all right?"

So many answers he could give her. Some started with
a "yes." Others were the opposite. He spoke none of them
as he stood and walked away before he could speak the
only one he really wanted to say.

Nothing could be right until she was his, but he would
not risk letting another woman into his life while he had
not avenged the death of the woman he had vowed to love
forever.

Elspeth strolled among the trees at the river's edge. The
River Alun hardly deserved such a grand name. It was as
narrow as the stream that ran through one corner of St.
Jude's Abbey. Maybe it widened as it reached the sea, but
from where she stood, she guessed she could jump to the
other bank without much effort.

It was the perfect place for a cursed rock because King
Henry could span the river with a single leap . . . and set
foot on *Llech-lafar* before anyone could shout a warning.
Merlin, whether he had been real or legend, had been the
inspiration for a devilishly simple scheme.

She looked to the west where the midday sun was turning the sea a pale white. She squinted because the light was
so piercing. The River Alun meandered past the ruins of St.
David's Cathedral.

"What are you doing?"

She whirled when she heard Tarran's voice. He stood

higher on the riverbank. Heliwr sat on his arm. The bird regarded her with a gaze as chill as its master's. But nothing could cool the blaze of longing inside her as she took in the sight of Tarran. Strong. Powerful. Brawny. The words filled her mind as she admired his easy motions while he climbed down the bank. Not even the bandage on his arm could detract from his aura of strength.

Every inch of her begged to be in his arms, but she was not sure which Tarran she faced now. Was it the icy-cold prince who thought only of the hatred that consumed his soul? Or was it the gentle lover who inspired such fantasies within her own soul? She could never be sure. She wished he would explain his odd behavior the previous night, but he had said nothing. He might be wise not to speak of it, because any discussion could lead them into a very different type of discourse, where words only got in the way. Did he know that she had tossed and turned throughout the night, unable to sleep, as her body roiled with craving for him?

"I am fishing," she said, then wished she had offered a different excuse.

"Without a hook or a string or a pole?"

She laughed, not at his question, but at the ridiculous situation. Painfully ridiculous. "I should have said I was hoping to find a pool to fish in."

"Good luck."

"Tarran?"

"Yes?"

"Would you be glad to have the Normans gone from Wales?"

He regarded her with another scowl. "That is an absurd question, and I am surprised you ask it."

"Then give me an answer, and I shall not have to ask it again."

"I would be very glad to see every Norman gone from Cymru. I would be even happier if none of them returned."

"King Henry would die before he allowed that to happen."

"I know." He started to walk past her, then jumped to the other side of the river. The bird squawked, flapping its wings before settling quietly on his fist again. He continued on his way upstream without looking back.

Elspeth fought her feet, which wanted to race after him. She bit her lip to keep from shouting after him to explain his baffling behavior last night. *He* had kissed her. *He* had been the one to walk away last night. Now he was walking away again.

Sitting, she fingered her quarterstaff. He had left when it struck him. Had he thought she used it against him on purpose? When he had pulled her to him, kissing her with a savage longing that overpowered her, she had forgotten it was on her lap. Now he acted as if they were strangers, as if he trusted her no more than he did Druce.

She muttered a curse that would have earned her a reprimand from the abbess. She had not been sent to Wales to ease Tarran's grief. If he wanted it eased . . . She could not keep from wondering if he had pulled away last night because he feared being anything but miserable. Her father had said more than once that no one wished to be unhappy, but maybe he had been mistaken.

"Oh, I thought I might find Prince Tarran with you."

Elspeth looked up from the river to discover Seith wearing an uneasy grin. "He went off by himself."

"What did you say to him?" His brows lowered in a stern frown he must have borrowed from Tarran.

"What I always seem to say. The wrong thing. I asked him if he would be happy to see the Normans leave Wales."

Seith snorted. "A foolish question."

"A question of loyalty!"

"We can be loyal to King Henry and respect his throne, even if we wish that he and the rest of you Normans would stay on the other side of Offa's Dyke."

"Thank you for making me feel welcome." She pointed to the trees across the river. "He went in that direction if you want to give chase."

"No." He squatted beside her. "If he wishes time to himself, I will not intrude on him."

"Was he always like this?"

Seith picked up a small branch and rolled it back and forth between his fingers. "Like what?"

"Without an inkling of humor in anything he says or does. Being so short-tempered when one fails to meet his expectations." She looked squarely at him. "He seldom smiles, and I have never heard him laugh with anything but disgust. It is as if he has forgotten how to be happy."

"He has." He tossed the branch into the river. "I hope he will remember again."

"Once Bradwr ap Glew's blood has been drained from his corpse?"

Seith glanced at her and quickly away. "Vala should not have told you what we do."

"She did not."

"Prince Tarran did?"

Elspeth nodded. "When he realized it was absurd for the rest of you to spend every minute guarding your words, he told me what I had already guessed."

"Then you understand why he is as he is. How could he have guessed Lady Addfwyn would be murdered by a man he considered his closest friend?"

"His *friend* killed her?"

"I thought he told you about her death."

"He told me she was murdered and that you are seeking Bradwr ap Glew. He never mentioned anything about a friendship with the murderer."

Seith appeared as if he were about to weep. "Do not tell Prince Tarran that I spoke of this to you. Forget I told you."

"How can I forget that Tarran was betrayed by a friend?"

He stared along the river. "None of us can forget it. Nobody could have foreseen such a tragedy, not even Prince Tarran himself. He and Bradwr ap Glew were closer than friends, for they were foster brothers. Their fathers were cousins, and more than one person thought, despite the differences in their heights, Prince Tarran and Bradwr ap Glew were twins."

She did not reply. Seith's words confirmed what she had guessed. Tarran was haunted by the fact that he was a warrior, born to the title of a leader of men and trained to be prepared for any battle. In spite of that, he had failed to imagine that his friend—a man he had trusted since he was a child—could have murdered his wife.

"But why would Bradwr ap Glew kill Addfwyn?"

"That is something only the traitor can explain. Prince Tarran will have the truth from him before he has the pleasure of slaying him."

Again she considered his words. The icy Prince Tarran would not hesitate to kill his wife's murderer. Nor would the tender man who thrilled her with his touch. But would his enemy's death put the pain within him to rest?

"Where will you go after we reach Tyddewi?" Seith asked into the silence.

"I am not yet sure." She saw no reason to lie. "Did Tarran ask you to ask me?"

Seith leaned against a tree and locked his fingers over his wide belly. "If *Prince* Tarran wished to know, he would ask you himself. Subterfuge is not his way."

"True."

"So where do you go?"

"I am not certain yet." She smiled coolly. "Where do

you go after Vala is delivered safely into the keeping of her granddaughter?"

"Where we can complete the task we have sworn to do."

"I understand." She almost added that she did because her answer was the same. She would go where she must to complete the task the queen had given her.

Branches rattled, and Elspeth reached for her staff as Seith drew his sword. Neither spoke as Druce, again holding his gold-colored staff, walked toward them, followed by his silent companion, Orwig.

"We will reach your destination before the rains over the western sea come ashore," Druce said. His pride suggested that he had arranged for their deliverance to Tyddewi himself. She guessed he believed that.

"Those are good tidings." She was lying, because when the big storms moved from the sea, the king would be able to sail from Ireland. She was aware of the passing of each hour. *Llech-lafar* might be along the River Alun, but where? She held her staff on her crossed legs and folded her hands atop it. Her skills with the staff were useless now. Why had the queen chosen *her*?

"I am pleased you are pleased. If you are not busy, I would speak with you."

Seith rose and nodded toward Druce. Even though the big man's steps were slow and even, Elspeth was certain Seith was eager to put as much distance as possible between him and Druce. Yet, she knew as well that he or one of Tarran's other men would remain nearby.

Druce sat where Seith had. Orwig chose a spot under a tree farther along the water. It was the most shadowed spot, she noted. Was he afraid of the sunlight? If that was the reason he did not lower his hood, he must be frightened of the moon too because he constantly wore the hood over his face.

"It is a surprise to see a Norman woman among the

Welsh," Druce said, and she pushed his companion out of
her mind as Orwig rose and walked inland along the river.

"Our paths lie in the same direction, so we thought it
wise to travel together." She kept her voice steady. If Druce
thought that she had been with Tarran and his party since
they left Castell Gwalch Glas, then she would not disabuse
him of that notion.

"What do you think of Cymru?"

"It is a lovely land."

"Many of your countrymen believe the same. That is
why they have claimed our lands as their own."

"Druce, I cannot speak about what others have done.
Only myself. I am here to learn what I can of your country.
There are many fascinating stories and legends."

He brightened. "I teach the old ways to those who are
willing to listen."

"What sort of old ways?"

"The tales that have thrilled our warriors since the first
dawn. Tales that have inspired them to great deeds to cre-
ate more songs." He flung out his hands. "Songs Cymru
can take pride in."

His ring glittered. The bead was not exactly like the
blue ones around his neck. It was clear save for three
strands of blue spiraling through it. She wished she could
examine it more closely. Maybe if she touched it, she
would recall where she had seen something similar. It must
have been at St. Jude's Abbey, because no one who came
to watch her parents perform would have been wealthy
enough to afford such a fabulous jewel.

"Teaching others," he went on, "is my duty as a descen-
dant of the greatest wizard of all time."

"Wizard?" she asked, astonished. Until now, Druce had
sounded as sane as Tarran. Now he was talking about
magic.

"Myrddin, who was born Emrys at Caer-Fyrddin."

"I have never heard of him."

He smiled. "Yes, you have. You Normans call him Merlin and his birthplace Carmarthen."

"Merlin? Do you know the story of *Llech-lafar*, the talking rock?"

He smiled. "I know all the stories about Merlin. How is it, milady, that you know of *Llech-lafar*?"

"I have heard others speak of the stone and its mystic qualities. When I asked for more about the story, I got few answers. People know of the rock, but not where Merlin hid it along the River Alun."

"He did not hide it. He left it where it could do what it must when the time was right."

"So you know where it is?"

Again he smiled. "One who studies the ancient tales quickly learns how much more there is to learn."

Elspeth fought not to sigh. For all his blustering and bragging, Druce apparently knew no more about *Llech-lafar* than anyone else.

"We are Merlin's descendants," Druce went on, "sworn to keep alive the stories of his greatest deeds along with the other tales belonging to this land."

"Other tales? What sort of tales?"

Druce leaned forward and lowered his voice until it sounded like the wind coursing along the forest floor, a deep rumble that flowed over and around her. "Tales that were old even when the great Merlin was a boy, for these are the stories that come from the first men to call Cymru home."

"Will you tell me?"

"There are too many to share before we reach Tyddewi." He smiled. "But I will tell you the ones I think you will enjoy most. Shall we start with the story of Prince Pwyll?"

"Who fought in Death's place?"

His smile wavered. "You already know that tale?"

"No, but I have heard of it. Tell me please." Maybe some part of the story would help her understand Tarran's ever-changing behavior. She did not want to admit, even to herself, that she hoped she would learn something to help her discover if his heart had a place for her in it . . . or if it was broken beyond any hope of loving again.

Chapter 13

He was dreaming.

Tarran did not recall falling asleep. It seemed only a moment before that he had been glaring at the moon that had risen to gleam in the river. It soon would be hidden by the branches overhead, but, for now, its chalky light glowed around the tree's trunks.

He was astonished he was dreaming, for sleep had eluded him so many nights. In the fortnight after he had discovered his slain wife, he had not wanted to sleep. He had tried to use every moment to find out who had killed her and why. The answer for the first he had gotten quickly, for his onetime friend had made no effort to hide his treachery.

When at last Tarran had to sleep a fortnight later, he had been set upon by nightmares. Some started out filled with joy. He could hear Addfwyn's laughter and watch her eyes light with love for him. But those swiftly became nightmares, and the echo of her laugh altered into the screams he had heard when he rushed into their home to find her bodyservant kneeling beside her.

Then Elspeth Braybrooke had burst into his life with endless chatter and passionate eyes. He did not understand why Addfwyn had returned in his dreams as his craving for another woman grew stronger.

To discover the answer, he must sleep. He must find Addfwyn in his dreams and speak to her.

And now he was dreaming.

Tarran recognized the massive chamber that would hold his family's manor house and have enough space for the stables and other outbuildings. Even then, the room would not be full. Great columns edged the room, but there was no roof. No roof was needed when rain never fell. Yet, all around him, greenery was lush and fragrant.

The old ways did not linger anywhere in Cymru except in the legends. He did not believe that King Arawn ruled in this land lit by a sun far sweeter and brighter than the one where men walked through their days, never knowing which one might be their last.

Despite that, he was within the great hall in Annwfn once more. Music curled around him, like a cat seeking his attention. Voices raised in convivial conversation while trays of food were set in front of those relishing King Arawn's feast.

He threaded his way through the scores of tables where great heroes found the reward for their bravery. None of the warriors seemed to notice him, and their faces were unfamiliar. Maybe it was because, after death, a man's visage did not remain the same. It was a puzzle he had no interest in solving.

He was there for one reason. He wanted to be with his beloved Addfwyn.

As if thought could convey him to her, he was standing beside the table where she sat. She was unchanged. So tamed, so sedate, her black hair had not a hint of curl like Elspeth's. When she turned to look at him, it stayed perfectly behind her shoulders instead of bouncing about as Elspeth's did.

Elspeth! Why was she in his thoughts *now*? He could not help comparing the two women. Addfwyn who quietly oversaw his home and anticipated his every need. Elspeth who was never quiet and anticipated danger lurking nearby even before he did. The two women could not be more different.

As she had before, Addfwyn motioned toward the empty spot beside her. "Prince Tarran ap Llyr, come and sit with me."

"Prince Tarran ap Llyr? You address me formally, Addfwyn, when you are my wife." He swung one leg over the bench and sat so he could admire her profile. Like her, it was gently drawn. Elspeth seldom was still long enough for him to enjoy looking at her. Like her quarterstaff, she moved with purpose and grace.

Get out of my head, Elspeth! He knew such an order was futile. He could not stop thinking of her. Even now, she was lying not far from where he slept. If he woke and went to her, would she draw him into her arms and grant him the powerful release he could find deep within her? His body responded to the thought, every muscle tightening until he struggled to breathe.

"Prince Tarran," Addfwyn said, and he looked at her. He had eagerly waited for this moment, and now he could think only of Elspeth.

"No longer am I your wife," she continued. "Our vows were until death did us part." Her sad smile softened her words. Facing him, she put her hand over her heart. "But there are some things that even Death cannot halt, for your love is a part of me forever."

"And I love you, Addfwyn." The words burst from him like a wounded man shouting for relief from pain. He *did* love her, and he did not want to fall in love again. He had told Elspeth that. *Elspeth, begone from my thoughts!* Desperation crept into his voice as he added, "My vows went beyond death."

"I know you intended that, but Death has rules of his

own." She smiled again, this one bright with happiness. "There is another woman in your life. A woman who insists that you put aside your grief and regain the gift of life that still is yours." She lifted a hair from his sleeve. "This tells me." She tossed the red hair into the air.

As it drifted back toward the table, it metamorphosed into the image of Elspeth. She held her staff with the ease that bespoke the skill he would never underestimate again. As she went through the steps he had seen her practice, the image floated down toward the table. The tiny Elspeth came to rest next to Addfwyn's hand.

"She is brave," Addfwyn said quietly.

"Yes, she is, but how do you know? Can you see the living world from here?" Had Addfwyn seen him take Elspeth into his arms? Could she know of the cravings Elspeth created within him? Guilt riveted him as strongly as if the staff had been driven into his gut.

"No, the veil between the world of the living and Annwfn is too thick for a mortal to look through. Only when you bring something with you from the world of men can I see." She smiled as warmly as she had when she slept in his arms. "That this woman can be seen in the hall of great warriors tells me that she is worthy to sit among them."

"She is courageous, even though she takes unnecessary risks."

"You always worried about that with me as well." She looked at the miniature Elspeth lowering one end of the staff to the ground and bowing to acknowledge her invisible opponent. "You are a man who wants to protect those in his life. Now you have met a woman who says she has no need for that protection."

He gazed at Elspeth's living picture. It was silent, but he could tell she was laughing as she wiped her sleeve across her forehead. Her hair flew about her, and he could think only of its sun-washed scent.

"She is skilled," Addfwyn said, "but the greatest danger for her does not come from an enemy she can beat back with her staff. She needs your protection from . . ."

"From me?"

"That you ask that question should show you that you already know the answer." She blew on the image, and it floated away, once again a single red hair.

He reached for it. As his fingers closed around it, he woke. His hand was empty, for he had lost what he once had while trying to grasp what he should not want to possess.

Tarran heard Elspeth laugh as he lashed his cloak around his neck. The sound was like a happy song, and it grated on his bones when he saw her sitting next to Druce as they prepared for another night along the river. She had spent the whole day talking with Druce. He had lingered by her side, his silent man always nearby.

Let Elspeth enjoy Druce! That kept her from turning her soft green eyes in his direction. As Tarran walked away from the others, climbing the hill toward a rolling moor that led to the east, he repeated those words to himself. Maybe during time alone, hunting with Heliwr, he could gain some perspective.

He must not be distracted, especially by Elspeth. Seeing her with Druce, he had to question whether she could be trusted. Not that he believed she would betray him on purpose. Hadn't he learned that only a fool trusted blindly? Addfwyn had paid with her life for unseeing faith in Bradwr ap Glew.

Tarran paused in the middle of a field partway up the hill. Except for one slash of woodland cutting through it, open land rolled away like waves frozen into the earth. In the other direction, the sea was covered with gray as storms between Cymru and Ireland stirred it up. Only beneath his feet was there stability. Any step he took could lead to quicksand where his hopes and plans would be sucked away by Elspeth's smile that drove every other thought from his head.

"She has infected me with madness, my friend," he said as he drew off Heliwr's leather hood and ran his finger along the bird's breastbone. By judging its sharpness and the size of Heliwr's crop, he could tell the goshawk was not overfed and was ready to hunt.

The bird gave him an impatient stare.

"You are fortunate, my friend. You think solely of the hunt and the unfortunate prey that will soon be yours."

The bird shifted on his hand, a sure sign that the hawk wanted to be released.

Drawing back his arm and then moving it forward quickly to keep it free of his cloak, Tarran sent Heliwr flying. The hawk soared to sit in a tree, surveying far beyond what Tarran could see. What freedom there must be in such flight! What simplicity there must be in a life where prey was found and dispatched with talons as sharp as the dagger at his belt.

He watched the hawk moving from tree to tree, always seeking a better vantage point, while he climbed the hill. When he reached the top, he saw a few houses along a headland lumped into the sea like a loaf of unbaked bread. The southwest of Cymru was different from his beloved mountains to the north. He missed their rough crags with rings of broken rock at their bases. As a child, he had scrambled over them, fighting great battles with imaginary foes. Now he had a real enemy.

With a screech, Heliwr aimed talons first toward the ground. Tarran raced toward where the bird was killing its prey. If he let the bird feast too long, Heliwr would be reluctant to fly more. The bird was tearing at the small rabbit it held beneath its spread wings. Tarran drew out a piece of meat and put it beneath the bird's beak. Heliwr grabbed it, and Tarran yanked the rabbit away, hiding it in his pouch. The hawk would think the rabbit had fled and search for other game, giving Tarran an excuse to loiter longer on the hill.

He put another piece of meat on the thumb of his glove and held it out. Heliwr jumped onto his glove and swallowed the treat in a single gulp. Once the bird was settled on his arm, he sent it aloft again. Heliwr soared, delighted to be free of the hood and hours of riding.

Tarran wandered along the hill. He paused when he saw large stones stacked atop one another. It was one of the ancient places built by the people who had first claimed Cymru as their own. Three upright stones supported the rear of a huge, flat boulder. A single stone was set beneath the front of the teardrop-shaped boulder. Several flat rocks were scattered around the standing stones.

He heard something rattling in the bushes beyond the stones. A beast anxious to find its herd? Rain began falling fitfully. He whistled to the hawk to call it in because the bird would not fly in a heavy rain.

He heard the sound again. Who was nearby? Elspeth? He silenced the burst of hope he did not want to feel. Everything that happened, everything he saw, everything he heard brought her to mind. But someone was coming toward him, and he could not imagine who else would climb the hill after him. Seith had not gained his generous bulk by exercising, and Kei and Gryn did not trust either Druce or Elspeth enough to leave them alone with their companions.

"Elspeth," he said, not softening his exasperation, "I have had enough—"

Helwir screeched from overhead.

Tarran whirled. Something slashed toward him. A sword! He fell backward to avoid it and rolled to his feet. Tossing his hawking glove away, he pulled out his sword. He raised it to meet a fierce downswing from the other blade. Edges shrieked as the two swords slid past each other.

He stared at his opponent. The man wore a simple robe, much like the ones worn by Druce's men. Why would one of them be attacking him? Were Elspeth and the others under attack, too?

He knocked the other man's sword aside before it could slice into his arm. Overhead, Heliwr shrieked again. Were others coming to assail him? He gritted his teeth so hard he heard his jaw crunch.

The splattering rain became a downpour. He blinked aside the water coursing down his face. The other man had the advantage because his deep hood protected him. But the other man might not be able to see as well to the side.

Tarran swung his sword, not directly at the man but in a wide arc from the right. The man's sword met it without hesitation, then thrust toward him.

He backpedaled. His boot skidded on a rock in the grass. His arms windmilled while he fought for his balance, and the other man slashed at him again. Pain seared Tarran's right arm. His sleeve turned a watery crimson, but he still had feeling in his fingers. The wound could not be deep.

He struck the ground hard. Shoving aside his cloak, he lifted his sword and parried the other man's blow. Just barely. The incision above his elbow was slowing him. When the other man jabbed at him again, he knew his opponent must realize the truth, too.

As he struggled to regain his feet, he was pushed back by the man's sword. He stared at the colors half hidden beneath the man's cassock. They were colors he had once welcomed. Now he despised the emblem of Bradwr ap Glew's family.

"Who are you?" he shouted.

"The one to have the honor of slaying you." The man swung at him again.

Tarran halted it once more, but his fingers almost lost their grip on the hilt. "Where is Bradwr ap Glew?"

"Waiting to learn you are dead!" He leaned forward to put his sword close to Tarran's throat. His eyes gleamed in anticipation.

"Tarran!" His name resonated along the hill.

Elspeth!

How had she found him? He heard Heliwr cry out again from above. Had his hawk called her? That was impossible. The bird cared for nothing but the hunt.

But the cry distracted the other man. Tarran kicked up with both feet and sent the man staggering. Jumping to his feet, he tried to swing his sword. The man laughed at his feeble attempt.

That laugh faded, as with a shout that rang in his ears like the hawk's, Elspeth ran forward. She swung her staff at the man, striking him in the back. He spun, but she was even faster. She lowered the staff, and he tripped over it. As he fought to regain his feet, she brought the staff up sharply, hitting him in the chest. He staggered back. His sword flailed, opening him to her next blow. She slammed the staff down on the wrist of his sword arm.

Tarran heard bone crack, and the man's sword fell to the ground. The man shrieked in pain and anger. He groped to pull his dagger. She lunged forward to halt him, but she was not quick enough. He pulled the blade and drew it back to throw at her.

Leaping forward, Tarran grabbed her around the waist with his uninjured arm. He threw her to the ground, falling beside her as the knife flew over their heads. The staff hit him in the knee just as the knife thudded into the ground inches past them. He heard her groan beneath him. Had he injured her in an attempt to save her?

She raised her head and spit out some grass. "Let me up!"

"Elspeth—"

She pointed toward where the man was fleeing down the hill toward some trees, dragging his sword awkwardly behind him. "I can catch him!"

"No."

"I can halt him." She tried to roll over onto her back, but he knew to allow her even that would risk having her slip away and go after the man.

He shook his head and scowled. "You would be at a great disadvantage among those trees. Even a sword would be difficult to swing among them."

"I know some tricks that can—"

"No, Elspeth." He tried to harden his voice, but it broke as he said, "I will never chance finding you dying, too."

Chapter 14

Elspeth sagged against the ground. "I did not realize—
that is, I thought Addfwyn was dead when you found
her. I am sorry, Tarran. I cannot imagine how horrible it is
to watch someone you love die."

"Be glad you cannot imagine such a sight!" Tarran
would not meet her eyes. Was he ashamed of his heartfelt
words?

Tears filled her eyes. "You must stop blaming yourself
for her death. Even if you had been sitting by Addfwyn's
side, your friend could have found a way to slay her."

"If I had been there, I would have fought him off." He
looked at his bleeding arm as dispassionately as if it belonged to someone else. "Addfwyn was no warrior like you,
Elspeth. You are like Rhiannon, who was more than consort
to her husband, Pwyll. Addfwyn resembled Blodeuedd, the
lady made of flowers."

"But Blodeuedd sought to betray her husband, and
Addfwyn would not have done that."

His brows lowered as he met her eyes for the first time.
"No."

"And Rhiannon endured a sentence for a crime she did
not commit. She sat in front of her husband's hall and had
people spit on her because they wrongly believed she had

caused the death of her son. Your Welsh women are strong and strong willed. Their glorious deeds match the tales of the heroes in your sagas. Why do you believe Addfwyn was different?"

"She was a gentle spirit who could not protect herself."

"How can you be certain? You said Bradwr ap Glew was seen with blood on him. Could some of it have been his own?"

"Who knows? We were not there. If I had been . . ."

"Tarran, I did not mean to add to your burden." The rain halted as if someone had plugged a hole in a dam, but her drenched clothes stuck to her when she moved.

"Nothing can add to my burden or take away from it. It simply is."

"Will you be able to put it down once you have had your vengeance?"

He stood and walked toward where his sword was lying in the grass. If he wanted to hide his pain, he failed. His whole body was weighted with his grief.

Coming to her feet, she brushed grass and mud from her gown. She paused when she realized she was smearing it across herself. "Let me check your wound."

"After I call in Heliwr." He whistled sharply.

Out of the clouds, seeming to materialize through the gray, the hawk flew toward his upheld arm. It settled on his left wrist with an elegance of motion that reminded her of Tarran.

Thunder crashed. It shattered the silence that had become as forbidding as the landscape. When another distant rumble of thunder rolled along the hills, Tarran cursed. "If we stay here, a single bolt of lightning could leave us burned embers."

"There is plenty of space beneath the standing stones." She gasped as lightning struck the water beyond the headland.

Bending, he picked up something before following her. His hawking glove, she realized, as the clouds opened again, sending rain down in sheets. Under the massive rock, it was dry. She knelt and leaned her quarterstaff against a stone supporting the one over their heads.

"From your knowledge of the old stories," Tarran said, "I can see you have been enjoying your lessons with Druce."

"Stories are all we share. You need not fear that I am betraying you."

"I had no concerns about that."

"But you growl each time I say I am going to speak with him." She held out her hand. "Let me examine your wound."

He moved his arm out of her reach. "My concerns are that he will betray *you*."

"Me?"

"You sound shocked."

"I am. Druce has suggested nothing other than I should learn more about your Welsh tales." She scowled. "Will you let me examine your arm?"

He shook his head. "In a minute."

"Tarran, it could fester. Let me—"

"In a minute!" He set his sword on the ground and balanced her staff over the hilt. He placed the bird on the staff before drawing his knife and opening the pouch at his waist. He sliced apart a dead rabbit. Cutting a piece, he gave it to the bird, who tore into it.

"Fortunate bird," he said.

"Yes, he could have been hurt if he had been called in when you were attacked."

He regarded her with the same expression the bird had when waiting with obvious impatience to be fed. It was a combination of desire and aggravation at someone too witless to understand that hunger. "That was not what I meant." He tossed another small piece of meat at the bird, who ate it enthusiastically. "A hawk is not expected to forego meat during Lent for a diet of dried and tasteless fish."

She laughed. Hard. His complaint was not that amusing, but the emotion that had built up in her since she saw Tarran being beaten by a well-handled sword came bursting out. If she did not laugh, she was going to weep.

He looked at her with astonishment before turning his attention back to the hawk.

As soon as he had wiped his hands on the wet grass, she said, "You have Heliwr fed. Now let me examine your wound."

"You are making too much of something of little consequence."

"It would be of great consequence if I were to faint at the sight of blood."

"You do not faint upon seeing blood."

"Not others' blood, no." She took his arm and settled it across her drawn-up knees. "Seeing your lifeblood streaming down your arm is different." More lightning crackled above, and even the stones shuddered as thunder pounded the hillside.

"Elspeth, don't say such things."

"Scold me if you wish, but there are some things over which you cannot rule, Prince Tarran."

"And one of them is you?"

She smiled. "Now you are beginning to understand."

With care, she tore his sleeve high enough to reveal the new wound. It was more than the span of her fingers above the previous injury, and she guessed his arm would grow stiff as the muscles healed. She was pleased to see the blood was already congealing.

"It is not bad," she said as she ripped off part of his sleeve to wrap over the wound.

"Just as I told you."

She smiled. "I have learned that, unlike Druce, who exaggerates everything, you tend to diminish things."

"I prefer not to complain."

"And you do not complain very well." She peeled the torn sleeve back a bit farther. "Save about me."

"True."

For a moment, she thought she saw a smile on his taut lips, but it must have been a trick of the dim light. She wondered what it would take to bring an honest smile to those lips. Why was she wondering? She knew the answer. He smiled when he held her close. For that short time, he was willing to lessen his hold on his grief.

"You are learning much about Druce." His voice remained unagitated, but she sensed his tension.

Tying the fabric over his arm, she replied, "I am learning much about the stories of this land. I am sure he has one about these stones that he would say could not possibly have been raised by men's hands, so it must have been by magic. Druce seems to believe the events in the legends really happened. Not that I would expect anything else from a man who avers he is descended from the great magician Merlin."

"Interesting."

"You do not sound surprised."

"Nothing about Druce or his odd companion would surprise me."

She shivered as she crept away to wash her bloody hands in a puddle past the shelter of the rocks. "Orwig unsettles me."

"Because he never speaks?"

"He seems to be watching you all the time."

Now she had surprised him. As she sat with her back against a stone, he asked, "Why would he be watching me? I have offered no threat to Druce, even though I have considered dunking him in the river and leaving him there while we continue on our way."

She laughed, trying to ignore the chill seeping from the rock and through her gown. "If you have said that to anyone else and Orwig chanced to overhear, that would explain his interest in everything you do."

"I have not spoken of this to anyone. I do not want to give him the excuse he could be waiting for to attack."

"I know." She rubbed her hands together.

He took her hands in his, wincing as he moved his wounded arm. "Help me, Elspeth."

"You know I will. You need only to ask." Did he realize she did not mean solely his uneasy truce with the hooded men? She wanted to help him set aside his sorrow.

"Be vigilant," he said, "and let me know if you gain an inkling of what Druce plans. His tale of guiding us across *his* lands is one he knows none of us believe."

"He might believe it as he believes the story of Pwyll trying to win Rhiannon's heart by following her white horse around the mountain without ever being able to catch her."

"Pwyll spoke plainly to Rhiannon in that old story, but I doubt Druce is so honest."

"I agree." She tapped her staff lightly, making sure she did not bother the hawk. "That is why I carry this everywhere." Her eyes widened. "Do you think he sent the man to attack you?"

"The man wore a plain cassock like Druce's men, but beneath it, he wore the colors of Bradwr ap Glew's family."

She stared, too horrified to speak.

"I can only assume," he said, "that I am getting close to where he hides."

"You must never be alone."

He cursed viciously. "I don't need to be watched like a child. I can fight off—" His mouth tightened. "Maybe you are right. I needed your help today to keep my heart beat-

ing inside me." He put his hand on her arm. "Thank you, Elspeth."

His shoulder was at the perfect height for her head, and
she did not resist. As his arm curved around her, she closed
her eyes. She wanted to lose herself in his warmth, but she
had to say, "Tarran . . ."

"What?"

"I don't think we should discount Druce's involvement
in the attack on you. I believe Druce was alerted to our
route by a bard who left Castell Glyn Niwl after we arrived."

"What?" He sat straighter. "Do you have proof?"

"They both wear glass beads around their necks. The
man at Castell Glyn Niwl tried to hide his, but I saw it." She
stared at the storm. "I know I have seen something like
those beads before, but I cannot remember when."

"Or where?"

"I have remembered where."

"Where?"

How witless could she be! She had been careful to keep
the truth of her life in the Abbey from him. "On the other
side of Offa's Dyke," she said, hoping that would be enough
to satisfy him.

It was not. "Where in England did you see such beads?
If Druce is an agent of the Normans, he must be halted."

She laughed. "Druce? A Norman agent? He thinks that
he possesses these lands, and he despises King Henry. He
derides the king on every possible occasion."

"Which an agent would do in hopes of diverting attention."

"True, but I do not think he is King Henry's agent."

"I agree. He hates the Normans as any loyal son of
Cymru should."

She asked softly, "As you do?"

"Yes, and as you would the Welsh if our situations were reversed and we were trying to claim England."

"But I would not hate the Welsh enough to kill the king to get them to leave."

Tarran regarded her as if she had sprouted horns and a pig's nose. "Are you suggesting that I want to see King Henry dead?"

"Without a strong leader, the Marcher lords could not hold."

"If the Normans leave now, Cymru will be in chaos. Too many Welshmen would be eager to lay claim to the lands of their fathers and grandfathers. I want the Normans gone, but at a time when we have a strong leader who will unite us."

"You?"

He twirled a strand of her hair around his finger. "I find enough challenge with you. You force me to look at situations with new eyes." He tapped the tip of the dagger she wore at her side. "I trust you know how to use this."

"I use it best when I am eating." She smiled.

He did not. He ran his finger wrapped in her hair along his cheek and then hers. "And what of your feminine skills, Elspeth?"

"You are changing the subject."

"I know."

"We need to learn what that man wanted when he attacked you."

"To kill me."

She scowled. "I know, but why would Bradwr ap Glew give him the honor of slaying you instead of doing so himself?"

"My enemy has no honor, Elspeth. He proved that when he killed a woman who had always spoken of him with the highest regard."

"If you had let me go after that man—"

He untwisted the hair from his finger and brushed her hair back. Putting his mouth close to her ear, he whispered, "Did I ever mention that you talk too much?"

"But the man tried to kill you!" She had to fight for each word.

"He is gone." He drew her earlobe into his mouth and teased it with his tongue. When she gasped as quivers shot through her, he drew back enough to say, "You are here."

"Such talk proves only that your head was not hit too hard, for you can see who is here and who is not."

"You have a quick wit, but wit is not what a man thinks of when he holds a lovely woman like you."

"You should let me go."

"And what will you do for me in return?"

"In return?" She searched his face burnished by sun and wind.

"You may think I need answers to why that man attacked me. What I *need* is for you to kiss me."

"What—?" Her question vanished beneath his mouth as it claimed hers. His fiery lips swept her into a storm more ferocious than the one exploding around the hill.

She slid her mouth along the rough, whiskery coolness of his cheek, and his breath caught. It was the most amazing sound she had ever heard. She wanted to hear it again and again. With a soft laugh, she took his earlobe between her teeth and gave a gentle nibble. She pushed him back against the ground, awed by the power to give him the pleasure he had offered her.

His skin tasted of fresh air and rain and sweat, a delicious combination. He writhed beneath her when her tongue curved up the outside of his ear. She gripped his shoulders while she sampled the softer skin behind his ear. It must be the only soft spot on his whole body.

Delighting in his reaction, she traced his feverish pulse along his neck. At the spot where it met his shoulder, she reached beneath his cloak to loosen the front of his tunic. She slipped her hand across his broad chest. Her fingers delved into the hair over his rapidly beating heart.

His right arm swept up her back, pressing him to her. When he spoke her name in a breathless whisper, his voice seemed more powerful than the thunder crashing overhead. She looked down at his face. It was not the face that he wore with others, because she saw so many emotions on it. Longing, uncertainty, sorrow. She had not seen him share those feelings with anyone else. Joy surged through her, even as tears filled her eyes once more.

"What can be amiss now?" he whispered, as he slipped his hand beneath her hair to curve around her nape.

"Nothing."

"But . . ." He winced as he moved his injured arm enough so he could wipe a tear from her cheek. "You are weeping. What is wrong?"

"Nothing." She laughed softly. "You accuse me of being silly when I am not. Yet when I have silly tears, you fret." She brushed one fingertip across his lips. "I am happy to be here with you."

"Then trust me enough to tell me the truth."

She drew back, startled by the sudden change in his voice. It had regained its raw edge. "What truth?"

"Of why you are here in Cymru. I must know if what you are doing will keep me from gaining my vengeance." His face had no more warmth than the stones around them.

Sitting, Elspeth turned her back on him. "You are right!" she spat. "I am silly. Silly to believe you think of anything but your hopes for revenge. Is that why you kissed me, Tarran? To woo the truth from me?" She stood, and the bottom of the uppermost stone brushed her head. "If you want to know why I am here, you needed only to ask."

"I am asking."

He got up, then scowled when he had to hunch his shoul-

ders. He captured her lips in a deep kiss that leaned her
back against the stones. As his hand came up to slip along
her breast, she turned her face away.

"Don't!" she whispered.

"Don't kiss you? Don't touch you?"

"Don't kiss and touch me when you are thinking of *her*!
I am not Addfwyn! I can never be a woman who waits for
her beloved hero to return to the perfect home she has made
for him. I am who I am. A woman who can take care of herself, who does not need a man to defend her."

"So you can stand alone against anything?"

"Yes." More tears filled her eyes, but she would not let
them fall except back into her throat, where they burned
like a hundred separate candles.

"Maybe you are right. You do not need anyone. You are
Elspeth Braybrooke, woman warrior. Tell me, Elspeth, does
a woman warrior have any compassion within her?"

His words stung, and she fired back, "More than you
have! You hold me. You pretend to want me."

"I was not pretending!" He pulled her against him. His
hands slipped down her hips to hold her tight to his hard
male lines. "I want you, Elspeth."

"As much as you want your revenge for *her*?"

"Don't ask me that."

She edged away again, even though she craved his body
against her. "Why not? You ask me dozens of questions. I
am asking you one!"

He swore before sitting again.

"Does that mean you will not answer me?" she asked.

"I don't have an answer for you."

She was unprepared for his abrupt honesty. She had
girded herself for another argument and had hoped that he
would tell her that she was mistaken and that he wanted her
more than anything else.

"Oh." She knelt, keeping as much space as possible between them. When the rain sprayed her on a gust of wind, she moved back closer to the center of the shelter.

"You have to decide what you want, too, Elspeth."

"I know what I want." *I want everything you can share with me, but I want you to want to share it with me without thinking of another woman.*

"Tell me."

"I don't think that would be wise." Turning, she looked out at the dark sky. "It does not look as if the rain will be stopping soon. We need to return to the others before the storm gets worse."

"Go, if you want to." He closed his eyes and rested his head back against the stones. "I will not risk Heliwr." He gave a taut laugh. "Don't chide me, Elspeth, for not saying I am worried you might get hurt, too. I know you consider yourself one great knight standing alone." Without giving her a chance to answer, he said, "Tell me how you came to be skilled with a quarterstaff."

No, she pleaded, *don't make me lie to you when I have asked you to be honest.* But she had to tell him something. "My father accepted that he would not have a son, so he had me trained to know what a knight should know."

"But you are a woman. You cannot fulfill your family's feudal obligation to the king."

"I know that." She was glad the shadows would disguise how strained her smile was.

You could have told him about your life before St. Jude's Abbey. She could not guess how he would treat *her* if he discovered her parents had been traveling performers. He had offered her the respect due a lady, and she did not want to lose that.

"Yet, your father had you taught to use a staff and a dagger." Tarran's words intruded.

"I believe it pleased him, even though his daughter could never hold lands or title."

"I see." He stretched out on the ground. "Thank you for being honest at last, Elspeth. Assuming you were honest." Without another word, he rolled so his back was to her and drew his cloak over himself.

She stared at him, shocked. Every instinct urged her to tell him the truth. She wanted to show him that she really did not want to be alone. She reached out a hand. As if he sensed it coming near, he drew in his shoulders.

Maybe you are right. You do not need anyone. You are Elspeth Braybrooke, woman warrior. His words reverberated through her head, each a painful accusation.

Lying down, she looked out at the storm. Water poured off the stones overhead even as new tears welled up in her eyes. She had sampled the happiness she could share with Tarran, and she wanted more.

I know you consider yourself one great knight standing alone.

Maybe so, because she had never felt so alone.

Chapter 15

Not knowing what to say was strange for Elspeth. She always had words to fill even the most awkward silence. A gift, her mother had teased her, that she got from her father, who was able to entice a crowd for their performances in the dreariest town.

But what was she supposed to say as she walked down the hillside beside Tarran? He had not even offered a good morning when they began as soon as the sun rose over the mountains to light their way. All night, while she had listened to his breathing and known that he too found sleep impossible, she had tried to think of something—anything—to say to him. What could she say that he would believe? She had had her chance to be honest, and she had let it slip past.

Everything was in disarray. She had found the River Alun, but not *Llech-lafar*. The storms last night were a reminder that the ones at sea were moving inland. The sea would calm, and the king could leave Ireland. And she still had not found the cursed stone. For all she knew, she could have already walked past it.

As they reached where the others had spent the night, Vala greeted them with a relieved prayer. Tarran's men rushed forward, but Druce and his companion remained by the remnants of the fire where they must have cooked their meal last night.

Elspeth's stomach rumbled, and she did not resist when Vala urged her to have some bread for her breakfast.

"With honey," the old woman said.

"Honey? Where did you get that?" Elspeth asked, glad to talk about anything. She could not stand the silence any longer.

"A pilgrim on his way to the holy sites near Tyddewi shared our fire last night. He traded the honey to me for a blanket."

Elspeth was reaching for the bread when she heard Kei ask with a laugh, "How did you get cut, Prince Tarran? Did she try to fight you off?"

Heat scored her cheeks, and she was sure she was blushing. Vala's face became white with anger.

"Be quiet," Tarran ordered as he set his hawk on the side of the wagon.

"Did she surrender in the end?" Kei snickered again.

Elspeth gasped when Tarran knocked Kei off his feet with a single blow to the chin. She took a step toward the men, but Vala caught her sleeve and shook her head.

Kei jumped up and swung at Tarran. He missed wildly, but tried again.

Tarran caught him by the front of his tunic and shouted, "Gryn!"

The other man rushed forward, his eyes wide as he looked from his cousin to Tarran.

"Douse his head in the river until he comes to his senses," Tarran ordered, pushing Kei toward his cousin.

Gryn caught him and kept Kei on his feet. He turned toward the river, but went only as far as the firepit. Dropping his cousin to the ground, he said something that Elspeth could not hear.

Tarran's eyes fired daggers in her direction; then he

turned to speak to Seith. He answered Seith's questions about what had happened on the hill.

"You were attacked?" asked Druce from by the fire. "Who?"

"I have no idea." Tarran took a flask that Seith handed him and tilted it back. She was not surprised when he added nothing more.

Druce's man whispered to him; then Druce asked, "Did you kill your attacker?"

"No." He took another drink. "The coward ran away."

Druce stood and stuck his hands into the wide sleeves of his robe. More than ever, he looked like a friar. More than ever, when he spoke, Elspeth doubted he was.

"I will contact my men, and they will capture the cur. You are under my protection while you travel my lands, and I will not abide with you being put in danger." He snapped his fingers, and Orwig shuffled forward. "Get a message to my men."

Orwig bowed and walked away.

"Make sure he is captured alive!" she called after him.

Druce repeated her order, then smiled. "Your tender heart is another sign of your sweet nature, milady."

"Do not be fooled," Tarran said, his voice as taut as his expression. "She wants her curiosity about his identity satisfied. She should be careful about what she wishes for. She might find that she gets what she wants, and it is not what she expected."

As he went to speak with Seith privately, Vala handed Elspeth the piece of bread lathered with honey. She took a bite, but it tasted like road dust. She wondered if anything could be right again when Tarran was shutting her out of his life.

Drinking by himself was a habit no man should develop carelessly.

Tarran thought of his grandfather's words as he tilted back his tankard of the ale that Druce's men had provided when they stopped for the night in a moonlit glade. From closer to the fire where the others had gathered, voices revealed both fatigue and wary camaraderie. He could not pick out the voices belonging to his men, but a lighter one rose above the others. Even though Elspeth's words were not understandable from where he sat beneath a tree at the edge of a wood, the sound of her lilting voice pierced him like a honed blade.

Nobody had come to ask him to join the conversation around the fire. He had not expected anyone to. His men had been distant, unsure if he would lash out at them as he had at Kei. Elspeth was as wary of him, but he had seen bafflement in her eyes that were as dull as his own spirits. Did they glow now when she was laughing at something one of the men had said?

Druce had fawned on her all day, and she had given Druce many smiles. Tarran had to wonder if she was accustomed to such treatment as a Norman lord's daughter.

Why hadn't he seen the truth before she mentioned her father while they sought shelter beneath the ancient stone monument? Her words about lands and title told him that she was the legitimate daughter of a Norman lord, recognized as a lady on either side of Offa's Dyke. His fellow Welshmen might address him as "prince," but to those who claimed lands to the east, Tarran would be considered the son of a bastard.

He had seen Elspeth look in his direction frequently during the day, but had pretended to be oblivious. Her rank was so far above his that he should ask permission to speak with her. To kiss her—that could not happen again. The ache within him at that thought hurt more than the wound on his stiffening arm.

A shadow moved toward Tarran. He reached for his sword, then relaxed when he recognized Vala.

"What are you doing out here?" he asked.

Instead of answering, she sat beside him and drew a needle and thread from her bag. She began to sew his sleeve closed, taking care not to touch the bandage on his arm.

"Why are you doing that now?" he asked.

"To vex you."

"What?"

Even in the dim light, he could see her smile with the coolness she had used when he was a naughty lad. "You can stamp about and pout as much as you want, or you can go after Lady Elspeth as you know you want to."

"It is not my place to pursue her."

"And why not?"

"I have my quest."

"That did not stop you before. What changed while you were up on that hill?"

"Everything. She is a lady, Vala."

The old woman did not raise her eyes from her stitching, but she gave a sharp tug on his sleeve. "Anyone with a pair of eyes could see that. She has the bearing and the generous heart of a lady raised to care for those who do not share her high status."

"So I have seen."

"As well you should, for you have looked at her enough." She stabbed the needle through the fabric. Glancing at where Druce was standing and waving his arms as he told a story, she added, "It would have been much simpler for you if she were of his ilk, wouldn't it?"

"She is nothing like Druce."

"You leap to her defense with rare fervor." She chuckled.

"This is no laughing matter." He fingered the hilt of his sword, but he could not slay his frustration with a blade.

"Nothing is a laughing matter for you any longer."

"Do not chide me, too, Vala." A yawn tickled the back of his throat, but he kept it from escaping.

"So Lady Elspeth has been scolding you about your dour attitude?" She smiled. "I knew I was right to admire her. And you are right. She is not like Druce. She is much more like you."

"Like me? You must be jesting."

"No." She took a few more quick stitches. "She is deeply caring, worrying about those around her more than for herself. That is like you. She is courageous and well trained with the weapons she wears. That is also like you."

"But she is giddy with words and never seems to know when to stop talking."

"I said she is *much* like you, not exactly. Although I do remember years past when you babbled like a squirrel trying to keep a bird from its cache of nuts." She knotted the thread. "But you believe there is something she has failed to tell you."

"Yes, for she would not meet my eyes when she told me of her past."

"She may not have wanted to mention a former lover or two."

He shook his head. The tentative naïveté in the first kisses they had shared suggested she had not enjoyed many, a fact confirmed as she quickly learned to return the ones he offered her. He thought of how she had been bold beneath the great stone. A groan cramped in his throat as he recalled her eager caresses. Again his body reacted to the yearning he could not control.

At the same time, another yawn tried to push its way out of his mouth. He had been awake all night, aware of Elspeth lying not even an arm's length away. If he had rolled over and gathered her into his arms, she would have welcomed his kisses. She had been astonished when he turned away.

"She knows," he somehow said in a calm voice, "the

ways of Cymru are much more open-minded than the ways of Norman England."

"Only on the subject of heirs, both legitimate and illegitimate. Here in Cymru, we are same minded as the Normans about love affairs for maidens of her class. However, you are the grandson of a princess. She may see you as a proper suitor."

Proper? A proper lady waited for her father or brothers to bring a suitor to her. She did not kiss him while lying on the ground as a storm raged around them and through them. Addfwyn had been a proper lady. Even though he had known her since shortly after she was born, she had insisted that he obtain her father's permission for their marriage. How delighted she had been when the title "lady" became hers, and how happy he had been to offer it to her. Elspeth did not need his name or his title, which would mean nothing in Norman England.

"What you are talking about, Vala," he said, "suggests a great deal of calculation on her part. She is artless."

"Yet you believe she is hiding something—something very important—from you."

He arched his brows. "And there, Vala, lies the source of my concern."

"It is quite a quandary." She bit off the thread and bent to put the needle and thread back into the pouch she wore beneath her gown.

"One that I cannot solve."

Tyddewi looked much the same as the other villages they had passed, save for a great empty space where St. David's Cathedral had been. Charred remains were tossed into piles, but plans to raise another cathedral and shrine in its place were underway. Great stones had been gathered in the empty field that edged the meandering River Alun.

A cluster of houses followed the cathedral's precincts.

Both cows and sheep grazed in the fields, but the common area at the center of the village was reserved for pigs.

Elspeth shaded her eyes. More than a mile of bank on either side of the River Alun awaited her exploration. But what was the point of looking when she had no idea how to identify *Llech-lafar* from the hundreds of boulders jutting from shore?

It was frustrating—almost as frustrating as Tarran's coolness toward her. She had hoped Vala would explain why he barely spoke to her, but the old woman had stated that the matter was between Tarran and Elspeth.

As they went down the hill, Elspeth looked toward the sea. The clouds continued to hang above the waves, which were wild with the storms beyond the horizon. She was grateful for every hour the storms remained at sea.

Just as she was grateful that Druce and his men had not come into the village. Instead Druce had bragged about bringing them safely through *his* lands. As she had listened to Tarran express his thanks to Druce, she had paid less attention to the words the two men spoke and more to the tension in their voices. She wished she could believe they had seen the last of Druce and his strange men, but she did not. Druce had been lying to them from the beginning. She could not imagine why he would be honest now.

She pushed Druce from her mind when Tarran drew in his horse before a cottage no different from the others along the hillside, dropping into an earthen bowl where the cathedral's scorched timbers stood, stunted and black. The stone cottage had a thatched roof, but the stones were stained with the same soot as the timbers. Elspeth guessed the house had burned along with the cathedral.

He swung down off his horse, but nobody else moved as he went to the door and knocked. The door opened immediately, and she knew their progress through the village had been watched.

The woman in the doorway could have been Vala forty years ago. Her smile as Tarran explained who they were held the same warmth that Vala's did. She wore a simple gown of unbleached fabric, her only adornment a pilgrim's cross that she wore with pride.

Elspeth helped Vala from the wagon, and the old woman hobbled on stiff legs toward the younger woman. They embraced.

"Come in, come in," urged the woman, who introduced herself as Modlen. She stepped back to let them into her cottage.

As Gryn and Kei, who had avoided Tarran since their fight, hurried inside, Elspeth assisted Iau out of the wagon. He was healing well, but complained more with every mile they traveled. He showed no ill will toward her, even though his brother, Seith, spoke to her only when absolutely necessary.

Food was on the table by the time Elspeth entered the small, dark cottage. Tiny windows kept out wintry winds, but allowed in little spring sunshine. Helping Iau to the sole empty spot on the two short benches, she drew in the aroma of fragrant soup from bowls on the table.

Potato and leek soup. A bowl was pressed into her hands. When Modlen apologized for not having enough spoons, Elspeth said, "I can drink from the bowl."

"You are very kind, milady." She reached past Elspeth, holding out another bowl. "You honor me by partaking of my simple fare, Prince Tarran."

Elspeth flinched, and hot soup splashed on her hands. She had not realized Tarran stood behind her. As Modlen apologized and Elspeth reassured her that she was fine, he said nothing. He remained silent while they ate. When Modlen brought bedding to augment what they carried with them, he thanked her, but added no more.

There would be scarcely enough room for the men to

sleep in the cottage's large room. Modlen warned that the tiny chamber beyond, where the women would sleep, would be as cramped.

Finally, after Vala and Modlen had gone into the other room for a private conversation, Elspeth could endure the silence no longer. She put her emptied bowl on the table before turning to Tarran. He wore no expression, and she wondered which strong emotion he was hiding.

"Modlen did not ask how long we were going to stay," she said.

"That is not the way of Welsh hosts." Tarran's voice was as passionless as his face.

"But—"

"It is simple. If you enter a Welsh home, be it cottage or castle, you are welcome for as long as you wish. You owe your host no explanation of where you have come from or where you are bound. In fact, you need say nothing. You are simply welcome, and food and shelter will be supplied for you as long as you remain."

"Lord de la Rochelle asked you many questions."

"He is a Marcher."

"You make that sound like an insult."

"Did I?" He put his bowl on the table next to hers. "You are hearing things."

"Maybe you have said so little in the past two days that I have forgotten how to interpret your words."

"There is nothing to interpret. I always speak the truth."

"I know."

"It is the truth that you are very skilled with your staff."

Elspeth almost gasped at how easily he changed the subject. "Thank you," she managed to say.

"I want you to teach me. I have seen how valuable having skills with a quarterstaff could be."

"A quarterstaff is not a prince's weapon."

"But I have many questions I would like answered."

"About the quarterstaff?"

He either did not hear her soft question or he ignored it. "Why don't you teach me?" He motioned toward the door.

"Now?"

"Why not?"

"Because . . ." A twinge ached in her when she realized he might see this afternoon as his last chance to learn from her. He had brought Vala to Tyddewi and now he could continue on his quest for vengeance without Elspeth Braybrooke.

"I will be glad to teach you," she said, "but only if you teach me something in return." She looked at the perch where Heliwr sat, hooded and silent. "I would love to learn to fly your hawk."

"It would take a long time to accustom him to fly for you. Heliwr is very temperamental. You must choose something else."

She hid her disappointment. She had watched him casting the bird into the wind and wondered what it would be like to have a hawk as her partner. Motioning for him to follow, she went out of the cottage.

Tarran helped search for a branch to use as a staff. There were no trees near the cottage, so they went down the hill toward the burned-out cathedral. As Elspeth had hoped, there were several long poles that once held up a section of the building. She gathered several and set them aside. With a bit of cutting to bring them to the proper length, they might prove to be better than the staff she was using.

She picked one up and tossed it to him. Lifting her own staff, she gave him a quick explanation of how to hold it. He asked questions, and she answered each with a demonstration, as she did with her students. She was surprised how much she missed teaching.

"There is more to using a staff than lunging at someone

or striking him," she said. "Sizing up one's opponent may be the most important part."

"That is simple. You are shorter than I."

"But is that an advantage or disadvantage? A staff is not the same as a sword. While you slash with a sword across your body, with a staff, you must be prepared to think of striking both high and low and to your left and right." She smiled coolly. "Go ahead. Attack me."

"Just like that?"

"Yes." She settled the staff across her shoulder as if she were carrying a bucket at each end and draped her hands over it. Putting her foot on a stone, she smiled. "What are you waiting for?"

"You are not ready."

"How do you know?"

"The way you are holding your staff. You said to hold it with one hand over and the other under and to bend your knees."

She lowered her foot and walked toward him. She did not shift the staff as she paused in front of him. "But there are many ways to prepare for a fight with a staff, Tarran."

"I don't see—"

He yelped as she swung her staff down from her shoulder and up against his thigh. She laughed, for she had not hit him hard. He tried to lift his quarterstaff between them, but she blocked the motion. It was simple because he did not have room to move the long pole well.

Stepping back, she said, "Do not underestimate any opponent."

"I would not underestimate you." He swung the staff.

She blocked it, not surprised at how hard he had swept it toward her. He knew she could halt it. Edging to one side, she jabbed her staff at him.

"Nor I you," she said when he grunted as the pole struck

him lightly in the chest. "Do not overly strain your injured arm."

"I know my limits." He directed another blow at her. When she put up her staff to stop it, he asked, "Do you?"

She gave her staff a twisting motion and knocked his out of his hands. It flew up in the air, and he stepped back to avoid its landing on his head. She ran forward and caught it before it could strike the ground. He stared in disbelief.

Resting both staffs on the grass, she said, "I know my limits, but I continually test them. Just as you seem ready to test yours while you travel to Lundy Island."

He walked toward her. "How do you know that is where we are bound?"

"While you were taking Heliwr out to hunt on that hill with the old stones, I heard your men talking about how a sea passage south might be difficult if the storms continue to raise the waves."

"My men talk too much."

"Maybe, but that changes nothing. Are you really going to Lundy Island?"

"Unless I discover my enemy is elsewhere. I may not have much time to find out."

"Not much time? What do you mean? You know where Bradwr ap Glew is?"

"I know where he may be." He looked toward where the river twisted toward the western sea.

"In Ireland?"

"Beyond it."

"Are you talking about the story of the Welsh prince finding a new land across the western sea?"

"Yes." He sat on a rock. "I believe, as many others do, that Prince Madoc has discovered a land far to the west."

"Lord de la Rochelle believes otherwise."

"A Marcher lord wishes to see the Welsh as weakhearted and weak-minded. The idea of a Welsh prince discovering a faraway land bothers him." Taking her hand, he drew her down onto the soft grass beside the stone. "De la Rochelle told you only part of the story. Let me tell you the whole story. Three years ago, King Owain of Gwynedd in the north of Cymru died. He left many sons, both legitimate and illegitimate. They fought for the throne, save for Madoc and one of his brothers. They decided to find a land of their own where they could live in peace. On two ships from Aber-Kerrik-Gwynan, they set sail. They went beyond Ireland and found a land with a great harbor. The people there offered welcome, even though they were very different. Two years ago, Madoc returned with tales of rich lands. He gathered ten ships at Lundy Island in the Severn Sea between Cymru and Cornwall. He invited those who wished to join him in establishing a colony on the other side of the western sea. The ships sailed away, and they have not returned, but another fleet is gathering to make the long journey."

"At Lundy Island?"

He nodded.

"And you plan to sail with them to find Bradwr ap Glew?"

Again he nodded.

"Why do you think he sailed with Prince Madoc? The man who attacked you must have done so on his orders."

"Those orders could have been given before he left. After he slew Addfwyn, a man matching his description sought passage to Lundy Island. He would have arrived there just before Prince Madoc set off with his ten ships."

"But you cannot be sure they reached that harbor on the far side of the sea again. Your enemy may be dead at the bottom of the ocean."

She was astonished when he ran his fingers across her cheek, letting them linger at the corner of her lips. He had not touched her since their argument beneath the stone monument. "I vowed to do whatever I must to avenge Addfwyn's death."

"Even if it leads you to your own death?"

He looked away. "I hope not, but if I must die, I shall."

"So you can be with Addfwyn again?"

She did not expect him to meet her eyes, but he did as he put his hands on her shoulders and drew her up to her knees. "There is no guarantee I will be granted a place among the honored dead."

"You are jesting! I know no man with more honor than you. You have given up the rest of your life to fulfill a pledge of vengeance."

"There was no honor in allowing my wife to be murdered. If I had been there instead of hunting with Heliwr, I might have been able to save her. Instead of being with her, as she had asked, I stubbornly went to join my friends and—"

"By St. Jude, Tarran, you could not have known what was going to happen."

"She asked me to stay."

"As she must have other times."

"Yes." The answer was reluctant.

"And you must have argued other times."

"We seldom quarreled."

She pushed his hands away and stood. Gathering up the staffs they had used as well as the others she had set aside, she said, "I find that difficult to believe."

"Why? Because you and I quarrel all the time?"

Answering that question could lead the conversation in directions she would be foolish to let it go. "I understand why your men call you 'prince.' Your sense of honor is admirable."

"A compliment?"

"I have been known to offer a few when they are due."

He took some of the staffs from her. She thought she saw

a smile on his lips before he climbed the hill toward the cottage. She followed, relieved that he had not asked what her plans were. Maybe he had accepted that she did not know herself. She looked toward the river. Her answer was there.

"But where?" she whispered.

Chapter 16

He was dreaming.

Why did all his dreams bring him to Annwfn and Death's court? But this dream was unlike the others. Instead of splendid music, discord struck him like a blow. He put his hands over his ears. It was futile because the music was inside him as well.

The warriors at the tables stared at him. He wanted to shout that he knew he did not belong among the honored dead. Didn't they realize that no living man could control the destination of his dreams?

The sky over the court was darkening as if some wickedness had come to hunt the dead. For a moment, hope filled him. Maybe his dream was telling him that he was getting closer to his enemy. At that moment, he would be able to confront the evil of a man he had dared to believe was a friend.

Then he saw her.

Not Addfwyn. He had come to expect Addfwyn to be waiting for him when he traveled in his dreams beyond the shimmering curtain that separated this world from the one walked by living men.

Elspeth.

She stood at the very center of the great hall. Her vibrant

curls streamed down her back as she stared at the sky. He wondered how he could ever have despised red. Yes, it was a reminder of Affwyn's death, but it was also the color that brushed his face when he drew Elspeth close. It was the hue in her cheeks when she faced a foe. It was the warm tint of her lips that she shared eagerly with him.

In one hand, Elspeth held her staff. It leaned against her right foot. Anyone who believed that pose belonged to an easy quarry would quickly learn a painful lesson.

Her clothing was not the luxurious fabrics worn by the valiant dead. Dust and caked mud stained her skirt, and her fingers closing around the staff were ingrained with dirt. Had she been digging in the earth? Why?

He walked toward her, his footfalls swallowed by the jarring music. Some sense must have alerted her, because she looked in his direction. Was her presence here, a Norman woman amidst the ancient dead of Cymru, causing the dissonance? She had shaken up everything in his life. Could she do the same to Annfwn?

"What are you doing here?" he asked.

"You brought me here, Tarran. I could not find the way myself, for my knowledge of the old stories is limited." She again gazed up at the sky. "Where are we?"

"In Annwfn."

"The lands held by Death?" Her green eyes widened until he could see white all around them. "Are you wishing we were dead?"

"I would not wish you dead."

She closed her eyes and sighed. "You did not answer my questions by the cathedral, but you have now. You wish yourself dead so you can be with Addfwyn." Opening them, she looked around the hall. "Which one is she?"

"She sits there." He pointed to where Addfwyn had spoken to him in his other dreams. He half expected that she would have vanished, but she was there. Even across the distance, he could feel her smile's warmth.

"You should go to her."

He saw how difficult it had been for Elspeth to say those simple words. A hunger filled her honest eyes, a hunger she wanted to sate with him. Or was he seeing his own craving for her reflected in her eyes? His fingers cupped her cheek, and she leaned against his palm. The motion was so trusting. Was that how she truly felt, or was his dream showing how *he* felt?

Pressing her even closer, he was thrilled by the swift motion of her breasts against him as her lips parted to let her rapid breaths stream into his mouth. She whispered something he could not understand as he held her with his thighs against hers. He could not think about what she said. All he could think of was the ache that would find relief deep inside her. As her hands stroked his back, he drew them down across his buttocks. He stared down into her eyes that were glazed with desire.

He cupped her breasts, which were the perfect size for his hands, and could not silence his moan. Her hands drove him up tighter to her as his thumbs caressed the very tips of her breasts, which seemed to be straining to escape her gown. He loosened the laces at the top of her gown as he tasted the eager heat of her mouth.

She turned her head away. "We should not . . . not here where . . . " Her voice faded into a sigh as his lips sampled the luscious skin along her neck.

"Where we could be interrupted?"

As if his words had been a request, a chill surged over him. When Elspeth shivered and stepped back, he pulled her to him and draped his cloak over her.

"What is happening?" she asked.

He did not answer as King Arawn, the lord of the realm of the dead walked toward them. Tarran reached for his sword, even though he was no match for Death. It refused to slide from its sheath. He watched in horror as Death's mighty sword rose. It was not aimed at him, but at Elspeth, who stepped away from the protection of his cloak.

She lifted her staff and faced a battle he doubted any living being could win. He had to help her. He could not move his feet. His hands were glued to his sides. He could do nothing but watch as Elspeth stood with her quarterstaff at the ready while Death towered over her.

"Stop!" Tarran shouted.

The sword raced down toward her staff. Elspeth leaped aside as the blade's edge wedged deeply between two stones. She dropped her staff and winced. Her fingers curled up in obvious pain, but she had not been struck.

"What are you doing to her?" he shouted.

"This is nothing to you, Tarran ap Llyr."

His name spoken in Death's voice sent an icy breath through him. He could not move as he watched Elspeth fall to her knees, staring at her fingers, which were as red as if she had scalded them.

"She is in my protection," he argued.

"She avers that she does not need your protection." With his mighty sword, King Arawn tapped her quarterstaff.

She reached for it while she slowly rose as though wading in water as high as her waist. She was fighting for the very air that seemed to have solidified around them.

"What would you have me say?" Tarran shouted. "That I cannot protect Elspeth either? Why do you want her? She is a Norman. She is not of Cymru."

"She has a warrior's heart." King Arawn gave a horrifying smile. "And a warrior's heart belongs in my hall."

"No!" he yelled. Somehow, he broke free of the invisible bonds holding him. He reached for his sword and drew it. He ran forward as Death's sword rose and fell toward Elspeth.

She cried out his name over and over, and the ground beneath his feet trembled. Darkness consumed the great hall, and he could no longer see . . .

Elspeth bent forward and whispered, "Tarran, Tarran, Tarran." With each repetition of his name, she shook his shoulder again. "Wake up! You are having a nightmare."

His arms thrashed, almost knocking her aside and atop one of his sleeping men. She caught one arm with both hands and pinned it to the floor. Ducking, she avoided his other one.

"Elspeth!" he moaned.

"Wake up, Tarran. You are having a nightmare."

He groaned again. He was awake, but mired in his dreams.

She heard the other men rustling beneath their blankets. If they remained here, someone else would wake up.

Putting her arm under his shoulder and using her body as a lever, she hefted him to his feet. She steered him out the cottage door. He cursed when his head struck the lintel, and he wobbled. She gave him a not-so-gentle shove toward the well in the middle of the village common.

He tripped on the uneven ground and fell. She went to the well and, in the moonlight, drew up a bucket. Without warning, she dumped it over his head.

He choked and swore before snarling, "What did you do that for?"

"Cold water makes the drunkest man sober." She put the bucket back beside the well and stepped around a pig sleeping in the mud beside it.

"I did not have anything to drink." He shook his head, spraying water in every direction.

"Then what were you dreaming about? You were shouting in your sleep and were going to wake up everyone in the village."

"Elspeth, it is you!" he gasped.

She knelt beside him and put her hand on his forehead, praying there would be no sign of fever. He grabbed her hand and pressed his mouth to her palm. At his touch, hot liquid seeped deep within her. She was ready to melt against him.

"You saved me," he whispered.

"What?"

"You were ready to fight Death to save my life."

"Tarran, you are making no sense." Before she had a chance to form another thought, his arm was around her. He pulled her down as he whispered, "I don't care if you are a lord's daughter or a shepherd's. I need your heat to force away the grave's chill."

She pulled back. "Are you still asleep?"

"Don't talk. I do not want to talk. I do not want to argue. I want you in my arms. You are wondrously alive, the balm for the nightmares that plague me. I want the balm you are. A living, breathing, sensual woman who never does anything halfway."

"Tarran—"

With a groan, he twisted her beneath him. Water dripped from his hair, but she paid no attention as her mouth surrendered to his fiery lips, and her eyes slowly shut. Her fingers reached up his arms as she guided him closer. She could not imagine resisting such a tempting offer, even though she knew every reason why she should. When he cradled her head in his broad palm, he pressed his lips to hers again, and she answered with a desperation she did not recognize in herself. His kisses were shattered by her frayed breath as he explored her mouth. She drew back, shocked by her own throaty moan.

"I did not mean—" she whispered. "That is—"

He gave her one of the rare smiles she adored. "Do not restrain yourself. Those eager gasps are the sweetest sound

I have heard after many silent months. Each is a separate note in an amazing melody I want you to play for me."

"But we are on the village common."

She almost laughed as he stared around in amazement. When a pig grunted, annoyed at being disturbed, her laugh slipped out.

"We do have too much company," he said as he scowled at the pig. "Let us find a more private place. Where you gave me a lesson with the quarterstaff this afternoon would do well." He tilted her chin toward him with one hand as his other rose from her waist to caress her breast. When she quivered, he whispered, "I promised to teach you a few lessons. No one will be there at this hour."

"I have a better suggestion. The riverbank would be more private with the trees edging it." She ran her finger along his sleeve that was spotted with water. She was amazed it did not sizzle away between them because every touch elicited more heat. "I want to see the moonlight dappled on your skin."

"An intriguing idea."

She smiled as he did. "I thought you might appreciate it."

"And I want you naked and alight beneath me." He groaned as he kissed her with the longing she understood too well.

He drew her to her feet and to him. Could he sense how every bit of her was eager to be even closer to him? As his hands stroked down her back to press her up against him so she could not doubt that he wanted her, she brought his mouth to hers.

A voice coming through the night intruded.

Tarran glanced over his shoulder. "It is Vala." He released her and squeezed her hand. "Let me assure her that all is well."

"I will meet you by the river."

He shook his head. "Stay here, and I will return for you."

"Stop worrying about me." She laughed. "I can take care of myself. I will meet you by the river." She boldly slid her hand down along his abdomen.

He caught her wrist. "Go any lower, and I shall not care if all of Cymru watches us right here."

Elspeth took his fierce kiss with her as she ran down the moonlit hill toward the river. She could hardly wait for him to join her there. Join her. She shivered in anticipation. Her sisters at St. Jude's Abbey had speculated about what a man and a woman shared. Memory flooded her mind. She remembered how her mother had glowed with happiness on a morning after Elspeth was sent to sleep under the wagon rather than within it. Only later had she realized what the soft, eager sounds from above her head had been. She wanted to glow with love as her mother had.

The moonlight on the river was like a silk ribbon. She wished she could gather it up and tie it around the moments to come, so she could treasure them forever. Stepping into the shadows, she looked for a place where there were no rocks.

She laughed aloud. Since her arrival in Wales, she had been obsessed with finding a particular stone. Now she wanted nothing to do with any of the ones around her.

Her arm was grabbed. Hard. She winced and started to ask Tarran why he was being so rough. Her voice dried up as a knife was pressed to her throat.

She held her breath, knowing she had only seconds to react. She used both hands to grab her attacker's arm and forced his arm down until the knife was flat against her chest. Bending her knees, she pulled on his arm. He flipped over her back. She heard his shout of surprise as he struck the earth, but she did not loosen her grip on his knife arm. She reached down to press her hand against his throat.

He stared up at her. He was balding or maybe he had shaved his head. Or was it a tonsure? A monk attacking her?

The idea was too outlandish even to consider. He shifted, and she saw a scar on his left cheek. It looked like a slice made by a knife. He was no older than Tarran. His hair and eyes were as dark as Tarran's. Beneath her, his clothing was simple and of rough fabric.

"Who are you?" she demanded.

He stared at her, silent.

"Tell me!"

He shook his head.

Her hand shifted on his neck so he could not escape. Her fingers brushed against a leather strand. She gasped when she saw a bead hanging from it along with a crucifix. Both glittered in the moonlight.

"Elspeth, where are you?" came Tarran's voice.

The man took advantage of her momentary distraction. He slapped her face, knocking her away. She grabbed for him. He reached for his knife, slashing it at her, and agony sliced into her leg. She kicked out with her other foot and sent him reeling. The knife flew from his hand.

Stretching out on her stomach, she grabbed the knife the man had dropped.

He stared as she raised it, then turned and ran.

"Elspeth, where are you?"

"Tarran, take heed!" she shouted back as the man vanished along the riverbank.

Tarran burst out of the trees from the opposite direction. He looked toward where the man had gone. She thought he would follow, but he knelt and helped her sit.

"Are you hurt?" he asked, pushing his wet hair back out of his eyes.

"Just scratched." She drew back her gown to reveal her bloody stocking. The wound stung, but the bleeding was already slowing.

When he pulled aside the edges of her torn stocking, her breath caught.

"I am sorry if I am hurting you," he said, pausing.

"No, you are not hurting me." She touched his cheek. "Quite the opposite. Tarran, I want to thank you for—"

"Thank me this way." He kissed her deeply.

She was tempted to forget the attack while they continued what they had begun on the village common. She guessed he was also trying to forget.

Yet, too quickly he drew back enough to ask, "What happened?"

"I was attacked. Tarran, he wore a bead around his neck as Druce and his men do. And he was also wearing a cross."

"Are you sure?"

"Yes. I saw both of them when I pinned him to the ground after he tried to slit my throat." She picked up the blade she had dropped into the grass when Tarran drew her to him. "He had this knife and—"

"Addfwyn," he choked like a drowning man reaching the surface for the last time. He took the knife from her. "This was Addfwyn's knife." He tilted it and pointed to engraving along the hilt. She could barely make out the letters of his wife's name. "It vanished the day she was killed."

"If she was killed with this—"

"She was not, but Bradwr ap Glew must have stolen it." His mouth grew taut. "Now he is using it to send me a message."

"What is he trying to tell you?"

"That he is willing to kill any woman in my life."

"But why?"

He held the dagger up so the moonlight glinted on its edge. "I don't know . . . yet."

Chapter 17

Impossible!" Druce said, striding along the riverbank as half the villagers watched. He almost ran over Vala, who had joined them by the river, refusing to let Elspeth out of her sight since she learned of the previous night's attack. Vala had insisted they contact Druce to find out what he knew about the man who had tried to kill Elspeth. Tarran's men had found him and Orwig not far from the village, confirming Elspeth's suspicions that Druce had been lying when he bid them farewell.

"It clearly was not impossible," Tarran said coldly. "The man was dressed as you and your men do."

"None of my men would have a reason to threaten Lady Elspeth with a knife." Druce paused in his pacing long enough to offer her a smile.

Elspeth tried to return it, but could not. Her leg smarted, and her face was bruised. She must have landed on her elbow, because it was skinned and sore. But none of those injuries hurt as much as the emptiness within her. She wanted to be in Tarran's arms, his lips against hers, his body stroking hers. She wanted him to want her because she was in his heart.

It was extraordinary. She had been certain that if she ever fell in love, she would be aware of the very moment when her heart decided to belong to another. She could not say for sure with Tarran. He had sparked something within her from the moment he had knocked her off the wall and insisted she listen to him.

Now, as she looked at Tarran standing by the river and gazing out to the sea frosted with gray clouds, she could not help wondering if she was even in his thoughts. He had been eager to make love with her last night . . . until the knife reminded him of his loss. She did not want him to forget Addfwyn. His heart could never be that fickle, but she longed to know if she had a place within it.

You were ready to fight Death to save my life. She should have asked him what he meant by those strange words. Not that it mattered—he had been caught up in a devastating nightmare. She wanted to be in his *dreams*.

"Such accusations are an insult," Druce snarled at Tarran's back.

Tarran did not answer.

"Nobody is accusing you or your men of being involved," Elspeth said. "We thought you should know that someone may be using your clothing and jewelry to hide his identity."

"You are showing rare wisdom for a woman," he replied.

She fought her instinct to bristle. Vala gave her a wink, and Elspeth let her bluster ooze away. She had not seen any women with Druce. Maybe their women were docile and silent, keeping their minds solely on their hearths.

Orwig, who, as always, was shadowing Druce, leaned forward and murmured something Elspeth could not hear. He hid his hands within his long sleeves and his face could not be seen beneath the wide hood. She wondered how he kept from tripping on exposed tree roots. Whatever he said must have been disturbing, because Druce began to toy nervously with the ring on his left hand. Orwig bent toward him again.

Druce nodded before saying, "The important thing is
that Lady Elspeth was not injured badly."

"But her attacker must be captured." Tarran's voice remained chill.

"The attacker wore clothing like *my* men, and the land
beyond the village is *mine* to oversee. I have told you that."
He made no effort to hide his annoyance.

"Then help us hunt down that bastard and see he pays for
what he did to Elspeth. Any other woman would have been
killed."

Druce opened his mouth to reply, then closed it when
Orwig whispered in his ear again. The two men bent their
heads together to confer.

Elspeth went to where Tarran stood, but did not put her
hand on his arm. She feared she could not restrain herself
from flinging her arms around him and telling him with a
fervent kiss how much she wanted him.

He glanced at her, then back toward the sea. Questions
burned on her tongue: Was he looking west in hopes of seeing Prince Madoc's ships returning? Did he think first of his
revenge and second of everything else? Did he even think
of Elspeth Braybrooke when she was not in his arms?

Sighing silently, she turned to walk away. She could not
remember being afraid to confront anyone ever before. The
feeling was appalling. Could it be that she had never had so
much to lose as she did now?

The queen has more to lose if you fail her.

The chiding words shocked her. She had not forgotten
her duty to Queen Eleanor . . . except when Tarran looked
at her with passion blazing in his eyes.

"Stop!" shouted Druce. "Lady Elspeth, stop!"

She heard Tarran curse and draw his sword. He lowered
it, scowling at Druce.

"Don't step on that stone," Druce ordered as he rushed to

her side. He pointed to a misshapen stone sticking partway out of the riverbank.

"Why not?" she asked, wondering if he had gone as mad as the situation around them.

"Behold!" He gestured toward the rock with his golden staff.

"Behold what?"

"Why, the work of the magnificent Merlin."

"Merlin? He is nothing but a tale." Elspeth laughed, even though she had never felt less like laughing in her whole life. Could he mean . . . Was it possible . . . She did not dare to hope. She barely dared to breathe. Could Druce, who was so familiar with the old tales, have the answer for the puzzle that had brought her to Wales?

"Are you sure he is only a legend?" He tapped the staff against the rock. "Then how do you explain the existence of this boulder?"

"I do not attempt to explain the existence of any of the thousands of boulders I have seen in Wales." She fought to keep her voice light and her eyes focused on Druce. If she glanced at the rock, she suspected her excitement would be visible.

"But this is not just any rock. This is *Llech-lafar*, a rock placed here by Merlin to guarantee Cymru's future." He raised his voice. "To ensure that Cymru will never be ruled by a *Sais,* the great mage ordered this rock to await a king who wishes to conquer Cymru and the land across the sea."

"King Henry!" Vala choked. "He left Cymru to go to Ireland."

Druce chuckled with glee. "And upon his return, King Henry will find that he pays the price for his greed."

As Druce's laugh dissolved into a giggle, Tarran drew his gaze away from the high waves marching toward the shore. They matched his roiling thoughts as he imagined what would have happened if he had been in this very spot last night when Elspeth's assailant attacked her. He would have halted the man. He could have asked questions, and maybe the answers he sought would finally have been his. Then he would not have to continue his quest. He could stay with Elspeth and discover what they had only begun to explore with each other.

But was she staying in Tyddewi? As he watched her while Druce continued to rant about the iniquities King Henry had enacted upon Cymru, her face was blank. She wore that mask each time she suspected her emotions would betray her.

As he did. Vala was correct. Elspeth was more like him than he wanted to admit.

He watched Elspeth's eyes shift again and again toward the rock under Druce's feet, moving away quickly as if she did not want anyone to guess she was fascinated by the rock. She had worn a similar expression when de la Rochelle had spoken of Merlin and rocks and streams. Could she be searching for *Llech-lafar*?

She must be. Such a quest explained everything she had done and said.

"What is this price you keep referring to if the king steps on the rock?" Tarran asked quietly, even though he knew the old story. If he let Druce ramble on, maybe he could discover why Druce had pointed out a rock that was supposed to be known only to its guardians.

"Death. The price to be paid is death." He raised his hands skyward as if awaiting a bolt of lightning to strike through him and into the rock. Lowering his arms, he clenched his fists. "Then Cymru will belong to us once more. Every *Sais* will be banished from our land."

Elspeth whispered while Druce continued to praise Merlin's foresight, "Do you believe an old legend will come true?"

"Do you?" Tarran asked as quietly.

"It does not matter what I believe." She looked at Druce, who was attracting a growing crowd as he shouted out the curses Merlin had placed on the stone. "The only belief that matters belongs to someone who wants an excuse to murder the king. Druce has just given everyone the means."

He could not argue with that.

Elspeth stood with her quarterstaff against the rock. "Are you really *Llech-lafar*? Or did I give myself away somehow while listening to Druce's stories? Is Druce trying to confuse us? Not that it matters any longer."

Half the village had listened to Druce's long-winded announcements by the river. The other half and most of the parish must have been told by now. By the time the storms cleared and the king sailed, the story could have spread from one end of Wales to the other.

"You are such a simple rock," she continued, knowing if anyone overheard her talking to it, they would think her mad. But its name meant *speaking stone*, and she *was* speaking to it. "If you are Merlin's famous rock, the least you could do is say so."

She knelt to examine the rock. It did have a few strange projections, eroded by the passage of water through the years, but so did many of the other rocks along the shore.

She stood and, leaning her cheek against the staff, gazed down at the stone. Tapping the staff on the rock as if to wake it, she sighed.

Rhan's voice echoed in her head. The old wisewoman at Castell Glyn Niwl had told her that she risked everything she loved if she did not turn back. If Elspeth had admitted defeat then, she could have returned to St. Jude's Abbey, saying that she had tried her best. It had been simpler to decide to go on when she stood in Lord de la Rochelle's castle. Then she had feared losing her home in the Abbey. Now she feared losing Tarran.

A footfall came from behind her. She looked up to see Tarran walking toward her. Her fingers tightened on the staff, but she did not move it.

"I thought I would find you here," he said. "But I did not expect to find you alone. I thought Druce would be holding court by Merlin's rock."

"Druce is being heralded in the village as the savior of Wales."

"In the village?" He glanced over his shoulder. "I thought I saw Orwig wandering around near the cathedral."

"You must have been mistaken. Orwig does not budge from Druce's side unless ordered to or he wants to find out what you are doing." She took a deep breath. "I don't want to talk about Orwig or Druce or the tales they are spreading."

"Which is why I am surprised you are alone. I thought others would want to come to see the wonder of *Llech-lafar.*"

"Nobody is interested in *Llech-lafar* while King Henry is in Ireland." She stared at the rock. "It seems so common."

"If one is putting a curse on something, it is best if the item looks ordinary."

"So the king could step on it without being aware of the danger until it was too late."

"Now you understand."

She slid her quarterstaff from the rock and prodded the ground around its edges. She heard the dull sound of earth and the sharper sound when the staff struck stone. "It is large, but not as big as I had feared."

"You have been looking for *Llech-lafar.*"

"I have." She would not lie when he had not made his comment a question. Why should he? The answer was obvious.

"Did your father send you to find *Llech-lafar* in an effort to obtain the king's favor?"

"No." She hesitated, then said, "My father is dead."

"Then who sent you?"

"The queen."

"The queen of what?"

"The queen of England!"

He grasped her arm and spun her to face him. Her staff struck him in the shin. He winced, but said, "Elspeth, don't lie to me!"

"I would never lie about a matter of such importance."

She could not keep from slipping her hand into his dark hair and uncurling her fingers around his head.

"Is *this*—" He tapped his foot on the rock. "Is *this* why you have not been able to tell me what you planned to do after we reached Tyddewi?"

"I could not tell you what I wanted to do because I was not sure myself until I found *Llech-lafar*. We cannot leave it here."

He bent down to look at the rock frosted with lichen. Running his fingers along the edges, he said, "Most of the rock is visible. Very little of it is beneath the ground. We should be able to pry it out."

"So you believe this is *Llech-lafar*?"

"It could be. The stone is as bearded as old Merlin was supposed to be. Do *you* believe this is the stone you have been seeking?"

"Yes . . . I think so. I am not even sure such a curse could exist."

Standing, he wiped his hands on his tunic, spreading bits of dirt across it. She should not notice how the pattern emphasized his muscles. She should be concentrating on the stone, not his rock-hard body.

"I am of Cymru," he said, drawing her eyes back to his face. "I know things exist in legend, even though I cannot see or understand them."

"Because you know the old tales."

"Yes."

"The old tales that haunt you in your nightmares?"

"How do you know that?" he asked.

She set her quarterstaff on the ground. "Vala interrogated me about what happened last night. When I told her what you said, she reminded me of the story of Prince Pwyll and his visit to Death's court."

"I said nothing of Pwyll."

"But you said that I was ready to fight Death to save your life."

"I did?" He looked puzzled as he put one foot on the stone. "Maybe the tales told by fathers to their sons beat within our blood as well." He tapped the stone with his boot. "You say the queen sent you. Why?"

"Because she does not wish her husband to die."

He gave a terse laugh. "From the tales I have heard of her fury at the king's affection for a woman named Rosamunde, I would think the queen might be pleased to see him dead."

"I suspect she does not believe her beloved Richard is of an age to rule his father's vast kingdom."

"King Henry the Younger is his father's successor."

"There is that as well."

"What sort of mother wishes one son dead so another may rule?"

She faced him. "I did not suggest that! I know only how devoted she is to Richard and how she wants him to have her lands in Aquitaine. Do not put words in my mouth."

"Then I shall put something else." He bent and pressed his lips to hers. When she gasped, surprised that he would kiss her in the midst of such a discussion, he slid his tongue into her mouth.

She pulled him closer as she trickled her fingers down his powerful back, then ran them up again. When he pushed her against a tree, her hands curved over his hips. She tilted her head as his mouth coursed along her neck. Hooking his finger beneath the top of her sleeve, he drew it down. Gentle nibbles across her shoulder sent quivers through her and clustered in the void between her legs. She needed to be so close to him that only their eager breaths would hold them apart.

With a groan, he released her.

"Tarran?" she asked, confused.

"We have our duties to fulfill." His voice sifted past his clenched teeth. "Letting ourselves be distracted would be wrong."

She nodded. She needed to fulfill her vow to the queen. But the price . . . She closed her eyes, unable to look at him when she knew the greatest curse of *Llech-lafar* could be denying her his love.

In an unsteady whisper, she said, "Then help me with my quest." She put her hand over his heart and was delighted to feel it thunder beneath her fingers. "Will you help me in my quest?"

"Elspeth, you know I have a quest of my own."

She closed the distance between them. "Your quest is to avenge a death. Mine is to prevent a death. Which is more important?"

"Now you sound as if you believe in the old legend."

"The queen does, and I will not fail her." She took another step toward him. "Tarran, I know how desperately you wish to see Bradwr ap Glew pay for killing Addfwyn, but help me save a man's life. I need your help." She took his hand and lifted it to her breast. "I need you."

His tense face tightened more. "Elspeth, I need you, too. Are you sure of what you are asking?"

"Yes." She doubted she had ever been more certain of anything. Preventing King Henry from dying on *Llech-lafar* could mean she would lose Tarran. She would not let another moment pass without enjoying what they had now.

"Are you offering yourself to me to obtain my help with your quest?"

"What do you think?"

His arm around her waist drew her to him. "I think I cannot forget how I held you last night." He bent to press his lips to her throat again. "I remember the sweet flavors of your delicious skin, and the memory makes me crave you more."

A tumultuous pulse rushed through her. "Tarran . . ." Words that had always been easy refused to form on her lips.

"I want to taste you," he whispered against her ear. "Not just your mouth, but your soft breasts. That would be only the beginning, for I want to explore the lithe lines hidden beneath your gown. I want to feel your curls brushing over my chest in the moment before we become one."

She stepped back. His eyes filled with sorrow again, but that grief faded when she held out her hand.

"We cannot do as you suggest here," she said with a throaty laugh she had never heard from herself before. "Who knows who might come to look at the infamous *Llech-lafar* and get a far more interesting eyeful?"

He handed her the quarterstaff before taking her other hand. Drawing her arm around him, he slipped his own behind her waist. Her knees almost buckled when his fingers stroked her breast.

"How do you expect me to walk if you do that?" she gasped.

"Do you want me to stop?"

Pausing in the thicker shadows, she whispered, "No."

He laughed as he jumped from the bank onto a stone in the middle of the river. It took only another couple of leaping steps to cross to the far bank.

She tossed him her staff before she followed him across the river. Taking his hand, she let him lift her onto the op-

posite shore. He drew her at a near run in the direction of
the sea. She was about to ask him where he was bound
when she saw tree branches reaching down toward the water.
Beneath was a bower, shaded and secluded and theirs.

"How did you know this was here?" she asked.

"I knew the pigs would not want to share their mud on
the common, so I sought another spot. I found this waiting
for us."

She laughed. "Do not tell me another Welsh legend
about how the trees are about to welcome us within their
branches?"

He turned her in to his arms. "I don't care if the trees
want us within them. I care only about being within you."

Her head whirled with the images filling it as he lifted
aside a branch and drew her into the shadowed bower. She
stared in disbelief at the thick blanket spread on the ground.

"This is amazing," she breathed.

He took her quarterstaff and put it back beyond the tree
branches. He unhooked his sword belt and set it to one side
before loosening her belt. He placed it atop his. Her breath
caught as she saw how the hilts of their weapons meshed.
She wanted to be entangled with him. Pulling off his boots,
he knelt on the blanket. He brought her down to her knees
beside him and undid her shoes and placed them next to his
boots. He combed his fingers up through her hair, drawing
it forward to surround them.

He buried his face in her curls. "Your hair smells of sunshine and of warmth and of you." Before she could reply, he
raised his head and whispered, "Elspeth, I fought my longing from the moment when you fell into my arms and lam-
basted me for intruding on your idiotic plan. I vowed never
to feel anything for another woman because I could not bear
losing my heart—and then losing her. You have upset all my
plans. You want nothing to do with any efforts I make to
protect you. You are confoundedly stubborn."

She laughed. "Are you trying to seduce me, or are you trying to convince me to leave?"

"Both maybe. Or neither. Can't you see? I once was clear about where I was to go and what I was to do; then you were there and nothing was clear any longer."

"You have intruded upon my own plans, you know."

"I know." He kissed her hard and with the craving of a man denied pleasure for too long. "I do not care if you are a lord's daughter or not."

She needed to be honest with him. She had let him assume something that was not true. She had to be honest now. "Tarran—"

He silenced her with another breath-snatching kiss. "I don't care who you are or why you are in Cymru or anything else. All I want to do is make love with you. Love me with every inch of your body." He gave her a roguish grin that sent her senses swirling anew. If he had shown her that expression before now, she would have . . . She did not know what she would have done, but she knew what she wanted to do now.

She drew his mouth to hers. His arms enfolded her so tightly she could feel his heart beating in tempo with her own. When he leaned her back onto the blanket, she drew him down with her. An excited gasp escaped from her when he pressed his lips to the valley between her breasts.

"You wear too many clothes," he growled.

"If you find them troublesome," she answered with the same mock intensity, "then you should do something about the situation."

"I shall."

He hooked his finger in the laces at the back of her gown. As he loosened them, his mouth found hers. She ceded herself to its tender assault. Her hand crept beneath his tunic's collar to explore. Sweeping upward, her fingertips moved slowly across his back, discovering how each sinew reacted to her touch.

He drew her loosened gown down, pausing only to let his mouth brand her skin with its heat. Delight coursed through her, a molten liquid that awaited him. She arched toward him when his hands pressed her breasts close to his face as his tongue laved the sensitive skin between them. A moan escaped her, urgent and pleading. When she put her hand over her mouth, shocked by her wanton gasps, he lifted her fingers away.

"Never hide your passions from me," he said, smoothing back her hair that was lathered to her forehead. "I want to know what brings you pleasure."

"I was not . . . sure. I am not sure what to do."

"Trust me, *cariad.*"

"What did you call me?"

"*Cariad.* Sweetheart."

Joy sent her heart soaring. The common word took on a precious meaning when he spoke it as, lying on his side, he entwined his legs with hers. Her thick dress separated them, but she forgot it amid the thrill of his lips.

He pulled her over him, and her gown dropped to her waist. His hands lowered it toward her hips. When she shifted to let him push it off, his fingers tightened on her.

"Continue moving like that," he said with a husky laugh, "and we will be finished far sooner than I had planned."

"I had no idea."

"I know. I told you that I would teach you."

"Then be quiet and teach me."

With another laugh, he yanked her dress aside, tossing it over their weapons. His hands swept up her thighs and beneath her long chemise. As his thumbs coursed along the insides of her legs, she could not hold her body still. She tried, but it was impossible. Her chemise rose higher as he reached beneath it.

She moaned when his mouth touched her right breast. His tongue slipped along it until he drew the very tip into his mouth. Even as he suckled, his tongue toyed with the tip. She was gripped by a frenzy of sensations she did not recognize. She could not sort out a single one because she was their captive while her bare thighs pressed against his tunic's rough fabric.

With the best speed she could manage when her body wanted only to succumb to rapture, she undid his tunic. She drew it over his head and threw it in the direction of her dress. He pulled off her chemise. She did not see what he did with it because his arms pressed her against his naked chest. Each wiry hair was a separate caress, and she wanted to savor every one.

When he rolled her beneath him again, she raked her nails lightly up his back. His eyes scorched her with their ebony fire as he lowered his mouth over hers. His kiss deepened as he rid her of her stockings and himself of his braies.

She stared at his unabashed virility. She was overwhelmed with a shyness she had never before experienced, but she refused to let it halt her from reaching out a trembling finger to stroke the hard shaft that would soon be sliding within her. It quivered at her touch, and he moaned.

His mouth pressed to her stomach as his hand settled between her legs. She gasped in shock as the craving grew even stronger. When his finger reached within her, she rocked in the rhythm he created with each motion.

"Now," she begged in a voice she had never heard coming from her lips.

"Are you in a hurry, *cariad*?" His voice was as unsteady as hers.

"I want you now."

"But I want you to feel this now." He shifted his finger slightly.

All her yearnings merged into a single indescribable explosion. It resonated through her body, consuming her in its power. She shuddered with its strength as everything collapsed into the blaze of sensation. Everything but the realization that he was with her, giving her a rapture she could not have imagined in her virginal dreams. Nothing would ever be the same again, for his touch had awakened parts of her that she had never known were there.

She opened her eyes as he rose above her. Locking her hands around his shoulders, she watched his face as he thrust himself into her. She gasped when pain eclipsed the pleasure.

"Forgive me, *cariad*. I should have remembered a maiden needs a special gentleness." His face bore the difficulty of his attempts to restrain himself. "But I want you so much."

She brushed his hair back from his forehead as he had hers. "There is nothing to forgive. Only to share."

He moved slowly, and she discovered she already knew how to respond. He had taught her, just as he had promised. When he claimed her lips, she matched his motions, each more powerful. She heard his gasps of gratification in the second before she was swallowed once more by the ecstasy of knowing she shared this moment with him.

Tarran had been sure his dreams that night would be filled with the memories of how he had initiated Elspeth into pleasure. Instead his dream was only of darkness. He was alone, not in the world of the living and not in Annwfn. He had called out Elspeth's name and then Addfwyn's. Neither answered, and he knew was completely alone in the void. Had he been banished from both worlds because he had let Elspeth distract him—for a single glorious afternoon— from his quest?

Being with her is worth banishment and more. Those

words were both in his head and hanging in the abyss around him.

No answer came to his defiance. The darkness never changed. It was neither living nor dead. It only was. He needed to escape it. He must! He must! He was covered in icy sweat. Was the dream a portent? If so, he had no idea what it might mean.

He woke and reached for Elspeth. His arms found nothing.

Sitting, he saw he was in the outer chamber of Vala's granddaughter's house. Everything looked as it should, for he counted the lumps that were his men who slept, fortunately unaware of his dreams.

One man rolled over, muttering something in his sleep. Tarran was shocked when he realized the words were in Latin. He peered through the dark. It must be Druce, who had been at Vala's granddaughter's cottage when he and Elspeth returned from their bower. Or it could be Orwig, he realized with amazement. He had never heard the hooded man speak.

He did not care if Orwig gave speeches in his sleep. He stared at the dark area where the women had retired with the coming of night. If he went in there and scooped Elspeth up into his arms, would she gaze at him with the longing he had seen in her eyes when he held her that afternoon? He had to know.

Edging around his men and the table, he drew back the curtain that separated the main room from the smaller chamber. His eyes were adjusting to the darkness that was not as absolute as in his dreams. He squinted, but could see only two forms in the room.

A finger tapped his shoulder, and he turned even as he was reaching for his knife. He discovered Elspeth standing behind him.

"Were you looking for me?" she whispered as she rested

one arm on his shoulder and slanted toward him. Her hair caressed his arms and bare chest.

"How did you know?"

"I don't know. I just woke and thought I heard you call my name." She traced a random pattern across his chest, and he wanted to forget about his latest nightmare. What could it matter when she was with him?

"I do not recall speaking it, but . . ."

She rested her cheek over his heart. "Let the nightmares go, Tarran."

"I wish I could, but I fear they will be with me until I have completed my vow of vengeance. How did you slip past me?"

Her soft laugh brushed his skin. "I came out here a few minutes ago. I did not want to disturb anyone, so I sat at the table until I saw you get up and walk over here."

"You do disturb me." He let his hand slide around her waist. "You bother me. You annoy me. You vex me."

"Do all Welshmen try to woo their women with insults?"

"It is the truth, just as it is the truth that I want you."

She stepped back and held out her hand. He took it as they walked out of the cottage to find a private spot to spend the remainder of the night in rapture. At dawn, they would have to consider their separate quests, but tonight, they would be together.

Chapter 18

"We must move *Llech-lafar*." Elspeth spooned more herbs into the soup cooking on the cottage's hearth. Aromas burst out, pungent and tantalizing. A hearty soup would be welcome because the day was chill and rainy. More of the storms that had held the king in Ireland were coming ashore.

Throughout the main room, she heard amazed mumbles from Tarran's men. Vala's granddaughter, who was slicing strips of dried fish for the soup, gasped and stared past Elspeth to her grandmother.

"A boulder of that size?" Vala asked. "It would cripple a horse to carry it."

"The oxen could pull it in the wagon."

Tarran was sitting by the door and polishing his sword. "Where do you want to take it?"

She wanted to hug him when he did not question her suggestion. She was uncertain how he would react if she were bold in the presence of his men. None of them treated her differently, so she guessed they had no idea that she and Tarran had become lovers.

A smile curved across her lips. For the past two nights after they had slipped out of the cottage, she had slept in his arms until he woke her with an urgent kiss. He had sought a haven within her, and she had welcomed him, ready to give whatever she could to ease the anguish that tormented him.

Did he guess that each time he touched her she heard Rhan's prophecy? If she could keep from loving him, maybe she would not lose him. That sounded simple, but how could she keep from loving him?

"Elspeth?" asked Tarran.

She turned to see everyone looking at her. She needed to reply before they thought she had been made mad by too much moonlight.

"*Llech-lafar* is dangerous where it is. We must move it somewhere where the king cannot step on it." She put the rest of the herbs on the table and sat across from Vala. That gave her a view of the village common.

For the first time since he had arrived in Tyddewi, Druce was not sitting by the well as he told stories for anyone who would pause and listen. He must have sought shelter in another cottage, perhaps the one with the young widow who always seemed to find excuses to pass by where he sat.

"We need to move it," she said again as she looked at the others in the room. "The best place would be amid other rocks where nobody can step on it."

"An excellent idea," the old woman said.

Elspeth smiled, then realized it was not Vala she had to persuade. Tarran must agree to help her. He had welcomed her into his arms, but he had never said if he would set aside his own quest to save a king he considered an invader. She was not sure what else she could offer him to persuade him to help. She would gladly give him her heart, but, even if he wanted it, that could be the very gift that would drive them apart. Cursing the wisewoman's prediction helped nothing.

"Absurd!" Seith exclaimed. "You cannot halt a curse by moving the stone."

"The king must *step* on it," she argued. "If we move the stone, King Henry cannot step on it. It is that simple, but we need to find somewhere to take *Llech-lafar* where he would not go."

"There is a place." Tarran slid his sword back into its sheath and dropped the polishing cloth onto the floor.

"Where?" She fought the excitement welling up inside her. If Tarran was willing to help her, King Henry could be saved and her obligation to the queen fulfilled. Then she and Tarran . . . She silenced the thought, afraid to let it form. Again she was astonished to feel fear's serrated grip around her throat.

What was wrong with her? She should be able to face anything. She was one of the queen's ladies of St. Jude's Abbey, trained to protect the queen, the Abbey and herself from all dangers. Until she had met Tarran, she could not have imagined faltering. Now each decision needed to be weighed with care because she wanted to serve both the queen and her own heart.

"St. Govan's Head," Tarran replied.

"Where is that?" She forced herself to focus on the problem of *Llech-lafar*.

"South on the peninsula reaching into the sea. St. Govan took refuge on a cliff on that bay hundreds of years ago, and there are remnants of the chapel he had raised."

"Or, as bards sing, the chapel was raised by Sir Gawain in the saint's honor," Vala interjected.

Elspeth did not want to hear any more about the legendary King Arthur and his knights and his magician. She wanted to agree with Tarran's plan. Not only would they be traveling in the same direction he needed to go in order to find his enemy, but they would also be spending more time together.

Yet she had to argue, "Pilgrims go to a chapel. The king might take the pilgrims' way back to England. He might stop in gratitude for his victories in Ireland."

Tarran rose and came over to the table. He sat beside her and stretched his arm behind her. His men exchanged uneasy looks, but he paid them no mind. He gazed deeply into her eyes, and she had to concentrate on each word. "Unlike the pilgrimages to St. David's Cathedral, one cannot cleanse one's soul by visiting St. Govan's Chapel. The devout go for healing, and I have not heard that the king was wounded in Ireland."

Kei stood. "I doubt many people go to St. Govan's Head. It is far from any settlement, and the pilgrims' road to St. David's does not pass near it."

She stared at him, amazed that he was participating in the conversation. Maybe he wanted to regain Tarran's favor.

"But," she began, "putting a rock in the chapel—"

"Listen, Elspeth." Tarran took her hands and folded them between his, which were gritty from polishing his sword.

She delighted in the texture of his strong hands. Until she had met him, she had never realized how fascinated she was with hands. She had taught the soft, untutored hands of her students. She had watched her father's hands while he juggled. Tarran's hands were skilled, whether holding a sword or cradling her face. They were tough and coarse, yet could be as gentle as a spring breeze. He used them to emphasize each word he spoke, even when keeping his strongest emotions under control. But when he released those passions, as he had during the night, those hands had brought forth feelings she had never imagined. His hands were an enthralling mirror into his soul, and she had been watching them all along without realizing.

"I am listening," she whispered, hoping no one else

would hear how her voice shook at the thought of his hands gliding along her.

"You must listen closely."

She reluctantly drew her fingers from between his palms. When his brow started to lower, she brushed her finger across one eyebrow, then the other, before clasping her hands in her lap. Whether he understood from her touch or from her tightly locked fingers, he nodded.

"The chapel," he said in a low, intense voice that assumed the rumble of the sea itself, rising and falling, "is built into a cliff overlooking the sea where the saint was pursued by those who wished him harm. It is said the rocks opened to conceal St. Govan. When those chasing him hurried past, the rocks reopened and this time did not close. A chapel was built at the spot where the miracle occurred. Its walls have tumbled down, so there is little more than an altar remaining."

"So hiding the stone within the chapel is impossible."

"Yes, but there is no need to hide it within the chapel."

Elspeth noticed Vala was watching him intently. Had she, too, noticed how his voice took on a bard's rhythm?

"The beach below the cliffs," he continued, "is littered with rocks broken off from the cliffs during storms. Among them, *Llech-lafar* would go unnoticed."

Elspeth stood. She could not sit still when excitement at completing her task battled with her heart, reminding her of what she could lose at the end. "And the cove offers no place for a ship to seek harbor?"

"There is a sandy beach, but the cliff faces are steep between the chapel and the headland. Scaling them is nearly impossible. Any ship would seek a safer harbor in Pembroke or near Tyddewi." Tarran stood and put his hands on her shoulders. "We can push *Llech-lafar* over the side of the cliff and let it become lost among the boulders on the shore."

"If there is any chance the king would go there—"

"Even if he did, no one goes beyond the bell rock." Kei gave Tarran a smile. "Tell her about it."

He looked puzzled for a moment, then said, "The chapel once had a bell." His voice took on a minstrel's meter again.

When he walked to where his men sat, Vala whispered, "It is good to hear him tell stories again."

Elspeth tore her attention away from Tarran's description of the sweet sound the chapel's bell had possessed. Sitting next to Vala, she asked, "Again?"

"He used to sing and tell stories and even write poems. That all ended when . . ." Her eyes filled with tears.

Grief tightened Elspeth's throat when she noticed how enthralled his men were. They had missed Tarran's storytelling as much as Vala had. Everything that had brought Tarran cheer had died with Addfwyn. A small bubble of hope filled her heart as she wondered if he was able to tell the story of St. Govan's Chapel because he had opened himself to her in the bower by the river.

"But that wondrous bell was almost stolen," Tarran said, his voice hushed and filled with a suggestion of doom, "so the saint concealed the bell within a rock. A rap with the knuckles on the rock will bring forth the sound of a bell. It is near the holy well. People will venture that far seeking healing, but rocks and the rough cliffs keep them from wandering farther."

No one spoke for a long moment when he paused.

Elspeth broke the enchantment. She must think of her task, not what had happened centuries ago. "So if we hide *Llech-lafar* among those rocks, it would be lost forever."

"Yes."

Elspeth smiled. "I cannot imagine a better place to dispose of this danger to the king. How far is it?"

"At least a week's journey." Tarran glanced toward the

window where rain splattered through the shutters and onto the sill. "A week in fair weather. If these storms continue, it could take longer."

"And we must assume that our passage will not go unnoticed." She tapped her thumbs together. "I wish we knew why Druce is still here in the village when he was so vehement that he—and only he—should look for the man who attacked me."

"You know the real reason he came here, Elspeth. He wants to rid Cymru of Henry and his allies."

"If he discovers what we are doing, he will try to halt us. We must find another rock to put in *Llech-lafar*'s place so he never suspects it has been moved." She stood and reached for her cloak. "Who is with me?"

Tarran's men stood as one. Tarran put out his right hand. His men put theirs on top of it. Stretching, Elspeth set hers over theirs. No one needed to speak. The pledge to save the king was now theirs as well as hers.

The rain made extracting a rock similar in size and shape to *Llech-lafar* simpler than Elspeth had dared to hope. The riverbank about a half mile from *Llech-lafar*'s location was muddy, and the earth fell into the river as they dug out the rock.

Seith proved that his girth was more muscle than fat when he pulled the stone from the bank and guided it onto the plank the other men held. The board was charred but only on the edges, so it had enough strength to support the stone as all five of them worked together to lift it into the wagon. Elspeth shoved the disturbed sections of the bank into the water so any sign of the rock's location disappeared.

The oxen strained and the cart creaked, but they were able to carry the stone along the river toward Tyddewi. Tarran sent his men ahead to make sure nobody was near, so the stones could be switched unobserved. Again the cold rain was their ally because it kept the villagers close to their hearths.

More planks were placed on the ground to keep the wagon wheels from cutting into the soft earth. Small rocks and debris could be used to cover the oxen's hoofprints. Nothing must divulge that they had been working by the river.

Digging out *Llech-lafar* was more difficult because they wanted to keep the riverbank looking untouched. Elspeth drew a line with her quarterstaff around the rock's edges, and Gryn and Tarran peeled back grass and earth. Using her staff as a lever, she loosened the stone. Once the grass was tamped down around the nameless stone, they lifted *Llech-lafar* into the cart and covered it with several old blankets given to them by Vala's granddaughter.

Elspeth watched Kei lead the cart toward the village. It would be left behind Modlen's cottage, where it had been since they arrived in Tyddewi. With luck, nobody would notice anything.

Luck had been with her since she had come to Wales. She hoped it would remain a while longer.

The rain had nearly stopped by the time Tarran strode through the wet grass at the bottom of the open vale where the cathedral had stood. He had heard it was a grand building, worthy of St. David's name, and that the building to replace it would be even more magnificent. That cathedral would take years to build, but it could be finished by the time he sailed to and returned from Prince Madoc's mythic land if he needed to follow Bradwr ap Glew across the sea.

He drew the dagger he wore next to his own. Addfwyn's blade could have spilled Elspeth's blood. As never before, he questioned his vow to see Bradwr ap Glew dead. It had been easy to risk everything for revenge before Elspeth

came into his life and into his arms. But he had made
Addfwyn a death vow, and he must carry it out, even if it
meant his own death.

Something near the cathedral caught his eye. Elspeth!
He could recognize her silhouette, which his hands knew
well. Striding through last year's knee-high grass that was
woven with much shorter fresh green blades, he said as
soon as he was close enough for her to hear, "You should
not have come here alone."

"I know." She looked toward the river.

He put his hand on her shoulder, and she leaned back
against him. The motion was trusting and innocent. There
was still much she did not know about him. He had not told
her about the dark nightmares he suffered before she had
started sleeping beside him. Those were gone, but during
the day he was afflicted with the idea of being separated
from her forever. Elspeth had said nothing about remaining
in Cymru once she did as she had promised Queen
Eleanor.

"What are you staring at?" he asked.

"The river. I cannot help but wonder if Druce was honest or lying when he pointed out *Llech-lafar*."

"Do not look for trouble when we already have more
than our fair share." He gave such an emoted groan that she
laughed.

"All right." She rested her head on his shoulder. "I will
assume we have the right stone, and we shall figure out a
way to persuade Druce not to go with us. Maybe he is enjoying the villagers listening to his stories enough to linger
here."

The wind blew rain into their faces, and she bent her
head forward as she raised her cloak's hood. The day was
not cold, but the crisp wind howled among the ruins as if
mourning the cathedral's destruction.

"There is an emptiness here," Tarran said.

"Like what you feel within you?"

He shook his head, then realized she could not see it. "What I feel is not emptiness. It is a hunger that will not be sated while Bradwr ap Glew lives."

"But what will be left when you see your enemy dead at your feet?"

"Triumph."

She turned to face him. "Triumph fades. What then?"

"I will—"

The grass rustled behind him. He whirled. He saw a flash of metal and drew his sword. At the same time, he shoved Elspeth away as hard as he could. He raised his sword. The man, dressed in the simple robes Druce wore, slammed his own into Tarran's.

He parried each blow, watching for the opening that would allow him to halt his attacker. He sensed rather than saw Elspeth creeping toward them, a staff at ready.

"Stay back!" he ordered.

"I want to help!" she shouted.

"Stay back!" Didn't she realize that she could not use the staff when he and his attacker stood so close? A single miscalculation, and she could strike Tarran instead of the other man.

He was astounded when the staff came down between them, not striking either of them, but landing with perfect accuracy on his attacker's sword. The man lifted his sword and brought it down on her staff.

The staff from the cathedral had been weakened in the fire. It cracked. He swung his sword again. She tried to move aside, but the edge sliced off several ruddy curls.

Blinded by his fury that the man had turned his attack on her, Tarran drove his sword into him. The man shrieked and collapsed, pressing his hand over the incision, which sent blood coursing down his robe and into the grass.

Tarran rushed to Elspeth. She was staring at the man, and when Tarran put a hand on her arm, she flinched and pulled away with a cry.

"Are you hurt?" he asked.

"You—you killed—" She turned and wobbled forward several steps. Dropping to her knees, she was violently ill.

He put his hand on her hair, not sure what to say. Looking back at the man lying on the ground, he said, "Elspeth, I must ask him what he knows while I can."

She nodded as she wrapped her arms around herself.

He did not want to move away while she retched, but he was not sure how much time the man had left. Going to where the man was lying on scarlet grass, he knelt and asked, "Who wishes me dead?"

"You know!" choked out the man, his bravado not flowing away along with his blood.

"If I knew, I would not ask." He heard the grass swishing again, and Elspeth walked gingerly toward them. Her face was as gray as the dying man's when she knelt beside him. "Who wishes me dead?"

"Bradwr ap Glew intends for you to pay for Addfwyn's death."

Tarran recoiled. "He wants *me* to pay? The crime is his."

"The crime is yours, Prince Tarran ap Llyr."

"Where is Bradwr ap Glew? Does he remain in Cymru, or did he sail with Prince Madoc?"

"My cousin is everywhere." The man gasped for breath, and Elspeth reached toward the man.

Tarran waved her away.

"But I may be able to—" she began.

"Be silent, Elspeth!"

She sat on her heels, dismay furrowing her brow.

He was tempted to comfort her, but there was no time. He bent toward the man. "Answer me! Where is Bradwr ap Glew?"

"Waiting to hear that you are dead, Prince Tarran."

"Where? Where does he wait?" His fist hitting the ground punctuated each word. "Tell me. Is he in Cymru?"

"He is where he waits to hear that you are dead." The man tried to spit at him, but choked again. "He will find you, Prince Tarran. I failed, but he has others."

"Who?"

The man did not reply. He groped for something at the top of his robe.

Tarran saw a leather strand there and pulled it from beneath the robe. As he lifted it, something popped out. Even in the rain, the bead glittered.

"Do you know Druce the poet?" Tarran demanded.

The man gurgled, and his head lolled to one side.

Elspeth gave a half sob as Tarran yanked the strand from around the man's neck before he lowered the lids over the man's unseeing eyes. Turning, he pulled her into his arms. She wept against his chest, trembling like a frightened child.

"I am sorry." Each of her words was broken by a sob. "I know you did what you had to."

"But?"

"I have never seen a man die like that before."

He stroked her quivering back. "But I had to halt you from chasing after the man who ambushed me while I hunted with Heliwr. What did you plan to do if you caught him?"

"Beat some sense into him." She shook hard. "I never planned to kill him."

With his thumbs under her chin, he tilted her head back. Gazing into her eyes that were as green as the new grass beneath him, he whispered, "Sometimes you have no choice."

"I hope it never comes to that."

"I hope so, too." Even as he spoke the words, he knew

how worthless they were. The dead man's warning echoed in his head. Bradwr ap Glew wanted to see him dead, and the attacks would not end until either Bradwr ap Glew or he was sent to dine with Death.

Chapter 19

"I will not tolerate such baneful actions on my lands." Druce puffed out like a frog getting ready to croak as he scowled at Tarran, who stood in the doorway of Modlen's cottage. He had repeated the same words for an hour, each time pounding his staff into the ground, but his ire had not lessened.

"Lord de Vay, who holds these lands for the king, will understand that I had to keep that man from killing Elspeth." Tarran's terse words could not hide his exasperation. "He will realize that we had to defend ourselves from attack."

Elspeth, sitting on the damp step below where Tarran stood, wanted to reach out and take his hand, but kept her fingers folded on her lap. Now that she was over her initial shock at the man's death, she had many questions. The most important ones were: What had Tarran done to make his onetime friend and foster brother despise him enough to blame him for Addfwyn's death? Could Bradwr ap Glew be innocent of the crime?

Druce frowned. "I want you gone from my lands."

"We will be leaving," Tarran said. "My errand to Tyddewi is complete."

"Good! I do not want to delay any longer returning to

my people who need me." He flung out his hands. "But I cannot leave the ones here to your murderous spree."

Orwig tugged on Druce's cassock, and Druce glanced at him. Unsure how any message could pass between them when Orwig's face was hidden beneath the hood, Elspeth said nothing. Druce's golden staff glistened as the two men walked away.

Tarran glanced at his men and nodded in the direction of the two men. With an anticipatory grin, his men slipped away to trail Druce and Orwig.

"I wish I could believe *that* problem was solved," Elspeth said as she stood.

Tarran nodded. "Anyone who trusts those men deserves to get caught up in their mischief."

"What sort of mischief?"

"Harmless, I hope."

"Do you really believe that?" she asked, shocked.

"I would like to believe it, but Druce and his cohort want something. Whether they realized we would not give it to them or whether their departure is only a ploy, it matters little. We will keep watch for them or whoever else might wish to intrude in completing our quests."

"I wish I could rid myself of this idea that it would have been better if Druce had *not* left."

"Why?"

"At least then we know where he is."

He took her hands as he faced her. "You could have tried to persuade him to stay. You said nary a word while Druce was snarling at me."

"Speaking when Druce is near is not easy." She tried to smile. It was useless because her lips wanted to quiver, and tears kept welling up in her eyes.

"What is it, Elspeth?"

"I keep thinking about that man saying Bradwr ap Glew blames you for Addfwyn's death."

"Why?"

She dampened her lower lip, for the words were not easy to speak. "What if he did not kill her, Tarran? What if someone else did and left clues to point to him?"

Raising her hands to his mouth, he kissed one, then the other. "Do not let his tricks confuse you, *cariad*. I know him well, and I recall how he often played pranks on others. His aim was always to baffle people so they did something they customarily would not do. He found that amusing. Now he is trying to do the same thing again, only with greater cost if one falls into his trap." He ran the back of his hand along her chin. "Elspeth, you have said nothing until now about the accusation that man made."

"That you had killed Addfwyn?"

"Yes."

"There is nothing to say. I have seen your sorrow, and I know it is genuine." She put her hand on the center of his chest. "I know the man within you. He is a man of honor, and he is a man who believes he failed the woman he loved and must rectify that mistake by being overly protective of everyone else around him. I know you did not kill her, but Bradwr ap Glew—"

"Killed Lady Addfwyn," said Vala as she appeared in the doorway. "I know that as surely as I know I am in Tyddewi. For a man who should have been good, he was wicked."

Tarran released Elspeth's hands and put his hand on Vala's quaking arm. "We know that, Vala, but Elspeth was right to ask. She does not know Bradwr ap Glew as we do."

"As we thought we did." She shook her head. Looking both ways from the door, she lowered her voice. "My granddaughter is growing nervous with the cart and its cargo behind her house. We must speak right away."

Elspeth followed the old woman into the cottage. Tarran closed the door after them. The soup cooking on the hearth offered a welcome, but Elspeth knew it was no longer for them. Modlen was right to be concerned about her home and her grandmother's safety.

"We plan to leave at dawn," Tarran said. "I will have another man stay with you if you wish, for Iau cannot offer you much protection if Druce returns." He glanced at Elspeth, and his mouth worked before he spat out, "Or if anyone else does."

"Take your men with you." Vala kneaded her lap with anxious fingers. "The danger goes with you. If anyone were to suspect what you plan—"

Elspeth sat beside her and put a consoling hand on the old woman's arm. "I have watched people walking toward the river to look at *Llech-lafar*. Nobody has raised an alarm."

"You must pass through Pembroke, and someone may demand to see what is beneath the blankets in the cart."

Tarran slammed his hand against the doorframe. "I had not given that any thought. The Marcher lords say they are acting on the king's behalf when they take their *taxes* from anyone passing through. How ironic that *we* are working on the king's behalf, and they could destroy everything with their greed."

"I have a suggestion." Elspeth swallowed roughly, wishing she had another idea. Any other idea. "There are others besides merchants who travel along the roads with carts."

"Who?"

"Traveling entertainers." She looked over her shoulder when the door opened and his men came in.

Seith gave a silent nod to Tarran before sitting on the floor. She hoped it meant that Druce and his companion were well on their way back toward wherever their people lived.

"You cannot be serious!" retorted Tarran, and she knew he was thinking only of her suggestion.

Elspeth wondered if he had any idea how endearing his honest emotions were, even bemusement.

"It makes good sense," Vala said, picking up her sewing and stitching in tempo with her words. "When you pass through Pembroke, no one will guess you have anything in the wagon but what minstrels would carry."

"So nobody will guess we are carrying Merlin's stone." Elspeth appreciated Vala's approval. Maybe the idea was not insane after all.

"But where will we find performers?" Seith asked.

She could say nothing and let the others devise a way to find people to entertain anyone who became suspicious. But hiring performers would take time, and they had little left.

"We have all the performers we need right here," she said quietly.

"Where?"

Vala smiled. "I understand."

"You do?" Tarran looked at the old woman. "Will you explain it to me?"

"*We* can be the performers," Elspeth said.

He scowled at her, then at Vala.

The old woman held up her hands and laughed. "Do not try to batter me down with that stare, which you learned from me, Tarran. *You* revealed your gift when you told the story of the chapel bell. The rest of us remember when you enjoyed singing and poetry." Her smile faded. "I recall the man you were before you found Addfwyn dead, and I wish you would recall that man as well."

"That man left his wife to the mercy of a murderer!" He stormed across the narrow room. "Why would I wish to resurrect that fool?"

"Because we need him."

At Elspeth's soft answer, he looked at her. She saw pain

behind his rage and craving for vengeance. He had tried to deny a part of himself, but failed.

She put her fingers on his shoulder. Softly, so softly she could barely hear the words herself, she said, "Tarran, I want to know the man you were. I want to see your mouth as expressive in conversation as when it is against mine. I try to imagine you laughing when we are sitting together. Not with sarcasm or disdain, but with happiness."

"I am not sure I remember how." He turned toward the hearth.

"You remember. Otherwise, you could not smile when you are with me. You must stop believing that if you tear down the walls of hate you will betray Addfwyn."

"How can I?"

"Tell me, Tarran. Tell me honestly. Would she have wanted you to banish all joy from your life? You have told me Addfwyn was a remarkable woman with a heart so generous that nobody was denied welcome within it. She loved you, and she must have loved your music and poetry. Why not? She was born in Wales. It is the way of the Welsh to exult in happiness."

He faced her, his eyes burning with the emotions he had vowed not to feel again. "I am happy when I am with you, Elspeth. Do not ask more of me, for I can never forget my death vow to Addfwyn. "

"I would never ask that of you." She put her hands on his arms. A mistake, she realized when she longed to draw them around her. She must think of the task ahead, not her yearning to be enfolded to within his arms. "But I ask you to help me with my vow to the queen."

Kei laughed as he walked past them to dip a bowl into the pot simmering on the hearth. "Pretending to be minstrels sounds like great fun, and it has been far too long since we have had any fun. Isn't that right, Gryn?"

His cousin frowned.

"I know," Kei retorted to the silent scold, "that we are on a quest, but must it always be dismal?"

Seith tapped his finger against his double chin. "We have vowed to do as we must. If acting the part of entertainers is what we must do, then we shall. What would you have us do, Lady Elspeth?"

Tarran's fingers itched to wrap around his friend's throat. Of all his men, Seith ap Mil was the most cautious. Shaking good sense into Seith was something he had never had to do. Seith shared his determination to see Bradwr ap Glew's blood; yet, Seith was agreeing to Elspeth's ridiculous plan.

"There are many entertainments you can provide," Elspeth was saying. "People like to see what they can do performed with greater skill, as my father was fond of saying when he was teaching me."

Her face blanched, and he knew she had said something she had not intended.

He looked at his men, motioned with his head toward the door, and they filed out of the cottage. Vala made some half-spoken excuse about something in the other room. She hurried in and drew the curtain.

Elspeth's head was lowered, and the ruddy curtain of her hair concealed her face. Her fingers were tightly clasped, a sign she was distressed.

"I thought your father was a Norman lord," he said in a low voice that would not carry beyond the curtain.

She shook her head, but continued to stare at the floor. "No, he was, as my mother was, a performer in a traveling show."

"So you lied to me?"

"Not so much a lie," she answered, raising her eyes, "as allowing you to continue to believe what you thought was true. Tarran, I tried to tell you beneath the trees when . . ."

Color rose on her pale face, and he was charmed by her shyness when she spoke of their first tryst.

"But I halted you."

"Yes."

He sat on the bench. When she sat beside him, he did not touch her. If he did, he would forget everything but how much he wanted to rediscover her, learning the tastes of her skin he had yet to explore, thrilling in her eager reactions, finding satiation of desire with her . . . only to want her more.

"Why didn't you tell me the truth in the first place?" he asked.

"I could say I did not think it was the place of the daughter of traveling entertainers to correct a prince's mistaken assumption."

"You could say that, but you never are content with so few words."

"True." Her smile was fleeting. "Tarran, you must understand that I did not lie to you in hopes that you would consider me close enough to your rank so we could be together."

"I tried to stay away from you because I believed you were a Norman lord's daughter, and your family would see me as nothing but the son of a bastard."

"Or at least half of that." Before he could respond to her teasing, she whispered, "I seldom speak of my parents. I am not ashamed of them, but after they died, I had to adjust to a new life."

"So you never grieved for them?"

"No." She blinked away the tears filling her eyes.

"How did they die?"

"There was a fever spreading through a town where we stopped. By the time my parents discovered the danger, it was too late. We left, but even if they had survived long enough, we would not have been allowed to enter the next town." She gnawed on her lower lip. "I could do nothing but put cool cloths on their brows and try to get them to drink cinquefoil, which I had boiled in milk. I was barely ten years old, and I did not know what else to do."

He brushed her hair back from her face. "You did as well as any physician. The Old Welsh would say their time had come to cross into the land of Annwfn."

"What is that?"

"You know. You were there when—" He cursed.

Elspeth drew back. "I was where? What is Annwfn?"

As he stood to walk away, she stepped in front of him. She planted her feet and crossed her arms over her chest.

"You might as well tell me," she said. "If you don't, I shall ask Vala or one of your men. We are not going to leave until morning, so you have the whole night to tell me."

"All right. Annwfn is the land ruled by Death."

"But you said I was there."

"In a nightmare."

"Tarran, I am sorry. I—"

His hands cupped her shoulders, then slid down her arms. When his fingertips brushed her breasts, she gave a soft moan.

"Now you know," he whispered. "And you should know that if we were to take this whole night for one thing, *cariad*, I would not want to spend it talking about nightmares." He pressed his lips against her neck, and his heated breath threatened to set her ablaze. "I would not want to think of the future, only of the night we have to share."

"We must think of the future." She stroked his face and smiled. "We must decide what you will do during our performances."

"Me? Perform?" He shook his head. "That is absurd!"

"Why? Because you are *Prince* Tarran?"

He walked toward the hearth. When she stepped in front of him again, he edged around her. She blocked his way a third time. With a curse, he picked her up and set her to one side. He took another pace before she grasped his arm.

Whirling, he said as he had so many time, "Enough, Elspeth. I have—"

"To listen to reason." She wrapped her arm around his head and leaped toward him.

"What are you doing?" he asked. Or he meant to ask, because the words vanished into a shout of disbelief as she threw her feet out in front of him. She pulled down on him even as her legs rose.

They tumbled toward the floor. She kept his head close to her as they hit. Before he could react, he was on his back and she was sitting over him, pinning his right hand to the floor.

The door crashed open, and his men peered in, alerted by the sounds within the cottage. They roared with laughter and pointed at him.

Vala pushed aside the curtain. Her expression of dismay became amusement when she saw he was not hurt.

Save for my pride. That was bruised after he was taken down by a woman a head shorter than he was. She was mad! Or was he the one who had lost his mind? As he saw her red hair bouncing around her shoulders and watched her breasts move with her quick breaths, he could think only of pulling her closer.

He yelped as he tried to move his right arm. Her thumb pressed into his wrist and refused to let him move.

"Let go!" he ordered.

"Not until you are agree to perform with us, Tarran!" Her chin jutted toward him.

If he wished, he could silence her with one blow, but he had no intention of striking her. *Even if you could*, he had to admit. He had never seen anyone move with such controlled speed as when she had thrown him off his feet.

"Is this one of your stage tricks?" he asked.

"It was no trick. It was a well-practiced skill." She leaned forward. "Will you help me?"

"Do I have a choice?"

"You do, but there is only one right choice if we hope to save the king's life." She released his right arm and stood, her legs still on either side of him. "You must ask yourself, Tarran, if you will regret more helping me or not helping me."

He grabbed her ankle. He meant to upend her, but again she was quicker than he was. Before he had a chance to react, she had seized his wrist and twisted it to the point just before it would be painful. He opened his mouth to retort, but she shifted her hold, and a twinge raced up his arm.

"Do not speak anything but an answer to the question of which you would regret more." She was not breathless, and listening to her, he would have guessed she was involved in nothing more strenuous than stirring soup. "Which is it?"

"Will you break my wrist if I give the wrong answer?"

That brought another peal of laughter from his men.

"There is no wrong answer," she said, still serious.

"I have said I would help you in any way I can, even if it means making a fool of myself from here to St. Govan's Head."

She released his wrist. As he sat, rubbing it, she squatted so their eyes were even. "That is the right answer, Tarran."

"I thought you said there was no wrong answer."

"There was not, but there was only one right answer."

"I surmise that I am going to regret giving you that answer."

She laughed. "I surmise you will." She leaned forward to press her mouth to his, then faltered.

"Nothing has changed between us," he whispered. "You are who you have always been, and so am I." He pulled her against him, and she softened beneath his kiss.

He must not let her guess, even for a moment, how he

hated that by helping her he was shortening their time together. Addfwyn had been taken from him too soon, and
once Elspeth had completed her task for the queen, she
would leave, too. He had thought losing Addfwyn to death
was the worst pain he could ever feel . . . until now.

Chapter 20

Tarran felt as out of place as a cloak on Heliwr's back as he walked beside the cart through the village of Pembroke. A canopy with curtains had been raised over the wagon, hiding *Llech-lafar*. Elspeth assured him that the cart now looked as if it belonged to true performers.

As the oxen edged down the steep hill, he saw a river ran between the walls of the castle on one bank and a priory on the far side. The priory was set higher on its hill, and he wondered if the lord within the castle wished to change places to have the higher vantage point in case of attack.

Elspeth had insisted he try to smile while he walked along the twisting streets. He tried, but his face was creased into a grimace sure to repel anyone who came too close.

He could not say the same of Elspeth. She was exulting in the chance to show her skills to anyone drawing near the wagon. She was calling to the villagers to come and watch as Kei and Gryn frolicked like two large children. Gryn, the bigger of the two, balanced his cousin on his shoulders. Kei was flinging his hands out as if he hoped to capture a cloud.

From the moment they had been able to see the wooden palisades surrounding the stone keep of Pembroke Castle, she had insisted they assume their roles. He guessed his men were enthusiastic, even though they were tired of practicing the tricks she taught each night after the long journey over the shore hills.

When Heliwr flapped wildly on his hand, Tarran calmed the bird's bating with soft words and a piece of meat. He motioned away villagers who were curious about the bird. If he had been certain the hawk's sounds in the wagon would have drawn no attention, he would have left Heliwr to guard *Llech-lafar*.

Children raced by, tugging on their parents' clothes. He watched as they ran to where Elspeth was holding two staffs in her hands. Not fighting staffs, but stilts, because they had crosspieces on them.

He gasped when she swung up onto them. She walked without a wobble, holding her hands up as she paused in front of the youngsters. They clapped wildly and pleaded for a chance to walk on the stilts.

"She has many unexpected skills, Prince Tarran," Seith said.

"Watch what you call me."

Seith apologized, his face reddening. "I will be glad when we are through the village and done with her quest."

"And with her?"

"Why are you asking *me* that?" The large man was taken aback. "The decision is yours."

"I would like your opinion."

"My opinion is that nothing would ever be calm when she is around." He walked forward to urge the oxen to a faster pace.

Tarran nodded. As usual, he and his most trusted man agreed completely.

Heliwr gave a shrill cry as the children ran toward them, following Elspeth on the stilts. When she jumped down, she offered them to the tallest child. A girl, Tarran noted, who climbed onto the stilts and promptly toppled into the muddy road. The children laughed with excitement as she tried again.

Elspeth smiled and waved to them as she walked to where Tarran followed the cart. Her face was aglow with happiness and her hair a red swirl around her. Even though the sunshine that seeped through the thickening clouds overhead was faint, it brightened her hair to match the fiery emotions in her eyes.

"Can you make the oxen move more quickly?" she asked beneath cheers as Kei jumped to the ground from his cousin's shoulders.

"Seith is trying to persuade them."

"We are running out of tricks. I have offered to take on anyone who wishes to challenge me with a quarterstaff."

"Do you think that is wise?"

She shrugged. "I cannot say, but I have to keep everyone amused until the cart is through the village."

"I can have Heliwr fly."

"Not unless we need to. Few traveling performers have the wealth to possess a hawk. We must make sure if someone looks down from the castle's walls, they will see only entertainers and people enjoying the performances."

"I will be glad when we are beyond the reach of the castle's archers."

She looked at him, feigning amazement. "But aren't you having fun?"

"No."

"You might enjoy yourself more if you smiled."

"At this silliness?"

"My family did not think it beneath them to bring joy to others. You should not feel too grand to help." She tapped the center of his chest with her finger. "In fact, you should be more willing to set aside your dignity in order to protect your liege lord."

He grasped her finger. "Keep touching me, *cariad*, and

we will give these people something truly memorable to
see."

"I like what you are thinking."

"How can you tell what I am thinking?"

She touched the spot between his eyes. "I can see it
here." Her fingers glided over his lips and chin and down
his chest. "And here."

When he caught them before they reached his belt, he
murmured, "Take care, for I need no persuading to throw
you into the back of the cart and make love with you."

"I will keep that in mind." Elspeth turned to go back to
where a boy was now trying to walk a few steps with the
stilts. She wanted to be certain none of the children would
get hurt.

"Elspeth?"

The gentleness in Tarran's voice compelled her to turn
around. She heard it so seldom, even though she was always
aware of his tenderness. "Yes?"

"I do not think these antics beneath me. If you think that,
I am sorry." He walked to her and stroked her face. "I never
guessed that you missed this life."

"Neither did I." Matching his steps as he turned to follow the cart again, she walked around a puddle.

"How long has it been since you last traveled like this?"

"I had seen only ten summers when my parents died."

"What happened to you then?"

Elspeth ached to tell him the truth, but it was sure to
complicate the situation further. Yet to lie was an idea so
distasteful, her stomach cramped.

"I buried them in the nearest churchyard in the middle of
the night. Or I intended to. The priest found me and offered
me shelter. He saw that I would never be happy in the village, so he sent me to friends who knew what to do with a
girl like me."

"A girl who dares to learn the skills a knight knows?"

She laughed. "That came later. I had much else to learn because my only lessons until then had been how to juggle and walk on stilts and—"

"Walk across a pole."

"My parents tried to teach me, but I kept trying later. Children like to learn things all by themselves."

He touched her cheek, the motion so caring her resolve to keep her grief in the past was almost undone. "And you learned to stand alone."

"Yes."

"One lady warrior standing alone."

"Aren't you one man standing alone against fate?"

"No. I have my men who share my longing for revenge."

She shook her head. "But they would not have set off on the quest if you had not asked. They will fight at your side, but since Addfwyn died, you have been alone. How long are you going to be alone, Tarran?"

He did not answer because Gryn rushed up to them. "Elspeth, come with me, please. They are asking for more entertainment, and Kei is too nervous. He keeps dropping the sacks he is trying to juggle."

She laughed. The cousins had been less than eager to master the tricks she tried to teach them, except juggling.

"I will stay with the cart," Tarran said. "Go and divert them." He grasped her arm before she could turn away. His kiss was both sweet and bitter at the same time, for it was tainted with the sorrow he carried in every heartbeat.

Elspeth eased away. Too often, her obligations drew her away. She wanted to linger in his arms until they could speak from the depths of their hearts and let passion banish their pain. But, as she went with Gryn, she knew it could not be today.

She looked back. Tarran was trying to keep his face blank. She wanted to urge him again to smile. While his heart remained broken, it would be impossible. She wished she could offer him sympathy, but had to remain in her role in their ruse. The burden of her obligation to the queen weighed as heavily on her as if she carried *Llech-lafar* on her back.

She continued with Gryn to where a group of spectators had gathered. Men and women and children wore the peasant garb of the village. She noticed a man in pale robes that must belong to the monastery on the other side of the river. Or could he be a member of Druce's group? She trusted Druce no more than Tarran did, and she wondered if he had set his spies on them. She would alert Tarran as soon as she caught up with him and the cart beyond the village.

Nobody was looking at her and Gryn. Neither were they, she was pleased to see, watching the cart as it went along the street that slanted down into the shadow of the castle where the river was not much wider than the River Alun.

The people were standing around a large boulder she had not noticed before. Not a boulder, she realized as she came closer, but a man who made even Seith look puny. He could have been one of the mountains rising in the distance. His head seemed small in comparison with the bulk of his body. People pointed, and he turned. In his hand was a staff as huge as he was.

Gryn swore. "Milady, you do not have to accept *all* challenges."

"I know." She glanced over her shoulder at the wooden palisades above the river. Sentries were watching their passage instead of walking along the walls. She must keep everyone distracted until the cart was on the far side of the river and climbing the hill past the monastery.

"I will tell him that you meant only that you would take challenges from other women," Gryn said.

"No." She grasped his arm to keep him from striding toward the giant. "If he creates a commotion because I refuse, those guards on the wall will come to halt it. Then we will face questions we cannot answer."

"Let me battle him, milady."

"When did you last use a staff?"

He shuffled his feet in the muddy street. "I prefer to use my sword."

"Which you cannot here." She pointed at the wagon, which was going around a corner as the street continued along the castle walls. "Bring my staff."

"He could kill you, milady!"

"I will concede the fight before that."

He gave her a tentative smile. "True. You do not have a man's honor to preserve."

Only the Abbey's, she wanted to fire back.

As Gryn ran to get her staff, Elspeth walked toward the enormous man. He eyed her boldly and laughed. She kept her expression serene.

She paused beyond the reach of his quarterstaff, which, she noted, had iron pieces on either end. Her makeshift staff was only wood. She had two disadvantages before the fight even began.

"You wish to accept my challenge?" she asked.

"Maybe you wish to withdraw it." His laugh was like a clap of thunder.

Gryn was panting when he returned and held out her staff. He started to speak, but she waved him to silence. Raising her arm, she threw the staff to her right.

The big man laughed again. "You are smart to quit, wench."

His laugh vanished when the staff hit a stone and bounced back into her hand. She had to show the man, right from the start, that she was as skilled as she had boasted she was. She swung it, hitting him hard in the shoulder.

"Maybe you wish to quit." Baiting him until he lost his temper might be her best weapon.

The man rumbled some answer. Towering over her, he balanced heavily on the back of his feet.

Elspeth rocked her quarterstaff between her two hands. She watched him step forward. His motions were slow and hinted at a strength earned by hard labor. As he took another pace toward her, the odor of manure and damp earth drifted from him.

He slammed his staff against hers. She was rocked back several steps. Only Gryn catching her kept her on her feet. She nodded her thanks and straightened.

"Do you always fight so gently?" she called. "Let me know when you are ready for a true contest."

"I am ready!" He whipped the staff around his head. "Are you?"

She wanted to shout, "No!" Instead she walked to where she could gauge every move he made. She jumped aside each time he swung the staff, which seemed as wide as a tree. If he struck her even once with it, he would crush her.

His movements slowed as she kept circling him, and she knew he was tiring. When she jabbed him with insults, he roared his defiance and tried to strike her. She heard some villagers calling to halt the fight. If he heard them as well, he gave no sign.

Her name was shouted. Tarran! Why wasn't he with the cart, guarding *Llech-lafar*?

The huge man's staff struck hers. She heard wood fracture, but the staff did not break. Then the man's staff hit her in the head. Not straight on, or she would have been killed. It bounced off her staff and grazed the side of her head. She reeled, then fell to her knees.

Sound assaulted her from every direction. None of the voices made sense, for she could not hear words over the clanging in her skull. Had the bell from St. Govan's Chapel been placed in her brain? Darkness closed in around her, and she found herself on the edge of a cliff dropping into nothing.

She raised her eyes. The huge man was standing a few feet in front of her. More shouts came, and she saw Tarran being held back by the villagers. Overhead, Heliwr screeched.

"You should have withdrawn," the man shouted. Or maybe he spoke at a normal volume. She could not tell. Everything went from loud to soft and back again.

"Elspeth!" Tarran called.

She blinked, forcing her eyes to focus as she grasped on to his voice to lead her from the rim of the abyss. She grasped her staff, which had fallen in front of her. She pulled it toward her, bouncing it off the rocks in the road. When she found one the right height, she let the staff teeter on it.

"Foolish wench!" The man smiled broadly and gripped his staff at one end, raising it to bring down on her. She heard shrieks from the onlookers.

"For St. Jude!" Jumping to her feet, she stepped on her staff. The other end rose sharply. His shout of triumph became an agonized groan as it struck him between the legs. He wobbled. His quarterstaff dropped from his fingers as he gripped himself and howled. When she pulled her staff from beneath him, he toppled over like a mountain tumbling into the sea.

Cheers rose from every side. Turning to where Tarran was pushing past others to get to her, she took a single step in his direction before darkness swarmed up to consume her. Her last thought was of Tarran's arms reaching out to catch her.

Chapter 21

Even with the blankets over the rock, *Llech-lafar* did not make a comfortable pillow. Elspeth winced as she opened her eyes. Staring at the makeshift canopy where rain pattered an intricate song, she wondered when it had started falling again.

She tried to push herself up. She only partly succeeded. A squawk came from her left. She saw Heliwr on his perch. He was regarding her with an expression that could mean disgust or sympathy or hunger.

"How do you feel?" asked Tarran from where he walked behind the wagon.

"Alive. Just barely, but alive."

"Did he pound some sense into your head?"

"Either that or knocked out every thought I ever had."

"How could you be so stupid? He was twice your size."

"I beat him, didn't I?" She grabbed the side of the cart and pulled herself up to sit. "How long have I been senseless?"

"Just long enough for us to get you into the wagon and to hie at the oxen's top speed past the castle."

"Past it?" She touched her tender scalp. "In the castle's stillroom, there must be something to ease my aching head."

"There probably is, but you would find scant welcome there."

"Why?"

"The man you defeated is a champion within Pembroke Castle. His fellow guards would probably chain you up in the Wogan."

"The what?" She inched toward the back of the cart.

"The Wogan. It is a cavern beneath the keep. It opens onto the river, and it could serve as a dungeon as well as a storeroom."

"Help me out."

His frown was comfortingly familiar. "You need to rest, so enjoy the chance to stay out of the rain."

"I am not going to lie here like an invalid if there is any threat to us leaving Pembroke."

Reaching in, he plucked her out as if she weighed no more than his hawk. He kept his arm around her shoulders when he put her on the road. She swayed, but was able to keep pace with him as the cart went slowly up the steep hill on the far side of the river.

"Your staff was cracked when we went to retrieve it," he said. "You are lucky it was not your skull he broke."

She nodded in agreement and wished she had been more cautious. "Once we have put a few miles between us and the castle—"

Tarran put his fingers to her lips. She sighed as the gentle touch teased her to plead with him to hold her until the world stopped spinning and the pain vanished.

"You cannot go much farther."

"But you said we would find no welcome at the castle."

"That is true, but Monkton Priory will open its door to us."

She looked at the heavy earthenworks that appeared more suited to a fortress than a holy house. Reminding herself that wars had been common before King Henry brought peace to Wales, she suspected the priory's residents had been grateful for those thick walls.

"Do you think you can walk that far?" he asked.

"I can if you can," she answered with mock cheer. "I hope they have some place that is warm and dry."

Tarran edged her around a thick pile of mud. When she careened against him, he steadied her. "Warm and dry. My thoughts exactly."

"Along with a place to sleep for hours."

His fingers stroked her side as he murmured, "And wake in your arms."

Elspeth glanced at him and quickly away. Although his seductive words tempted her to forget their predicament, she needed to concentrate on stumbling along the road leading to the priory.

"This is absurd," he said.

He lifted her into his arms. Tenderly, his mouth journeyed across hers, soothing, enticing, urging her closer. She leaned in to him. The simple motion almost sent her back into the eddy of darkness. Or was she being swept away by his kiss?

"*Cariad*," he murmured, "let me take care of you. Just this once."

She closed her eyes and nestled against his chest. His heartbeat was the most wondrous lullaby she could imagine, and she let it take her to a place somewhere between sleep and wakefulness.

Tarran led the way through the open gatehouse constructed of stone. The priory's brightly lit chapel was a straight line along the hillside. Barns and outbuildings surrounded it like sycophants waiting to do its bidding. Only one other building was lit in the stormy afternoon.

From the chapel came the sound of a choir singing vespers. A wave of happiness washed over her as she listened to beloved hymns. She could almost believe she was at home at St. Jude's Abbey, except that the hymns were being sung in deep, resonant voices. She had not guessed how much she would miss the simple day-to-day passage of time at the Abbey.

Her happiness tempered. Once she returned to the Abbey, she would never be close to Tarran again. She could not have the two things she loved most—Tarran and her life at the Abbey. Was this quandary what Rhan had meant with her warning?

Soon her quest would be finished, but Tarran's might be only beginning. He had been willing to help her. She could not hold him back from completing his. Nor could she hold back her heart, which would go with him, whether he wanted it or not.

Tarran halted before a simple door. Setting her on her feet, he kept his arm around her while he lifted a discolored brass knocker and let it fall against the door. The dull thud reverberated through the courtyard. As if it had a life of its own, the thick door opened.

A mousy face peered out. Surrounded by a dark brown hood, the man's face was almost hidden by whiskers. Bright eyes of the same, warm color regarded them with friendly curiosity. Beads on his thin belt rattled against his cassock as he smiled and held out pudgy hands in a greeting.

"A blessing on all who arrive at Monkton Priory. Do you seek something from us?" he asked.

Tarran kept his arm around Elspeth's shoulders as he said, "We seek haven from the coming night."

"How many of you?"

"We are five, and we have two oxen. In addition, I am traveling with a hawk, so if there are mews on the ground, he can shelter there."

The brother's smile broadened. "A hawk? We have a dovecote, but if you were to put him there, we would have dead doves by dawn. Fear not, we will find a place for him."

He pushed the door open farther. "Come in. I will have some of my brothers take your cart and beasts to the barn. There, sir, you can tend to your hawk."

"Thank you." Tarran gave her a slight push forward as the brother moved aside.

Elspeth stepped onto the smooth stone floor as Tarran gave their names to the monk. The odor from the candles set in niches along the corridor smelled like the ones at St. Jude's Abbey. The hushed sound of simple slippers and the rattle of beads was an embrace welcoming her home.

Tarran's arm tightened around her as the brother gestured for them to follow. She was astonished that Tarran's face was an expressionless mask again. What could be upsetting him in the priory?

"We should have gone to the castle anyhow," Seith muttered behind her.

Kei did not bother to lower his voice. "If she stays here, we can go to the castle. You do not need to be here where—"

"Silence!" Tarran snapped. "I told you before I would accept no argument about my decision."

His men exchanged wary glances, but subsided.

Elspeth was astonished. For his men to protest an order a second time—because they must have debated his command while she was unconscious—was inconceivable.

Rain struck windows along the corridor while they walked behind the brother, whose dreary robes blended with the shadows. No stained glass lessened the severe beauty of the building. Everywhere she looked was the same stern stone. Even the benches set before the windows were made of the gray stone.

When he opened a door and stepped back, the brother said, "If you will wait here, sir, with your lady, I will send for a brother from the stillroom."

"Thank you, Brother—"

"Leopold," he answered with a smile. "If your men will

come with me, I will take them to where they may rest until the evening meal."

Elspeth went into the small chamber, and she could almost believe she was in St. Jude's Abbey. The austere cell with its simple bed and single bowl on the floor reminded her of her room. A wooden chest by the door was larger than the one in her cell. If there had been a rack to hold her staff, she could have believed she had been transported to the Abbey.

"You should sit, Elspeth," Tarran said as he steered her toward the bed.

It was too narrow to hold both of them, she noted sadly. She sat and tried to slow her breathing. She had not realized until now that she was panting as if she were fighting that giant again.

"What is upsetting your men?" she asked.

"If you were they and could stay in a castle with eager wenches or in a priory with rules of chastity, which would you choose?"

She took his hand. "Tarran, you know it is more than wanting to bed a serving lass. Be honest. Please."

"If you will lie down and rest."

When she stretched out on the bed, he went to the chest. He opened it and lifted out some thick wool the same color as Brother Leopold's robes. He slashed off several lengths. Going to the bowl, he dipped one in and wrung it out before setting it on her forehead.

"Better?" he whispered as he sat beside her and folded her hands in his.

She lifted it off. "This is dark brown."

"So?"

"The man in the crowd was wearing a light-colored cassock."

"Man?" His eyebrows lowered toward each other. "Which man?"

She started to explain what she had seen, but he halted her while he put the cloth back on her forehead. She sighed as she sagged into the bed.

"I will send Kei and Gryn to the village to see what they might discover," he said. "I cannot say I am surprised that Druce may be watching us."

"We must get *Llech-lafar* to St. Govan's Head. Right away."

"We will be leaving with first light. It is too dark to travel now, even if you could. Rest while I speak with Kei and Gryn."

She reached for his hand. "Before you go, tell me what is disturbing your men about this priory."

"You must be better. Your impatience has returned. Rest."

"Tarran!"

"I must send the men back into the village to find out what they can. I also have to tend to Heliwr. I will come back as quickly as I can. Then you can pelt me with questions."

She nodded as he left. Finding out about the man in the pale robes was more important than easing her curiosity. She closed her eyes and let the minutes drift by uncounted. When Tarran returned to sit on the bed and hold her hands again, she was not sure how long he had been gone. It mattered only that he was there with her.

Elspeth was fading into sleep when a knock sounded. The door opened, and a tonsured head peeked in. It was not Brother Leopold, but a shorter, thinner man.

"It *is* you, Prince Tarran!" The monk came into the room, his dark brown robes flapping around his legs with a sound like the hawk beating its wings. "I was sure I was mistaken when I heard Brother Leopold tell the prior that a man with your name had come to Monkton Priory."

Tarran embraced him, being careful not to spill the contents of the cup the monk carried. "Brother Dewey! It is good to see you."

"Brother Twm in the stillroom asked me to bring this potion to you. It is to relieve pain. Are you hurt, Prince Tarran?"

"It is for Lady Elspeth." He took the cup and tilted it for her to drink. As she did, he added, "Brother Dewey was fostered by my parents. He came to live with our family soon after he was weaned." He clapped the monk on the shoulder as he handed Brother Dewey the empty cup. "He always preferred quiet to hunting and games."

"Do you still hunt, Prince Tarran?"

"I fly the best hawk ever. Heliwr is the smartest bird I have ever flown. I would show him to you if I had the time."

The monk's expression became grave. "So it is true. You seek vengeance for your wife's death."

"You know about that here?" asked Elspeth, taking the cool cloth off her head and sitting. "I would not have guessed such worldly matters would reach past your walls."

"It would not have except that Bradwr ap Glew has been named the murderer. I knew he had much anger within him, but I thought he had learned to restrain it while he was here."

"He was a monk?" she gasped.

"Until he left Monkton Priory about three years ago."

She put her hand over her mouth, but there was no need. Every word she had ever known had fled from her mind at the thought of a religious brother slaying Addfwyn.

"Brother Dewey," Tarran asked, "have you ever seen anything like this?" He held up the leather strand and glass bead. She recognized it as the one that he had taken from the man who had tried to kill them.

He shook his head. "No. Does it belong to Brother Bradwr?"

"A man who claimed to be his cousin was wearing it

when he tried to kill Elspeth. He revealed that Bradwr ap Glew wants me dead. I had hoped you would know what it might signify."

"It is nothing worn by the brothers of my order."

"Did you ever see him with something like it?"

Brother Dewey started to answer, but was interrupted by a bell clanging. "I must go. Vespers are coming to an end, and I need to return to my cell for meditation and prayer. Prince Tarran, I never saw Brother Bradwr with such a bead." He looked from her to Tarran. "I will pray for you."

He rushed out before Elspeth could thank him.

"Now you know," Tarran said as he held the bead out on its strap and let it rock back and forth, "why my men do not want to stay within these walls. The stench of our avowed enemy's treachery lingers amidst the holiness."

The glow from the room's single candle caught on the glass, sending bluish light cascading against the wall as one bead had at St. Jude's Abbey. Voices burst out of her memory. The abbess's voice and Sister Avisa's as they discussed a similar glass bead that Sister Avisa had brought to the Abbey.

"I know what it means!" she gasped.

"It?"

"The bead!"

"Tell me." He sat beside her, holding the bead tightly.

"It is an old story, which may be why Druce wears glass beads like this one. The beads are supposed to contain a great power."

"All of them?"

She closed her eyes, trying to bring forth the memory that had eluded her. "One bead is supposed to be strong enough to grant its wearer the power to rule Wales. That magic can defeat any army."

"Is it this bead?" He opened his hand.

"No, that one is solid blue. The special one has blue laced through clear glass."

"And the bead is safe in England?"

"I am not sure. I think she gave it to someone for safe-keeping."

"She?"

"Avisa de Vere. She was also a sister at St. Jude's Abbey, and—" She moaned as she realized what she had disclosed.

"Sister? St. Jude's Abbey? Are you saying that you belong to an abbey?"

She searched his face, wanting to discover how he felt at such a revelation. "Yes, but—"

He threw back his head and laughed.

She could only stare. Maybe her head had been hit harder than she had guessed. Or maybe the medicinal potion was stealing her wits. How else could she explain what she was seeing and hearing? Since she had met him, Tarran had never laughed as he was now.

"Tarran . . ."

He looked at her and laughed harder.

With a grimace, she started to stand. Her knees refused to hold her. She sat back on the bed and groaned. The room spun again, and her head was feeling oddly light.

He wiped away tears of amusement. "Lie back, Elspeth. Let me get the cloth wet again while you tell me more funny stories."

She leaned back with care. She closed her eyes and sank into the softness. The damp cloth eased the ache across her forehead. She opened one eye and said, "It is not a story. It is the truth."

"You? A cloistered sister?" He chuckled again. "What sort of nun masters the quarterstaff and knows how to walk across a pole? Do you expect me to believe that you were taught your amazing tricks to disarm a man in a convent?"

"It is an abbey. St. Jude's Abbey." She grasped for his

sleeve. Her fingers missed on her first attempt, but she managed to close them on his sleeve on her second try. "It is not something we speak of beyond the Abbey, but I want you to know the truth. St. Jude's Abbey is not like other religious houses. It is different. The sisters within its walls are different."

She began to explain what was kept hidden behind the Abbey's walls. He was silent until she was finished; then he stood and went to the door. Was he going to leave without saying anything?

She held her breath as she waited for him to speak. When he put his hand on the latch, she was pierced by a pain more severe than the one in her head. It came out of her heart, which yearned to be his.

He lifted the latch, and she bit her lip to keep from begging him to turn around and come back to her.

"Your story explains so much," he said without looking at her. "But it does not explain one thing."

"What is that?"

"Why these doors have no locks." He stepped away from the door and shoved the chest in front of it. "I don't want to be interrupted tonight."

She was suffused with happiness as he walked back to the bed. Sitting beside her, he brushed his fingertips against her cheek.

In spite of herself, she winced. He lifted his hand away, but she took it. "Don't stop touching me. I want you here with me."

"And I want to be here with you. I want to hear more about these ladies of St. Jude's Abbey." He drew off her shoes and put them by the side of the bed. "But in the morning. For tonight, you need to rest so you may heal."

"Stay with me, Tarran."

"I will. I will sit here and talk to you until you fall asleep."

"No, don't talk to me. Vala says you sing beautifully. Sing to me."

"A lullaby?"

"No, sing me the story of one of your legendary heroes." She laughed. "Just nothing that has to do with Merlin and some enchanted stone."

He nodded and drew off his boots. Stretching out his legs beside hers, he tilted her across his chest. She wondered why she had thought the bed was too narrow for two of them. He began to sing about how Prince Pwyll, in the guise of King Arawn, defeated Death's most dangerous foe.

She let his wondrously warm and resonant voice carry her into that enchanted land where anything was possible . . . even his loving her for the rest of her life.

Chapter 22

The wind blew water in straight lines across the flatlands near the cliffs. It was not raining hard. Most of the moisture was sea spray, creating a mist that clung to everything and everyone. The oxen bent their heads as they plodded toward the cliffs.

Elspeth pulled her cloak more tightly around her. The needle-sharp drops cut into her cheeks because she could not keep her hood on her head. Gusts tore it back. She leaned more heavily on her staff.

"Slow the cart!" Tarran called from its other side. His voice seemed little more than a whisper over the crash of the waves, whipped up by the storm, on the shore below the cliffs.

His shoulders were straight, for even the fierce wind would not make him bow. With his hair blowing back on the wind and Heliwr sitting on his left wrist, he could have been a hero out of the old tales. A man unbent by the trials the ancient gods had subjected him to again and again. He had not escaped unscathed. As they had traveled south from Pembroke through the sparsely populated peninsula sticking out into the Severn Sea, no nightmares had assailed him, but she wondered if they ever would truly leave him until he satisfied his vow to Addfwyn.

When the cart came to a stop not far from where the ground fell into the sea, Seith unhooked the oxen. As he led them away, Kei and Gryn grasped the shafts at the front of the cart and began moving it back toward the cliff's edge.

Once the cart was set in place, she leaned her staff against its side and walked toward where Tarran stood several yards away. He put out his arm to halt her as she neared. She understood why when she saw raw cliffs in a squared-off semicircle in front of her. The ground dropped off as if someone had sliced it away with a massive knife, leaving crumbs behind to tumble into the sea. These crumbs were boulders that dwarfed *Llech-lafar*.

"We are ready," she said.

"We cannot get rid of the rock yet." He pointed toward the boulders. "Pilgrims."

Elspeth saw forms moving partway down the slope. She could not tell how many people were gathered just beyond a flat surface, because they melded together in the mists. "How long will they be here?"

"I don't know, but until they leave the holy well, the stone must remain in the cart."

She glanced behind them. "If Druce's man is following us, he could be hiding anywhere in this fog."

He put his hand on the hilt of his sword. "We are as prepared as we can be." Putting his other arm around her shoulder, he said, "What is left of St. Govan's Chapel is there."

She was amazed to see grass growing around what appeared to be steps leading down to the flat rock floor about halfway down the cliff. She squinted into the grayness at a block of stone against the cliff wall. It was about as high as her waist, and she guessed it was about eight-feet long.

"The altar for St. Govan's Chapel," he said as if she had asked what the block of stone was. "Good! The pilgrims are moving toward us. Once they are on their way, we can fig-

ure out how to get the stone down among the others without any sign of its passage."

"It is steeper than I—"

"Tarran, beware!" came a shout from behind them.

She spun as he drew his sword. Seith and Kei were lying
facedown on the ground, and Gryn's sword clashed against
another. Forms were pouring from the mists. She heard
footsteps pounding up the slope. The pilgrims! Would they
help? Would they—She choked back a curse as the pilgrims
topped the cliff, and she recognized one by the golden staff
he carried.

"Druce!" she cried as she rushed toward the cart.

"Keep her from getting her quarterstaff!" Druce shouted.

Her arms were seized, and she was yanked nearly off her
feet. She started to free herself as Nariko had taught, then
paused when she saw more men emerge from the swirling
mist. Escaping from one grip would be useless if she was
instantly recaptured. She must save what Tarran called her
"tricks" until she could put them to best use.

Gryn was herded toward the cart where Tarran stood surrounded by a half-dozen men. When she was shoved in that
direction, too, she pretended to stumble forward and waved
her hands as if she needed to fight for her balance. She
grabbed the canopy over the cart and Heliwr flew skyward,
vanishing into the low clouds. Planting her feet, she yanked.
The fabric toppled over some of the men.

"Tarran!" she cried. "Now!"

Something stuck her in the back. She was knocked from
her feet. Her breath burst out of her as she hit the ground.
Before she could move, the back of her gown was grasped.
She was jerked to her feet and away from the cart. She saw
the flash of a sword.

"No!" bellowed Tarran and Druce at the same moment.

The sword lowered as her arms were grasped by two different men. She fought their hold to test their grips. Despair sank through her. They were both strong.

Druce pushed aside one section of the canopy with his staff as he advanced on Tarran and the wagon. "Thank you for bringing *Llech-lafar* to us." He tore back the blankets and ran his hand along the stone. "You may rest assured that we will give it the opportunity to do the work the great mage planned for it."

"How do you know *that* rock truly is *Llech-lafar?*" Tarran asked, contempt in his voice.

"What other rock would you bring from Tyddewi?"

"There are many miles between Tyddewi and here. We had many chances to rid ourselves of the rock."

"In Monkton Priory?"

"Your spies are skilled, Druce," Elspeth said, hoping to turn the men's attention to her. Tarran was closer to her staff than she was. If he could reach it, he might be able to stun some of the men long enough for him to escape and finish their task. "Was it your man I saw in Pembroke?"

Druce walked toward her, every step a swagger. "I am not surprised, Lady Elspeth, that you saw my man while you were fighting in Pembroke. Your cunning is remarkable."

"Then you should know that my cunning would extend to noticing your spies when they followed us."

"Yet, you came directly here from Tyddewi."

"Yes, directly here, which should tell you something."

Druce faltered, and Elspeth smiled triumphantly. A few moments of hesitation might be enough.

"Ask yourself, Druce," she said, again testing the grips the men had on her arms. They were not loosening, so she must continue talking and keep Druce off balance with a tale that was woven through with enough truth to make it plausible. "Ask yourself why we would go through Pembroke when King Henry could have arrived there. Would *I* take

Llech-lafar to where the king could step on it and die? Have you seen me do anything that is not completely logical?"

"No." The answer was reluctant.

She wanted to look at Tarran, to give him some sort of signal, but she did not dare. Did he have a plan? If so, she knew he would not initiate it until there was a chance of success. He did not intend to relinquish his last breath until he had his revenge against Bradwr ap Glew.

"She is lying." Orwig pushed forward.

She gasped. Druce's hooded crony had never spoken aloud. His voice was educated and deep . . . and familiar. But where had she heard it before? At St. Jude's Abbey? Impossible! Then where?

"The rock within the wagon is *Llech-lafar*," Orwig continued. "It is ours." He raised his hands as Druce had while standing on the rock by the shore. "It is ours! Its curse will be the bane of our enemy. Combined with the power within the bead you wear on your hand, we shall rule Cymru."

Druce lifted the hand where he wore the silver ring with the glass bead. Blue spirals caught the strengthening sunlight.

"Tarran, that is the ring!" Elspeth cried out in horror.

"You are right, Orwig," Druce said, ignoring her. "I shall not let her baffle me with lies." He walked over to Elspeth and slapped her hard.

Tarran tore his arm away from his captor. His fist drove into his captor's face. He leaped forward to grab Druce by the hood. Swinging the man around, he raised his hand and struck the man as he had hit Elspeth. Druce careened back several paces, then shouted to his men.

"Elspeth!" Tarran called.

"I am all right." She tried to hide her pain. "Tarran! Behind you!"

He whirled as a man raced toward him. He bent, striking him in the middle and sending the man flying over his back.

Elspeth screamed out his name, and one of the men holding her shook her and snarled in Welsh. The other man snapped what must have been an order. They started arguing.

She leaned forward as if feeling faint. As she bent her knees, the men tilted toward her, still quarreling. She sank toward the ground, and one released her arm, grasping onto her cloak instead as his voice rose with anger.

With an ear-blistering cry, she jumped up and jammed her elbow into the man's chin. He folded on the ground.

The second man tried to jerk her toward him. She drove the side of her foot into his stomach. As he clutched his middle, she kicked again, this time in his face. He was senseless by the time he landed on his back.

She ran toward the cart and her staff. Where was it? She had left it by the cart. If someone had thrown it over the side of the cliff . . . no! There it was in the cart. She pulled it out.

Her hair was seized as a man growled, "Put that down!" He shoved her against the cart. "Put it down now!"

"Tarran!" she cried.

The man snickered and reached out for her.

She threw the staff over his head, hoping she had judged the aim correctly. The stone she needed to hit was on the very edge of the cliff. If she was off even an inch, the staff would sail onto the rocks below.

"You threw away your only weapon!" the man sneered. "Are you so scared of me?"

"*You* should be scared!" She cheered as the staff struck the rock and bounced toward Tarran.

He caught it with ease and rushed forward.

The man grasped her arm, swinging her between him and the quarterstaff. She rammed her elbow into his gut. His moan became a shriek of pain when she drove her foot into his knee. Bone broke, and he fell to the grass.

"Good work," Tarran said with a smile. He tossed her the staff.

"Heliwr?"

"He is safe."

"Where are the others?" She looked around to see both Seith and Kei's prone forms were gone.

"Over there!" He pointed along the cliff. "They need my help."

"Go and protect them," she urged.

His quick kiss held the promise of many more that would not be as cursory.

Elspeth watched him vanish into the mists that were slowly lifting away, leaving the beach below in sunlight. Keeping her staff at the ready, she looked as far as she could see in every direction. She could hear voices, but, save for the unconscious men, she seemed the only living person on the cliff.

"Elspeth!"

Was that Tarran or someone else? The crash of the waves distorted every sound, and the cloying mist warped the landscape into shapes it could not have.

"Elspeth!"

She took a step, then paused. She must stay with *Llech-lafar*. She could not risk its falling into Druce's control. The wagon. Could she push it backwards? She put her shoulder to it and shoved. It did not move.

"Elspeth!" The voice sounded desperate, but she could not identify it.

"Tarran?" she called back.

"Elspeth!" came an answer not far behind her.

She looked over her shoulder. Someone exploded out of the mist. She saw something rise. Something gold. She tried to block Druce's staff with her own, but she was not fast enough. It struck the back of her head.

She did not remember falling. Just pain. Pain that reverberated through her head. She needed to get up and fight the giant. No, she had defeated him. She was fighting someone else. She was . . .

Everything rocked as if she were on a ship being buffeted by wild waves. Digging her fingers into the dirt, she prayed for the ground to stop moving. She wanted to close her eyes, but the whirling became more intense when she did.

"Stop! Don't hurt her!"

Tarran!

She had promised to watch over the cart with *Llech-lafar* for him . . . for the queen . . . for him . . . She was no longer sure. She had to find her staff and protect that accursed rock. Yet, all she could do was clutch the ground.

Someone grabbed the back of her gown again and lifted her like a bedraggled kitten. She was slammed against the cart. Grasping it, she kept herself from falling. She squeezed her eyes shut, then opened them, hoping they would focus.

They did. On the golden staff held close to her face. She looked along the staff to the hand holding it.

"Druce," she moaned.

"Where did you learn to fight as you do?" he demanded. "My men could use those skills to battle the Normans we shall drive from Cymru. You will teach them."

She spat in his face. "Go to hell! Not your Welsh hell in the hall of King Arawn. Go to Satan's hell!"

He laughed. "You know nothing of the old ways beyond a few stories." He held up the ring with its glass bead. "With this and *Llech-lafar*, we cannot be defeated."

"Tarran will—"

He snapped his fingers.

Elspeth moaned when Tarran and his men were pushed out of the mist. They were splattered with blood, but they were able to stand, so she guessed most of the blood was not theirs. Surrounding them were men in light brown robes. As the sun burned back the mist, its light sparked off the whetted edges of the blades Druce's men held.

One of the men stepped forward. "Druce, we await your orders."

"Kill them," he ordered with no more emotion than if he were selecting a piece of bread.

She locked eyes with Tarran and wished she could offer him some hope of escape. She had led him to this moment, and now he would die without obtaining his vengeance. She had failed the queen and the Abbey, but, even worse, she had failed Tarran.

When his lips tilted in a smile, her heart thumped against her chest. Did that mean he forgave her? Did it mean that he *loved* her?

"Throw the bodies over the cliffs," Druce ordered. "The scavengers will have a feast."

"Wait." Orwig came around from the other side of the wagon, where she had not noticed him. "First . . ." He lowered his hood. A scar disfigured his left cheek, and she recognized him. He was the man who had tried to slit her throat in Tyddewi. No wonder his voice had sounded familiar!

Tarran choked, then snarled, "Bradwr!"

Bradwr? She stared at the scarred man again. Save for his tonsure, he *did* look enough like Tarran to be his blood brother. Blood. She shuddered. Bradwr ap Glew had slain Addfwyn. He would not hesitate to murder again.

"You seem surprised, old friend," Bradwr mocked.

"I foolishly believed the story you must have started yourself," Tarran replied, his composure in place once more. "The story of sailing to the west with Prince Madoc to escape my vengeance."

Bradwr fingered the scar on his cheek. "I had no wish to escape it. I needed only time to heal so I might complete what remains unfinished. The she-cat scratched me deeply."

Elspeth bit her lower lip when Tarran glanced at her. She smiled sadly, glad that he had learned Addfwyn was as brave as one of the women in the old sagas.

"So are you ready to face justice for killing my wife," Tarran asked, "or do you plan to flee to meet the new fleet at Lundy Island?"

"To go across the ocean? Let Madoc sail off into the endless tracts of the sea. He may have nothing here, but I do."

"What?"

"My vengeance."

Tarran laughed sharply and twisted against the men's hold on him. "I think you have it backwards, old friend. I am the one who seeks revenge."

"I never meant to kill Addfwyn. I meant to kill *you* and take her as my wife. She should not have been your wife." Bradwr motioned for the men to release Tarran. Drawing a knife from beneath his robes, he said, "She was meant to be mine."

"Until you chose a life within the church because your father denied you and refused to give you a share of what your half brothers received."

"But she was promised to me!"

"Until you chose the church over her."

He guffawed. "So she had no choice but to turn to *you*."

Elspeth held her breath, waiting for Tarran's answer. He had taunted Bradwr enough to take the man's attention from the wagon and *Llech-lafar*. Not just Bradwr's attention, but the other men as well. It was an incredible story, and the Welsh could not resist listening to it. But the wrong word could mean Bradwr's killing Tarran immediately.

"She was frightened of you, Bradwr. She asked me to give her my name so I could protect her."

"But you did not."

Tarran reached toward his sheath, but it was empty. "Because I never suspected my most trusted friend would betray both of us."

Bradwr motioned for Druce to step aside. When Druce complied, Elspeth wondered who was the real leader. Raising the knife he held, Bradwr placed it just below her ear, where her pulse was pounding so hard it must be visible through her skin.

"This is the knife that slew the woman you dishonored, *Prince* Tarran." He made the title an insult.

"It cannot be! There was a knife in Addfwyn when I found her."

He scraped the knife up Elspeth's throat, nicking her ear. When she drew in a sharp breath, he smiled. "But *this* is the knife that dealt the death blow when she attacked me with her own dagger." He touched his scarred cheek again. "Now you dishonor Addfwyn's memory by bedding a *Sais.*"

"Loving Elspeth is no dishonor."

She gasped again, this time at how easily Tarran spoke of loving her. Bradwr scowled, but a wicked delight sparkled in his eyes. He was enjoying every moment of forcing Tarran to watch him hold a knife to her throat.

"Neither was it a dishonor to marry Addfwyn," Tarran continued. "But your killing her was."

"She would be alive now, if you had not forced her to marry you."

"I needed no force." His eyes narrowed. "Not as you did, Bradwr. If she truly had loved you, do you think she would have remained with me?"

Bradwr shoved Elspeth back toward Druce as he leaped toward Tarran. She reached out to halt him, but Druce's staff pressed her against the wagon.

Slashing his knife at Tarran, Bradwr laughed when Tarran edged aside.

"There is nowhere you can flee, Tarran ap Llyr," he

taunted. "You will die here today along with your kins-men."

"And Elspeth?"

He swung the knife again, backing Tarran toward the cliff. "Druce wants her. Druce can have her while he lives out his grand dreams."

"Or until you betray him, too?"

Elspeth strained for Bradwr's answer, because she wanted Druce to hear it. The wind swept it away. She watched Tarran and his foe step in and out of the fraying mist in a deadly dance along the cliff.

She cried out a warning when Bradwr rushed forward, swinging the dagger at Tarran. Jumping aside, Tarran fought for his balance on the edge. She screamed when he tottered and fell, crashing along the steps toward the chapel.

Bradwr shouted with triumphant glee and ran down the steps.

Druce's men pushed forward to see the end of the fight.

With a shriek, Elspeth grabbed Druce's right wrist, smashing it against the side of the cart. He screamed in pain. She reached for the staff, but he put up his arm to block her. Her fingers found the ring instead. She plucked it off his hand. Dropping it to the ground, she stamped on it. Glass shattered, and she winced as a piece cut through her shoe.

Druce screeched madly. His men turned to see what was wrong.

Tarran's comrades broke away. Fists hit dully against flesh, and swords slashed the air. Seith and Gryn ran toward her. They grasped the cart's shafts and shoved the cart. Kei hurried to help them.

"Here, milady!" shouted Seith.

She caught the staff he threw to her. It was not hers. It was longer, but she would make it work. Spinning it until it was a blur, she stepped between the wagon and Druce's

men. She fought them off. Knocking the staff against heads,
she sent one man after another to the ground.

The cart teetered on the rim of the cliff as Tarran had.

"No!" she cried. "Tarran is down there!"

His men exchanged horrified glances. They tugged on
the wagon. It was too late. The rock slid from the back and
the cart toppled over.

"Tarran!" she shrieked. "Look out! *Llech-lafar* is coming!" She prayed he was still alive to hear her.

Then the stone crashed against the ground. It tumbled
down the hillside, driving other rocks before it in a rocky
deluge. They bounced like a child's toys. Over the noise,
she heard the unmistakable sound of a bell clanging.

The echo of the crash was swept along the shore. One
wheel bounced against a cliff wall, skimmed a pile of boulders, and vanished beneath a stone arch. The rest of the cart
broke into splinters scattered around the chapel's floor.

Elspeth pushed past Tarran's men, and Druce, who was
on his knees by a rock, where pieces of glass glittered in the
rays stabbing through the clouds. He was weeping.

She stepped around him and edged over the cliff. Her
stomach cramped and she fought not to be ill when she saw
Bradwr lying on his back, staring at the sky. He was dead,
his body broken, for his arms and legs were twisted at impossible angles. *Llech-lafar* must have struck him as he
chased Tarran. She looked up at the ragged top of the cliff
and was astonished how many stones must have been
pushed down the steep slope.

"Tarran . . ." she whispered as she stared at the devasta-
tion around the chapel.

She heard a shriek from overhead. Heliwr! She scanned
the sky and saw the hawk dive down toward what was left
of St. Govan's Chapel. She watched, barely daring to
breathe, while a hand rose from behind the altar. As the
hawk landed on it, she raced down the steps. Skidding to a

stop on the flat floor of the chapel, she rushed to where Tarran was sitting up in the narrow space behind the altar.

She knelt beside him. His face was covered with scratches, and blood seeped through his sleeve not far from where the bird sat on his left wrist. He put his right arm around her shoulders and drew her closer.

"Bradwr?" he asked.

"Dead."

"Addfwyn is avenged," he whispered.

"Just as you promised her."

"*Llech-lafar*?"

"Lost among the boulders below us."

He shifted and grimaced. "Your pledge is fulfilled, too."

"Yes." She added nothing more as his men reached the chapel and began to congratulate him. Stepping back, she stared up at where Druce was weeping. *Llech-lafar* was gone; his glass bead destroyed; his men dead or fleeing.

Tarran stroked her shoulder as she whispered, "He has lost everything."

"He lost nothing, Elspeth," he replied while his men climbed the cliff. Heliwr screeched and bated, clearly unhappy to be carried by Seith. "He lost nothing, for he had nothing but malevolent dreams. He remains enmeshed in them."

"Then we should pity him."

He turned her to face him. Blood was matted in his hair and stained his tunic, but she could see only his eyes that glowed with emotions he did not try to hide. "*Cariad*, I have learned that a man's nightmares are of his own making. He can let them consume him, or he can escape by choosing to let love back into his heart once more."

"Don't say you love me," she whispered.

"Elspeth?" His face hardened. "Are you saying you do not love me?"

"No, but I am saying that if you love me, I will lose you."

"That is nonsense."

She shook her head, then winced. "I went to Lord de la Rochelle's castle to find Rhan, an old wisewoman. When she gave me information on *Llech-lafar*, she warned me to turn back from my quest. If I continued, I would lose what I loved."

"Did you love me when you spoke with her?"

"No." She searched his face, hoping he had an answer to the dilemma that had haunted her. "I thought you were an arrogant, obnoxious, overbearing brute who—"

He put his fingers over her lips. "Enough, Elspeth!" He smiled. "What did you love then?"

"My service to the queen. My life at St. Jude's Abbey."

"So the old wisewoman was right." He slipped his arm around her waist and brought her to him. "You will be losing those things you love if you stay with me in Cymru. Will you stay, Elspeth?"

Memories flooded her mind—beloved memories of her life in the Abbey, of teaching her students, of receiving her task from Queen Eleanor—but she did not hesitate to whisper, "Yes."

Epilogue

Easter morning was splendid. Around the ruins of the cathedral in Tyddewi, people had gathered to enjoy Mass at the rising of the sun. St. David's Cathedral would also arise again soon, and the rains had passed to leave the day a glory to be celebrated.

But every voice stilled when a group of men walked down the hill toward the River Alun. They were conferring on some matter that had nothing to do with the holiday because they wore mail beneath their tunics. There was no mistaking which man among them was the king. Disheveled and salt stained, he walked with the assurance of a man who knew he was one of the most powerful in the world.

Among the trees by the river, Elspeth sat between Tarran and Vala. They had been waiting for this moment since they had heard the king's fleet had landed near Tyddewi.

"Now," Elspeth whispered to Vala and gave her a bolstering smile.

The old woman stepped out from beneath the shade of the trees along the river. Holding up her hands in a pose she had stolen from Druce, she called, "Beware, great king! Beware of the doom that will come your way if you tread upon *Llech-lafar.*"

King Henry's forehead rutted under his mail hood. "Old woman, what nonsense do you speak?"

"Beware of *Llech-lafar*!"

One of the men whispered to the king, and he nodded. "Old woman, I do not believe in such ancient tales, and I shall prove that to you."

"*Llech-lafar*," Vala cried loudly as a crowd gathered to watch the curse invoked, "bring your vengeance now!" She looked down at the rock by the river. "Bring your vengeance now!"

King Henry laughed and stepped upon the stone as he crossed the river. He came back to the same side and said, "Old woman, your Merlin has been proved a liar."

Elspeth hurried forward at the best pace she could with her sore foot. The shards of glass from Druce's ring had cut deeply into her heel. She put one hand on Vala's arm. "Forgive her, your majesty. She is not always in possession of her wits. Forgive her, for it is Easter morn."

The king's eyes narrowed. "I have seen you before."

"It is possible." She drew her staff from behind her back and leaned it against the ground.

Again he smiled, and she knew he recalled her from his sole visit to St. Jude's Abbey. "It seems I may have another ally from a most unexpected quarter, Lady—"

"Lady Elspeth," she replied.

"And you helped her?" The king looked past her.

She did not have to glance over her shoulder as wondrously familiar fingers settled on it. Even with the bandages on his face and around one knee, Tarran was surely the most compelling man by the shore. More so even than the king.

"I did," said Tarran.

"You are . . . ?"

"Tarran ap Llyr, son of Prince Llyr."

She heard sharp intakes of breath at Tarran's identification of his father with a title the Normans had never acknowledged.

If King Henry heard them, he showed no sign. "A wise king knows to be grateful for every faithful subject, and no one has ever called me a fool." He looked down at the stone and then back to them. With a nod of his head, he continued with his men toward the village.

The villagers followed, leaving the three of them alone by the river.

Elspeth laughed.

"What is funny?" Tarran asked.

"Didn't you hear the whispers? They are saying that King Henry could not have truly conquered Ireland if *Llech-lafar* failed to bring forth its curse when he stepped on the stone."

"We of Cymru do not surrender our old ways easily, even when facts discount them." He smiled at Vala. "Thank you for your help. Nobody will ever question if that rock is *Llech-lafar*. No one will go looking elsewhere for it."

Vala kissed him on the cheek, then did the same to Elspeth before she walked toward her granddaughter's house.

Elspeth smiled when Tarran took her hand and strolled with her along the river, where flowers were pushing through the grass. Her smile wavered when he said, "I give up."

"Give up? What?"

He paused and faced her. Folding her hands in his, he brought them up between them. "I give up trying to protect you, Elspeth Braybrooke. Not only can you protect yourself, but I discovered at St. Govan's Head that trying to keep up with you can be a rough task."

"I could say I told you so."

"And I assume you will. Often." He leaned his forehead against hers. "You should know that last night I had a very pleasant dream."

"Really?" Her heart pounded with elation. "What was it?"

"A dream of my future life. Not a simple life because you were part of it." He chuckled softly. "If it is a harbinger of what is to come, I must say that, from this day forward, I will let you protect yourself unless you ask me to help."

"And what will you be doing?"

"Loving you."

She gazed into his dark eyes that were filled with the passions they had just begun to explore. "And I will spend all my time loving you in return, Prince Tarran ap Llyr." She gave him a saucy smile. "Yet, what if one of us needs protecting?"

"Then I guess we will have to defend each other." He tapped her nose. "Both of us instead of you insisting on being one knight standing alone. How does that plan sound?"

"Wonderful."

"For the rest of your life?"

She gave him her answer in a slow, luscious kiss that said more than mere words ever could.

Read on for a preview of the next book
about the Ladies of St. Jude's Abbey

A Moonlit Knight

Coming from Signet Eclipse in June 2006

An icy smile pulled at Saxon Fitz-Juste's lips. "I cannot believe that *you* are the one the queen has come seeking."

Mallory de Saint-Sebastian drew in a quick breath to keep anger from tinting her voice. "The queen trusts the abbess to make that decision. As her man, you should do the same."

"You are right. However, as the queen's man, it behooves me to serve as her eyes. You do not have the stance of a skilled warrior. If *you* are the best in St. Jude's Abbey, maybe the queen's faith in the Abbey is misplaced."

Was he trying to make her despise him? If so, he need not try so hard. She already loathed his arrogance. He could look down his aquiline nose at her all he wished. That did not do more than vex her, but she was furious at his disdain of her beloved Abbey.

"If you wish," she said, knowing she should have waited for the abbess's permission to speak, but too angry to keep quiet, "I will be very glad to show you the extent of my training."

"That exhibition must wait for the queen." Again his gaze slid up and down her. "She must see something in you that I do not."

"I agree."

"You do?"

She smiled as she set her quiver back on her shoulder. "She must see something in *you* that I do not."

He said nothing, and she wondered if she had shocked him speechless. Maybe he had not expected a cloistered sister to speak her mind, but she could not allow him to denigrate the Abbey . . . and the queen! Queen Eleanor deserved their respect and more.

When he turned and went back toward the horses, she smiled. That smile vanished when he pulled a quiver off the saddle and withdrew two arrows. They were several inches longer than the arrows she used. To use them would mean readjusting her stance and draw, and even that might not be enough. She had never practiced with arrows of that length.

"You would do well," Fitz-Juste said, "to guard that whetted tongue in the queen's presence. She is unlikely to have patience with your attempts at wit, considering what is going on."

Mallory's brow ruffled with bafflement. What was occurring beyond the Abbey that would distress the queen?

As if she had asked the question aloud, he focused his dark eyes on her and said, "Surely you are not so isolated here that you are unaware of how the young king and two of his brothers have risen up against King Henry the Senior."

"We are aware of the revolt." She tried to put as much haughtiness in her voice as he had in his. "If the king had not been determined to guarantee his heir the throne by coronating him three years ago, his son might have enough patience to wait until the throne is rightfully his with his father's death."

"Sister Mallory," said the abbess.

Mallory turned, horrified, to see the abbess's scowl. Not

wanting to know what was on the queen's face, she lowered her eyes, knowing she had spoken in a way that could bring shame on the Abbey. Heat scored her face, and she was glad the moonlight would bleach any color from her cheeks.

When Queen Eleanor spoke, there was no hint she had heard anything said by either Mallory or the abbess. "Where do you teach others, milady?"

Her finger shook as she pointed beyond the abbess's house.

The abbess frowned at her again before gesturing more graciously for the queen to come with her. As they walked away, the four dark-haired men fell in line behind them with practiced precision.

Fitz-Juste copied the abbess's motion toward Mallory. He said nothing, but he did not need to. In addition to speaking openly of the king's demise, she had been rude not to answer the queen aloud. She could not fault him when he had been successful at infuriating her to the point that she did not guard her words. It had taken her five years to learn to control her temper, which had flared too often at her father's indifference to her mother's suffering. Five years of restraint, which had been negated within minutes by Saxon Fitz-Juste's taunts.

She flinched as she hurried to follow the queen and the abbess. The queen had suggested he knew what to do. Had his words been a test of some sort? If so, she had failed completely, shaming herself and, more important, the Abbey.

The familiar targets that were set against short stacks of hay offered Mallory no comfort as she rounded the corner of the abbess's house. Other footfalls came from behind her, and she knew the sisters, awakened by the voices, were coming to watch. Hadn't she done the same, peering over the kitchen garden wall, the first time the queen came to St. Jude's Abbey and challenged Sister Avisa to prove her skills? Mallory had wished then that she could have been chosen. Now she would have gladly traded places with any of the sisters following quietly behind to see what the queen proposed.

"There," Queen Eleanor said. "The target farthest to the right, Saxon."

He gave Mallory a smug smile before crossing the open area to the target half-concealed by darkness. Easily he drove one arrow and then the other into the target before stepping aside.

"There is your target, Lady Mallory," the queen said.

Mallory stared in disbelief. The moonlight and shadow dappled across the yard made more difficult a shot that would have been challenging in the sunlight. The arrows were barely the breadth of her arrow apart. For so long she had been training others in the Abbey, and she had not spent much time in practice.

Silence filled the courtyard, but she was aware of everyone looking at her, waiting to see if she could accomplish the task given to her by the queen. Setting the arrow to the string again, she turned so her left side was to the target and raised the bow, then lowered it. She heard whispers all around, but neither the queen nor Fitz-Juste spoke. He simply watched her with that same self-satisfied smile. She wanted to warn him that he would not be wearing it long.

She slid her quiver off her back, leaning it against her right leg. The murmurs vanished when she lifted the bow to aim again. Slowly she drew the string back until it touched her lips and the middle of her chin. As she had hundreds of times, she let her fingers ease off the string and let the arrow fly.

It arched at what seemed an impossibly slow pace. She held her breath, not wanting to disappoint the queen and the abbess, even as she reached for two more arrows, sending them after the first. As it reached the top of its arc, the first arrow seemed to speed toward the target. It struck the target with a dull thud, directly between Fitz-Juste's two arrows. Right after it, Mallory's other two arrows hit, one on the outside of each of the arrows jammed into the target. All five arrows quivered with the impact.

Mallory lowered her bow and picked up her quiver so that nobody would see her relief. Or, she had to admit, her own smug smile if she looked toward Saxon Fitz-Juste.

"Well done, Lady Mallory," the queen said.

Straightening, Mallory delighted in the queen's praise. "I have been taught well."

Queen Eleanor continued as if Mallory had not spoken, "You shall travel to my court in Poitiers, where I have a task that you are well suited for."

Excitement and uncertainty battled within her, but she kept her face serene. "I am eager to serve, my queen."

"You will travel separately from us."

"As you wish."

"I would wish that you could journey with me so you could tell me how you learned to be so accomplished." The queen's smile wavered for only a moment. "One must be cautious not to show one's hand in these parlous times." She motioned to her men to return to their horses.

As the four dark-haired men obeyed, Queen Eleanor expressed her thanks to the abbess. Neither woman could have noticed the lecherous smiles the four men wore as they eyed Mallory anew.

She raised her chin and looked away, dismissing them with the dignity the queen had shown. Her pose was threatened when Fitz-Juste walked toward her, carrying all five arrows. He held out the three shorter ones to her.

"Thank you," she said quietly.

"You would have been wiser to miss." He walked away without giving her a chance to answer.

Which was just as well because she had no idea what she might have said.

About the Author

Jocelyn Kelley has always had a weakness for strong heroines and dashing heroes. For as long as she can remember, she's been telling stories of great adventures. She has had a few great adventures of her own, including serving as an officer in the U.S. Army and signing with a local group of Up with People. She lives in Massachusetts with her husband, three children and three chubby cats. She's not sure who's the most spoiled.

Learn more about Jocelyn and her future books at www.jocelynkelley.com.

Jocelyn Kelley

*For one lady of St. Jude's Abbey,
love is seductive...*

A Knight Like No Other

In twelfth-century England, St. Jude's Abbey is
no ordinary holy sanctuary: it trains young
women in the knightly arts.

When Avisa, the most skilled of them, is asked
by the Queen to safeguard her royal grandson,
the honor is both dangerous and seductive.

0-451-21438-2

Available wherever books are sold or at
penguin.com